Hebrew
Day School
of Ann Arbor

בית הספר העברי

באן ארבור

presented to

MARA METLER

Upon Her Graduation

from the

Hebrew Day School of Ann Arbor

June 14, 2012

24 Sivan 5772

Mara,
Study hard, enjoy life, and
give back with Joy. You are
great! Stay in touch with
your heritage - and with me!

Tina

The Brothers Schlemiel

This book and its illustrations

by Zevi Blum have been supported

in honor of Ida Faye Pucker, may her memory,

her love of life, and her warm Yiddish heart

be preserved in the spirit of

the Brothers Schlemiel.

Sue and Bernie Pucker

Gigi and Michael Pucker

Leslie and Ken Pucker

Marcie and Jon Pucker

Sharon Pucker Rivo and Elliott Rivo

Lisa E. Rivo

Jessica Millstone and Steve Rivo

Rebecca Rivo

And all of her great-grandchildren

The BROTHERS SCHLEMIEL

MARK BINDER

Illustrated by Zevi Blum

2008 • 5768
The Jewish Publication Society
Philadelphia

The Jewish Publication Society
2100 Arch Street, 2nd floor
Philadelphia, PA 19103
Design and Composition by Alexa Ginsburg
Printed in China

Library of Congress Cataloging-in-Publication Data:
Binder, Mark.

The brothers Schlemiel / Mark Binder ; illustrated by Zevi Blum. -- 1st ed. p. cm.

"The Brothers Schlemiel was originally serialized in the Houston Jewish Herald-Voice. The first episode was run in February of 2000. One-hundred installments later, the novel was concluded on January 16, 2002."

Summary: Born in Chelm, a small Jewish settlement known for being full of fools, identical twin brothers Abraham and Adam are alike in so many ways that they, themselves, are not always sure who is who, as they grow to adulthood encountering gypsies, thieves, kings, and love along the way.

08 09 10 11 12   10 9 8 7 6 5 4 3 2 1
ISBN 978-0-8276-0865-8

[1. Brothers--Fiction. 2. Twins--Fiction. 3. Identity--Fiction. 4. Jews--Poland--Chelm (Lublin)--Fiction. 5. Chelm (Lublin, Poland)--Fiction.] I. Blum, Zevi, ill. II. Title.

PZ7.B51165Bro 2008

[Fic]--dc22

2007036044

Contents

1. Oy . . . Lost Dad . . . Sunset Sunrise   1
2. Bris   12
3. Termites on the Brain . . . After Dark   16
4. Gossip . . . Coming Home . . . Found Father   23
5. The Question Is Answered   33
6. The Rom   37
7. Growing Pains   44
8. A New Teacher . . . The Plot . . . The Demon Is Banished   47
9. Separation Time . . . Adam Alone . . . In the Black Forest   59
10. Thieves, Caught   70
11. The Robber's Story   79
12. Trouble   84
13. The Man Who Complained Himself to Death . . . Training   88
14. The Governor's Palace—in Pinsk   94
15. Let's Not Talk about It . . .   105
16. Summer Day   109
17. A Girl   115
18. Breaking the Good News   119
19. The Eighth Light   124
20. Drudgery   128
21. Early One Morning   132
22. Double Bar Mitzvah   136
23. Bad News . . . The Curse of the Schlemiel . . .
    A Schlemiel Grows in Brooklyn   140
24. The Prank   149
25. Guess Who's Coming to Chelm   157
26. Macarooned   160
27. Much Ado   163
28. Where Does Rum Come From?   165
29. Oops, Wrong King   170
30. A Visitor   175

31. An Innocent Walk   179

32. A Very Schlemiel Wedding   184

33. The Wisest Rabbi   189

34. The King and the Carpenter   193

35. Breathless   198

36. Broken   201

37. Well, Well . . . A Half-Bucket of Tears   204

38. Signs in the Forest . . . Two Soldiers   211

39. No, You're in Trouble   218

40. Over a Barrel   222

41. Home . . . Goodbye, Adam   227

42. Becoming Abraham   234

43. Another Schlemiel Wedding   238

44. The Importance of Being Mud   243

45. Where the Wind Blows . . .   247

Publication Note

The Brothers Schlemiel was originally serialized in the *Houston Jewish Herald-Voice*. The first episode was published in February of 2000. One hundred installments later, the novel was concluded on January 16, 2002.

Excerpts also have appeared in:
Western Jewish Bulletin
Jewish Journal Boston North
The Jewish Advocate & Jewish Times
Washington Jewish Week
Jewish Free Press
Chicago Jewish Star
Ohio Jewish Chronicle & Senior Times
Connecticut Jewish Ledger
American Jewish World

Author's note

Villages like Chelm live in the footnotes of history. In this work of fiction, history lives in the footnotes. And there are occasions when the historical facts accidentally get in the way of a good story.

For example, mention of the construction of The Brooklyn Bridge sets the book near the end of the 19th century, but at that time Poland didn't exist. Furthermore, there was no king in Poland during this period, so several of the major turning points of the book seem to have been completely invented.

They say that history is written by the victors. If so, the Schlemiels lost.

Those who leave Chelm end up in Chelm.
Those who remain in Chelm are certainly in Chelm.
All roads lead to Chelm.
All the world is one big Chelm.

—I. B. Singer

CHAPTER ONE

Oy . . . Lost Dad . . . Sunset Sunrise

"Oy!"

"Push!"

"Oy!"

"Push!"

"Jacob, stop that!" Rebecca Schlemiel snapped at her husband. "We're moving a table, not giving birth. Not yet anyway."

"I'm practicing," Jacob laughed. "It's going to happen any day now."

They both looked down at Rebecca's bulging belly. It was huge, the size of a boulder and just as heavy.

"I can only wish," Rebecca said. She looked around the crowded kitchen and not for the first time wondered how they were going to fit another person into their lives. The house was tiny. In fact, calling it a house at all was a gracious compliment. Two rooms—a bedroom and the kitchen, plus a privy out back. "Do you think the crib is really going to fit between the table and the cupboard?"

"Relax," Jacob said. "I measured it myself. The first knuckle of my thumb is exactly one inch long. The distance between the cupboard and the table is . . ." He began measuring again.

Rebecca looked at her husband, inching his thumb along the floor, shook her head, and put on a pot of water for tea. This was going to take a while.

Jacob and Rebecca Schlemiel lived in the village of Chelm, a tiny settlement of Jews known far and wide as the most concentrated collection of

1

fools in the world. Chelm was celebrated in Yiddish jokes, shaggy dog stories, foolish songs, and the occasional ribald limerick. If someone in Moscow did something stupid, it was blamed on Chelm ancestry. A silly accident in Warsaw begged the question, "What part of Chelm did you come from?" And when a new politician promised revolutionary change, he was laughed down as "another wise man from Chelm."

Now, the villagers of Chelm did not think of themselves as doltish, stupid, slow, or otherwise mentally impaired. They kept to themselves, rarely traveling further than Smyrna for market day. If they were aware at all of the outside world's low opinion of them, they ignored it. Or perhaps they took it as a compliment. After all, as the learned Rabbi Kibbitz once said, "Wisdom shmisdom. What good is knowing everything if you can't laugh?"

All of this is a roundabout way of saying that Rebecca Schlemiel didn't think it at all unusual for her husband to measure a four foot space with his thumb. She saw it purely as an opportunity to rest her aching feet.

This pregnancy business was much more difficult than she'd bargained for. When she'd complained to her mother about back pains, swollen toes, and hair falling out, her mother had laughed. "You think you have problems? When I was pregnant with you I couldn't get out of bed. Your father had to use the hay winch to hoist me up in the mornings. Three days before your were born, he had a hernia. Now those were problems."

Those were also the kinds of things mothers rarely told their daughters about in advance. Or if they did, they were ignored as nonsense. This was probably for the best because otherwise the human species might never reproduce. Rebecca wondered what else her mother hadn't warned her about. For several months now, as her belly swelled, she found herself remembering the troubles she'd gotten into as a girl and shuddered at the faint echoes of her mother's shrill curse, "Just wait 'till you have children of your own."

"Foo!" Jacob spat. "Rebecca, is my right thumb bigger than my left? You know, I'm not sure the crib is going to fit."

Rebecca nodded. "I told you that before, but you didn't believe me. No, we had to move the kitchen table to see. Even if it did fit, I wouldn't be able to open the silverware drawers."

Jacob was a wonderful carpenter, the best in all of Chelm. In the workshop that he rented from Reb Cantor, the merchant, he had built a beautiful crib of the finest polished oak. Unfortunately, he had forgotten to take measurements in the small house before construction. To be honest, he wasn't even sure the crib could fit in the front door. This he didn't dare tell Rebecca, especially not after moving the heavy table back and forth across the kitchen seventeen times.

"What about next to the stove?" Jacob asked.

"Wonderful," Rebecca said sarcastically. "I'll be making a pot of chicken soup, I'll sneeze, the pot will spill, and boiling water will pour on the baby . . ."

"Enough!" Jacob interrupted. "We could hang the crib from the ceiling. He'd be out of the way then."

Rebecca snorted. "I am not going to have my child suspended above me like a bird in a cage. Besides, how do you know it's going to be a boy? My mother had seven daughters and her mother had seven daughters. I'm the seventh daughter of the seventh daughter. You don't think that means something?"

"I need boys to help me in the shop."

"Boys are clumsy and slow," Rebecca said. "Girls are careful. Imagine what wonderful work you could do with seven lovely assistants."

"I'm sure they would do wonderful work," said Jacob, putting his hand to his heart. "All I know is that I am not going to have seven daughters. Not unless you let me hang seven cribs from the ceiling."

Rebecca laughed. "Let's not talk about seven. I'm worried enough about this one. Do you think we're doing the right thing? The world is cold. Nights are dark and long. People get sick, there are robbers . . ."

"Don't think of such things." Jacob stood and put his hands on his wife's shoulders. He began rubbing them softly. "In the spring when the flowers come up, are they not the most beautiful and delicate things in the world? On a cold night a fire is warm. And as for robbers, what do we have to steal? I have you and you have me. A child is a blessing."

Rebecca sighed. "It's so quiet tonight. You know, after she is born, you and I will never be alone again."

"He," Jacob emphasized, "has to sleep some time." Rebecca looked so beautiful. He leaned down to kiss her forehead.

"Oy!" Rebecca said.

"You know, we don't have to move the table right away," Jacob said. "We can try again in the morning."

"Oy!" Rebecca moaned.

"All right," Jacob shrugged. "I'll push and you pull."

"OY!" Rebecca screamed.

"Oy?" Jacob said. His eyes widened. "Oy? Oy! Oyoyoyoyoyoyoyoyoy-oyoy!"

And thus he ran shrieking out of the house to get the midwife.

The moment he was gone, Rebecca burst into laughter. She wasn't due for another week. It wasn't exactly nice to get Mrs. Chaipul out of bed to play a joke on Jacob, but Rebecca would make it up to her with a walnut strudel.

Rebecca looked at her nice neat kitchen. Even with the table wedged nearly against the far wall, it was clean and tidy and well-kept—a good place for a daughter to grow up and learn how to cook.

The water on the stove came to a boil, and Rebecca began the slow process of hoisting herself up out of her chair.

"Oy," she muttered. Then her eyes widened. "Oh!"

It seemed that Mrs. Chaipul wasn't going to be wasting a trip after all.

Only in Chelm could a father get so lost going to fetch the midwife that he misses the birth of his first child. Or perhaps only Jacob Schlemiel. If he'd turned right instead of left as he ran out of his house, who knows, perhaps his entire life would have been different. At the very least he never once would have heard his wife utter the complaint that would haunt him until the day he died, "And your father couldn't even bother to be present . . . ."

He didn't do it on purpose. Who would do such a thing on purpose? He was on his way to the restaurant that Mrs. Chaipul, the midwife, owned. Her establishment, which served the finest chicken soup with the heaviest lead-ball knaidels, was less than two hundred yards from Jacob's house. He had been there hundreds of times—only last Thursday for corned beef on rye with a dab of mustard.

But Jacob Schlemiel was in such a panic at the thought of Rebecca giving birth that he decided to take a short cut. Never mind that his short cut was in exactly the wrong direction. At the moment he made the decision to turn left, he was certain—absolutely certain—that he was going the right way.

Even then, all could have been well. Chelm is not such a large village. There are fewer than eighty houses clustered around seven or twelve streets (depending on whom you believe and how you count). You could crawl from one end of Chelm to the other in fifteen minutes. Twenty if you got stuck in the mud. Thirty if you enjoyed playing in the mud, as most of the children of crawling age did. So, it was quite reasonable that after a moment of confusion, Jacob Schlemiel would have realized his mistake and looked over his shoulder to get his bearings.

Which is exactly what he was doing when he had the good misfortune literally to run, shebang, into Reb Shikker, the town drunk. The two men met, collided, rebounded, and sprawled into the mud.

Now, for many years Chelm did not have a town drunk. Every other village, town, and city had at least one, if not dozens. So, naturally the people of Chelm put an ad in the regional Yiddish newspaper, and in a matter of months the position was filled. Chelmites no longer felt excluded when a visitor from Smyrna boasted of their drunk's exploits. "Why that is nothing compared to our Reb Shikker," they would answer, their voices trailing off mysteriously. For none of them were quite sure what it was that the town drunk was supposed to do.

Truth be told, it wasn't easy being a drunk in Chelm. No one else in the village imbibed, except on Sabbath and holidays and festivals. No one made vodka, so Reb Shikker had to import his vodka from Moscow. And that was expensive, so he had to work. As it turned out, Reb Shikker was a skilled bookkeeper, but he couldn't keep his figures straight when his head was fuddled. And then there was his marriage to the rebbe's niece, Deborah, who sneezed at the smell of alcohol. So, although he had been fully qualified for the position, it was now quite rare for Reb Shikker to take even a sip from his flask.

In fact, the first words he uttered after finding himself sitting and splattered were, "I'm not drunk!"

"Nor am I," answered Jacob Schlemiel. "I'm sorry. It was my fault. My wife is about to give birth . . ."

"Mazel tov!" said Reb Shikker.

They helped each other to their feet, and then Reb Shikker remembered his vocation. "Would you like a drink?"

"I'm about to become a father," said Jacob.

"All the better," said Reb Shikker. "Once you are a father, you can't drink around the children. Besides, vodka will steady your nerves."

Reluctantly, Jacob accepted the offer of the flask. He took a long pull and then gasped.

"Good, isn't it?" laughed Reb Shikker. "But it's not good to drink alone. You have a drink for me. I can't, because I have to go back to work."

"All right." Jacob took another. This time his face went as red as borscht.

"You, my friend," said Reb Shikker, taking his flask, "have had enough for both of us. I'm not about to lose my reputation."

With that, Reb Shikker clapped Jacob on the back and trotted off.

After only two drinks on an empty stomach, Jacob Schlemiel was thoroughly kafratzed. He stumbled off and knocked on the first door he came to.

Esther Gold, the cobbler's wife, opened the door. Jacob started to explain that his wife was in labor, and that's as far as he got because Mrs. Gold had been preparing a noodle kugel for just this occasion, and she only had to wrap it in a towel for Jacob to take home. Five minutes later, he was standing outside again with a warm kugel in his hands, still wondering which way to turn.

At every house it was the same. Reb Cohen, the tailor, gave Jacob a teeny tiny suit of clothes. Reb Cantor, the merchant, presented him with a live chicken. And so it went. Everyone was so happy for him and cheerful. Some gave him tea, others gave him wine. The baker gave him a challah. It was only when, still struggling with boxes, bags, and the fussing chicken, he arrived at the home of Rabbi Kibbitz that Jacob remembered that he was supposed to fetch Mrs. Chaipul.

"Rebbe, Rebecca is in labor and I'm looking for the midwife!" Jacob blurted.

"Isn't she at her restaurant?" asked the rabbi.

"I don't know," answered the carpenter. "I forgot to go there."

"Well, then we'd better hurry."

The rabbi pulled on his coat, and the two men rushed back toward the center of Chelm.

On the way, they naturally passed right by the Schlemiels' small house, where they heard a peculiar mewling sound.

"Isn't that interesting," said Rabbi Kibbitz. "That sounds just like a child crying."

"Yes," agreed Jacob Schlemiel. "And my wife is supposed to be having a baby."

He stopped in his tracks. "She'll kill me."

Jacob Schlemiel Heads Home

"Nonsense," said the rabbi. "You're the father. If she killed you, she'd probably be executed as a murderer and the last thing she wants is to give birth to an orphan."

"Come in with me," Jacob begged.

"Not a chance." The wise old man shook his head and backed away. "You're on your own."

So, overburdened with packages and drink, Jacob stumbled through the door.

There was Mrs. Chaipul, in the kitchen, stirring a pot.

"I've been looking for you," Jacob said. "Rebecca's gone into labor."

"I know. Go on back," Mrs. Chaipul said, nodding toward the bedroom. "Hurry."

Jacob dropped the kugel, challah, and various packages on the kitchen table. The chicken ran behind the stove.

Meekly, Jacob peeked his head into the bedroom. There he saw Rebecca, looking tired but beautiful. And wrapped in a blanket was the smallest and loudest creature he had ever seen.

"It's been six hours!" Rebecca said. "You couldn't even bother to be present?

"I'm sorry. I got lost," Jacob answered. "Is it a boy?"

Rebecca smiled. "It's . . . AiEEEEEE!"

"What?" Jacob shouted. "What?"

"AIYEEEEEEE!"

The next instant, Mrs. Chaipul was back in the bedroom. "Get out of the way," she said, shoving Jacob into the kitchen. The door closed behind him.

"What?" he said. "I said I'm sorry . . ."

A few moments later, Mrs. Chaipul returned with the newborn babe wrapped in a blanket.

"Here." She handed him the bundle. "Hold this."

Jacob stared at the package. He held it in front of him in both hands like it was a brisket on a platter. "What am I supposed to do?"

The midwife stared up at him. "What, you never held a baby before?"

Jacob shook his head. "No."

Jacob was an only child born to a thirty-nine-year-old mother. He had grown up without young cousins and nephews. Although he had carved rattles for every family in Chelm, this was the first time that he'd ever actually held an infant in his arms.

"Ai yai yai," Mrs. Chaipul chuckled. She showed him how to hold the infant close, how to support its head and neck. Then a shriek from the bedroom summoned her back to her patient.

And so, Jacob was left staring at the tiny red ball of a head cradled in his elbow. It was asleep. The whole face was sort of bent and smooshed in, as if someone had flattened it like a pancake.

"You are ugly," Jacob thought. He would never say such a thing aloud. "I hope you are a boy, because if you're a girl you're going to have some big problems finding a husband."

Outside, it was dark. The sun had just gone down, and the only lights were from the stove and a single candle that Mrs. Chaipul had lit on the kitchen table. In the bedroom, Rebecca's cries subsided, and the small house was suddenly very quiet. Jacob could hear the crackling of the coals in the stove and the occasional footstep of Mrs. Chaipul in the bedroom.

Jacob looked at the little one. "So, you want to play cards?" he whispered. "I'll teach you canasta."

No answer. Of course not. The little one was asleep. Besides, if the face was so small, how tiny would the hands be? Canasta would keep.

Then there was a shriek from the bedroom. Jacob was so startled he nearly dropped the bundle. The scrunched-up face opened into a look of surprise, followed immediately by a bellowing yell that was surely heard all the way to Jerusalem.

The baby's screech was ear piercing. It stabbed through Jacob's skull like an ice pick into a summer melon. He had drunk too much vodka and not enough of anything else. Jacob lurched toward the bedroom to ask Mrs. Chaipul what he should do, but another shout from Rebecca stopped him cold.

"Make it stop!"

Something was going wrong and that frightened him more than anything had in his whole life. Just that afternoon he and Rebecca had been happy and joking. Yes, they'd bickered a little about where to move the kitchen table in order to fit the crib. Now, with his child screaming in his arms and his wife screaming in the bedroom, Jacob Schlemiel came face to face with the idea of a life he couldn't bear to imagine. What if . . . Life without Rebecca? What if . . . His wife and his love? He stood frozen, suspended in fear.

It was the infant crying in his arms that brought Jacob back. The tiny life in his hand, red as a beet and bawling, reminded him that there were other things to do.

But what?

"What can I do for you?" he asked the yowling child, but he could barely hear his own words. "Are you hungry? You must be hungry."

Jacob's eyes darted toward the bedroom, but he was more afraid of interrupting Mrs. Chaipul than he was of the infant's cries.

So, he did the only thing he could think of. He began to pray. And as he prayed, he davened, rocking back and forth, and the baby started to calm a little. But it felt funny, awkward, as if he was going to fall forward or drop the baby by accident, so instead, he began to daven from side to side, the way Rabbi Kibbitz sometimes did. A moment later, the little one was asleep, relaxed in his arms.

The candle burned slowly. Cries from the bedroom rose and fell like the waves of an ocean. Sometimes all seemed calm, and sometimes the fear rose in Jacob's heart, but still he rocked and prayed. Somehow during the night, he managed to switch the baby to one arm long enough to take a drink of water. Then, inspired, he dipped the end of a clean napkin into his glass and watched in pleased surprise as the baby took the cloth and began to nurse.

As the red glow of morning rose from the east, Jacob noticed that his legs ached and his throat was hoarse from prayer. Still, the baby was quiet, sleeping and sucking on the tip of the napkin. Slowly, ever so slowly, he lowered himself down into a chair.

Suddenly, Jacob saw the baby's face twitch.

"No! Please don't cry," he whispered. "Hush, hush."

Then, in the dim light of dawn, Jacob saw the baby's blue eyes open for the very first time, and he fell in love. What a perfect child! How wonderful.

He barely noticed as Mrs. Chaipul put her hand on his shoulder.

"You have another boy," she said.

"A boy," Jacob nodded, smiling back at the tiny one. "So that is what you are."

Then a wrinkle passed over his face. He turned to Mrs. Chaipul. "Did you say, 'another'?"

The midwife nodded and held out another red-faced bundle. "Twins," she said. "As identical as I've ever seen."

And they were. Now, Jacob Schlemiel held two babies in his arms. When he looked from one to the other, the only difference that he could see was that the first one was a little bit cleaner and a little less smooshed.

The two brothers stared at each other for a moment, and then with one voice they began to howl to the heavens.

"Rebecca?" Jacob shouted over the din as he jumped to his feet to resume his rocking. "How is my wife?"

"She's fine! She's asleep!"

"She's the lucky one!" Jacob grinned. "No, that's not true. We're all lucky!"

And with that, Jacob Schlemiel began to dance. He danced until, exhausted with joy, he and his two boys crawled into bed with their mother.

The crib could wait another day.

Soon, everyone was asleep, and the Schlemiel house was quiet.

For about ten minutes . . .

CHAPTER TWO

Bris

"You want what?" Rabbi Kibbitz stared at Jacob Schlemiel. Had he heard correctly? "You want me to perform the circumcisions differently?"

"Well, they're identical," Jacob said.

"Twins." The rabbi nodded. "Yes. They frequently look alike."

"No, Rabbi," Jacob said. "These two are exactly the same. I can't tell them apart. Their own mother can't tell them apart. There aren't any birth marks. Their eyes are the same. They both have ten fingers and ten toes."

"That's good."

"But I don't know which one is which."

"Why is this a problem? They can't be getting into trouble yet."

"But when they do," Jacob said, "how will I know who to blame?"

"You're going to make them drop their pants?"

"I don't know, Rabbi." Jacob Schlemiel put his hands over his eyes. "I just don't know."

Then he began to weep.

The rabbi sighed. The interview had gone relatively well up till then. When Jacob Schlemiel had knocked on the door to his study, the rabbi had given him warm congratulations and asked after the health of Rebecca and the new boys. Yes, Jacob had looked tired, but who wouldn't three days after the birth of one let alone two infants?

It was only when Rabbi Kibbitz drew out his paper and pencils to jot down the details for the *bris* that the confusion began. Usually, it was just a matter of scheduling. According to Jewish tradition, the ritual circumcision celebrating God's covenant with Abraham took place eight days after the child's birth. But, with one boy born at sunset and the other born at sunrise the next day . . . . That was tricky. You might be able to say that they were both born the same day. After all, didn't all the holy days begin the evening before? Still, Mrs. Chaipul wasn't sure whether the first was born just before or just after sunset, and there were the local authorities, who would never understand . . .

So, naturally, the rabbi had stalled by asking about the catering. It was clear that Jacob hadn't given it a thought, perhaps because he hadn't had time for more than a quick bite in days. The rabbi had suggested that Mrs. Chaipul handle the whole thing. Jacob had nodded and shrugged.

"So, what are their names going to be?" Rabbi Kibbitz had asked.

"We thought we'd call the first Abraham," said Jacob. "After Rebecca's great uncle's cousin on her mother's side. And then we'll call the other Adam, after my father's brother's father."

Rabbi Kibbitz scratched his head. "Your grandfather?"

"Yes," Jacob nodded.

"Why wouldn't you call the first one Adam, since he was the first human?" Rabbi Kibbitz asked. "Although I suppose Abraham was the first patriarch of the Jewish people . . ."

"Rebbe," Jacob said. "I would call the first one Adam, or I would call the second one Isaac. I would even call them One and Two. But who can be sure? When I first held them in my arms, I knew which was which. But the next morning, they both looked the same."

That was when Jacob had taken the rabbi's hand and asked if the rabbi could help them figure out which boy was which—surgically.

Rabbi Kibbitz rummaged through his pockets until he found a clean handkerchief, which he passed to the poor weeping carpenter.

"Listen, Jacob," he said. "What you're asking isn't so easy. All my life, ever since I was trained as a *mohel* so many years ago, I have striven for only one thing during a *bris*—consistency and perfection. Two things. It's not like building a table, where if one leg is a little short you saw off the other three to even things out. There's not a lot to work with. I perform the circumcision the way my teacher taught me, and it's not something you want to experiment with. Nu? You know?"

Jacob sobbed loudly.

"But wait!" said the chief and only rabbi of Chelm. "I have an idea. We'll bring in another rabbi! I'll do one boy, he'll do the other. We'll do them both at exactly midnight.* And then it won't matter which was born first. One will be Abraham, one will be Adam. And you should be able to tell the difference. Like a signature."

His cheeks still wet with tears, Jacob Schlemiel's face broadened into a smile. "Thank you," said Jacob. "Rabbi Kibbitz, you are wise like Solomon."

"Nonsense," the rabbi blushed. But when the carpenter left, he admitted to himself the possibility. "And Solomon," he chuckled, "had only one baby to cut!"

In a big city, rabbis are a dime a dozen, but in the tiny village of Chelm there was only Rabbi Kibbitz. He sent a note to his friend, Rabbi Sarnoff of Smyrna, but it seemed that there had been a baby boom in Smyrna, and the learned rabbi of that town would be unable to assist. So, Rabbi Kibbitz put a free advertisement in the Yiddish newspaper and hoped for the best.

Every day he went to the post office to see if there was an answer, but every day he was disappointed. He didn't dare tell the Schlemiels. Why worry them? They were busy with the babies. Besides, who knew what would happen at the last minute?

Finally, the night of the *bris* arrived. It was a strange event, even for Chelm. Usually, circumcisions were scheduled in the family's home during the day when there was plenty of light, but in this case the ceremony would have to be performed by candlelight. Since the Schlemiels' house was so tiny, the rabbi had argued that with all the guests (the mother alone had six sisters, six aunts, and at least thirty-six cousins) the synagogue's social hall would be a better setting. Now, in those days candles were expensive, but

---

*It has been noted by scholars that the circumcision ceremony is traditionally performed during the day. Furthermore, since the new Jewish day begins at sunset it would make better sense to perform one bris before sunset and the other just after. However, and this is an important point, word had reached Rabbi Kibbitz that, on the very day that the Schlemiels were born, the territory that included Chelm had been traded by the king of Poland to the czar of Russia for fifteen pounds of caviar and two boxes of Cuban cigars. Ultimately, the rabbi thought that for legal reasons it was crucial that the boys be circumcised on the appropriate days according to the Prussian and the Russian calendars.

everyone in Chelm was glad to bring a candle or two with the promise of one of Mrs. Chaipul's delicious *bris* brunches. Chopped liver, corned beef, pastrami . . .

Rabbi Kibbitz wiped a speck of drool from his lips. He was hungry. He was also nervous. So far, there was no spare rabbi. Perhaps at the last minute . . .

But it was not to be. Rabbi Kibbitz waited outside the shul until five minutes before midnight. At last, wearing his best and most confident smile, he went in to perform this most delicate of duties.

The two boys were held, one in each of their grandfathers' laps. He gave them some wine to quell their cries and set his instruments on the table. Rebecca Schlemiel nearly fainted right then, but her mother propped her up.

"You know," Rabbi Kibbitz said to Jacob, "as the father, it is your duty to circumcise your sons, but you may delegate this duty to me. Under the circumstance, perhaps you could do one and I could do one."

Jacob Schlemiel nodded solemnly, then his eyes rolled up into his head and he fell to the ground with a crash.

"It was just an idea," said Rabbi Kibbitz. He shrugged and began the procedure as Jacob was quickly revived.

But which one should be done first? Which was Adam and which was Abraham? Did it even matter? He had to pick one to start, so he chose the one on his right.

A moment later, the baby began to scream, and the rabbi gave him another sip of wine.

Now, on to the second. Perhaps he could try something a little different . . .

"Oops," the rabbi said.

The town of Chelm gasped. "Oops?" Rebecca Schlemiel screamed.

Jacob collapsed to the ground again.

"Relax! Relax!" Rabbi Kibbitz shouted, quelling the near riot. "Nothing's wrong! They're both the same. That's what the 'Oops' was. I couldn't do it differently!"

Of course, in the chaos, the babies were switched once again, and not even Rabbi Kibbitz could tell which was which.

So, one was named Abraham and one was named Adam, but it would be many, many years before anyone in Chelm could tell the difference.

Chapter Three

Termites on the Brain . . . After Dark

To say that Jacob Schlemiel went temporarily insane after the birth of his twin boys might be overstating the matter. The poor man certainly had a breakdown. His spirit, which had been as strong and as straight as a nail, was bent. It was as if the mule pulling his wagon down the road of life had suddenly kicked him in the head.

You couldn't really blame him. Jacob had been raised as an only child, which was a rare thing in those days. So, rather than growing up in an atmosphere of barely restrained chaos, he had grown up in a house that had been quiet and calm. His late father had been a great scholar, and Jacob's earliest memories of his mother were the soft hushing noises she made when he cried. In his parents' house, everyone spoke in a soft whisper.

It had, in fact, come as a complete surprise to Jacob's parents when he'd taken up carpentry. "How can you stand the racket?" his father had asked after he had confiscated the wooden mallet five-year-old Jacob had borrowed from a childhood friend. Eventually, the racket had gotten so bad (and Jacob's love of banging so great) that they'd been forced to send him away from Chelm for his apprenticeship.

Jacob couldn't explain that the noise was something that his heart and ears longed for. The pounding of nails into wood, the harsh rasp of the saw, the repetitive burr of the plane . . . They were as calming to Jacob as a chapter of Talmud was to his father. He especially loved early mornings, when he unlocked the quiet carpenter's shop, picked up a hammer, and began whacking away with unrestrained glee. The instant transition between silence and din was delightful.

Children, however, were another matter entirely. Hammering at least was under his control. The inconsolable screams of two hungry babies with wet diapers were more than the poor man could stand. For one thing it never ended. No sooner was Abraham fed and cleaned than Adam was filthy and hungry. Jacob barely slept a wink at night. Even when the babies were calm, there were dishes to clean, laundry to do, and dinner to make.

Rebecca, bless her soul, was still flat on her back from the effort of twelve hours of childbirth. And of course she had to feed the twins herself, a task that took far more energy than Jacob could imagine.

You would have thought that one or two of her six sisters or six aunts or dozens of cousins might have been able to lend a hand from time to time, but not all of them lived in Chelm, and the ones who did had families of their own to care for. The grandmothers tried to help, but that was mostly during the day. He could see the feverish look of relief on their faces when he came home from work. The two of them were out the door almost as soon as he took off his coat. So, not only did the carpenter spend a good ten hours a day making the finest furniture for all of the villagers of Chelm, he spent an additional fourteen hours a day taking care of the boys.

"If I could fill the bags under my eyes with gold," he joked to a customer, "I could retire a rich man."

Actually, it was a wonder he survived those first weeks with all his fingers. One day, while hammering together the shelves of a bookcase, he actually dozed off in mid-blow. He only woke up when the hammer landed on his foot. He didn't dare use his largest two-handed saw for fear of lopping off Jacob's arm.

Jacob's day-to-day existence faded into a numbing blur. One morning he woke up, put his pants over his head, dumped a pan of scrambled eggs into his shoes, and didn't notice until he got to work, reached into his pocket for his keys, and found he was still wearing his nightshirt. An ordinary man might scream in frustration at such an occurrence (or conclude that he must still be asleep, having a nightmare from which he'd soon wake up). Jacob Schlemiel shrugged, pulled the keys out from the pocket next to his ear, and went into his shop as usual.

For the first few months, his friends and customers didn't say anything. They knew that Jacob was suffering, but the transition between no children and children was something they'd all been through themselves. Yes, having children was difficult, one of the hardest adjustments of their lives. But you got over it. You got used to it. You muddled through.

It was when Jacob presented Reb Stein, the baker, with a brand new work table that only had one leg that they began to worry. Even a two-legged table might have worked, if it could have been nailed into a wall. But the single leg was in the middle of the table. Reb Stein raised his eyebrows and started to object, but Jacob had fallen asleep on his way out the door. (As it turned out, the table actually worked quite well as a kneading board. Reb Stein gave his four apprentices a huge ball of dough, and they made quite a game of trying to keep the table from tipping onto their side while pushing it over to somebody else's.)

But not all of Jacob's new creations were so successful. The milking stool with the legs sticking up from the seat, for instance, could only be used upside down. And the dowry chest he made for Reb Cantor's oldest daughter, Leah, had seven lids and no walls. Jacob tried to explain that he intended it that way—so that it could be opened from any angle, but Reb Cantor knew that the poor man was blithering.

Still, the villagers of Chelm were nothing if not polite and patient. They knew that sooner or later Jacob Schlemiel would get the hang of living and working and taking care of himself and his newly expanded family. They could wait for their carpenter to return to normal.

But one afternoon, Reb Levitsky, the synagogue's caretaker, pushed on the door to Jacob's shop and was surprised to find it locked. He knocked and peered in the windows, but the shop was dark and silent. Perhaps one of the children was sick. He decided to stop by the Schlemiel house and try to cheer them up with a song.

It was a warm day, so the door to the house was slightly ajar when Reb Levitsky arrived. Inside the house he found Rebecca standing by the stove, stirring a pot of stew.

"Shh, the boys are asleep," she whispered.

"It's good to see you're feeling better," Reb Levitsky said. "Is Jacob napping also?"

"No," she said. "He should be at his shop."

"But I just came from there," said Reb Levitsky. "The door was locked."

"Didn't he leave a note?" Rebecca asked. "He always leaves a note. I wonder where he's gone . . ."

"Don't worry," Reb Levitsky said. "He probably went for a walk."

"Of course," Rebecca agreed. Now that she was feeling better, she had to get the house in order and care for the boys. She didn't worry until it got dark.

During the warm light of day, it hadn't seemed possible that something unfortunate might have happened to Jacob, that he might vanish forever into the foggy wilderness that surrounded the small village of Chelm. No, after Reb Levitsky had gone, she had remained quite calm, stirring her stew and taking care of Abraham and Adam. But then the sun went down. And Jacob was still nowhere to be found.

At night, when there is no moon and the sky is full of clouds, Chelm grows very dark. If you wandered away from the soft glow of hearth fires, lanterns, and candle lights the night became as black as the bottom of a dry well that has been sealed by a boulder. No one went out after dark without a lantern. You might trip over your own shadow. You could walk ten yards from your house and never find it again. And the only lantern the Schlemiels owned was at home with Rebecca and the boys.

When it was time to light that lantern Rebecca started to panic. She had waited long enough. And now she couldn't escape the thought that her Jacob might be lost somewhere in the woods, hurt and helpless.

Chelm is not a very large village. In fact, the civilized portion is quite small. Surrounding the motley collection of well-kept houses, well-swept huts, and a few well-loved businesses is a thin ribbon of cleared farmland, and surrounding the farmland is the Schvartzvald. The ancient Black Forest made a wonderful setting for scary stories told in front of a warm fire on a midwinter's night, but in truth the forest was a fearful wilderness that a man could disappear into without a trace.

Perhaps Jacob had gone into the Schvartzvald to cut some wood. Usually he bought his wood from a woodcutter, but maybe he needed something special, a wide board for a table, or a particular length of branch for a chair. Such trips were rare but not unheard of. If he had tripped over a tree root and dashed his head against a stone . . .

There were still bears in the woods. And wolves. Packs of wolves. Mothers told stories of those wolves to scare their children into behaving.

Rebecca had only to imagine Jacob lying unconscious on the forest's moss floor while one wolf sniffed at his feet and another licked at the small stream of blood oozing from his forehead! She gave a little shriek and immediately bundled the boys into warm blankets. She couldn't manage the boys and a lantern at the same time, so she left the lantern at home and carried one baby in each arm, feeling her way along the dark streets.

Chelm is not a rich city like Warsaw or even Smyrna, with street lights at every intersection helping late-night travelers reach their homes safely. No, in Chelm there was only one street light, directly in front of the synagogue. It was a well-known fact that if you lost something at night that was the place to look for it because everywhere else it was dark.

At last Rebecca saw the reassuring glow of the synagogue's street light. Someone was there, standing right next to the pole! She hurried closer, her heart lifting with every step.

"Jacob?" she said, a smile on her lips.

The man turned, and in an instant Rebecca's hopes vanished like a candle snuffed in the wind. It was only Rabbi Kibbitz, who was smoking a cigarette that he immediately dropped and began stubbing out with his shoe. Thin wisps of panic began to float like smoke through Rebecca's mind.

"I was enjoying the night air," the rabbi hastened to explain, "but I'm a bit afraid of the dark."

"Jacob is missing," Rebecca said. Abraham (or was it Adam) began to cry. She bounced him gently against her hip.

"Nonsense," said the rabbi. "Misplaced, perhaps. Lost, possibly. But missing? No. How could that be?"

If he wasn't in his shop, and he wasn't at home, and he wasn't here in the light, Rebecca asked, where could he be?

"Jacob has parents," the rabbi said, reassuringly. "He has friends. Perhaps he went to someone's house for a visit and has lost track of the time."

"But he didn't leave a note. He didn't tell me where he'd be."

"Child," the rabbi smiled sadly. "Sometimes a man needs to get away on his own."

"But whenever he leaves the house he always tells me where he's going and when he'll be back."

"Ahh," said the rabbi. "Then won't you feel foolish when you arrive back home to find him waiting and wondering where you've gone?"

"He's at home now?" Rebecca's face brightened.

"Of course," said Rabbi Kibbitz. "Have I ever been wrong?"

Actually, Rabbi Kibbitz was famous for being wrong, but no one in Chelm had the heart to tell him. And at that moment, Rebecca was so eager to believe everything was all right that she accepted the rabbi's statement at face value.

Streudel, But No Father

Together they hurried down the dark streets back to the Schlemiels' house.

In Chelm, one small house looks much like the other. After sunset, and without a lantern, who can tell one door from another? So, of course, Rebecca and the rabbi walked into one wrong house after another. It was a natural and common mistake, and the surprised neighbors tried their best to make the frightened wife and confused rabbi comfortable.

As was only polite, Rebecca and Rabbi Kibbitz accepted the offers of tea and strudel at the Golds', of Turkish coffee and cake at the Kimmelmans', and so on. In fact, so kind were the neighbors that (after a snack) each and every one offered to help Rebecca find her way home.

It was quite a parade that finally managed to find its way back to the Schlemiels' house. By then, Rebecca's stew was done, perfectly cooked and ready to be served. Since no one in Chelm could ever refuse a free meal, the table was set and the feasting began.

In their later years, Adam and Abraham claimed that evening was their first memory—the warmth of the fire, the laughter of the villagers, the smell of their mother's rich stew, and the underlying sense of terror and dread. Despite the false laughter and pretend good cheer, everyone in the house was terribly frightened. Jacob Schlemiel was still not home.

And, one by one, as the hour got late and the guests made their apologies and got up to leave, each and every visitor had the same unbidden notion.

"What a wonderful party," they thought. "It's too bad Jacob's not here."

One good thing did come of the celebration. With all the excitement, with so many neighbors taking a turn playing with Adam or bouncing Abraham, the boys slept soundly.

Rebecca was not so fortunate. She stood by the window, looking out into the dark night and whispering prayers until the glow of the morning sun began to rise.

CHAPTER FOUR

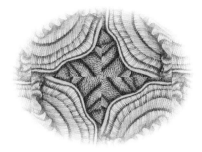

Gossip . . . Coming Home . . . Found Father

Three days passed, and there was still no sign of Jacob Schlemiel. Where was he? That question was on the lips of every man, woman, and child in Chelm. When he'd been late for the birth of his first child, everyone had laughed. "He's just gotten lost again," they'd joked at first. "He probably turned left when he should have turned right." Now that he'd been missing for three days, it wasn't funny any more.

You see, in Chelm, nobody gets lost for very long. It's not a big place. When a child runs away from home, he usually gets only as far as Great Uncle Mordechai's house, where Tante Nora feeds him cookies and milk until he decides to go home for a nap. But Jacob Schlemiel's Tante Nora and Uncle Mordechai had emigrated to America long ago. So where was he?

Chelm is nestled in a valley. To the north are two small round hills that are known on maps as West Hill and East Hill, which the townsfolk some-times call Sunset and Sunrise. A small stream meanders west of Sunset, down the valley, and through the farmland, skirting the edge of the village. An offshoot of the great Bug River, this shallow brook makes a somewhat revolting gurgling and coughing sound that gives it the name Uherka.

Jacob could be in The Schvartzvald, but that was one possibility, not to be seriously considered. Even though visitors to Chelm saw the forest as a bleak and blighted place filled with wolves, bears, and snakes, at least during the daytime, most of the time, it wasn't really so bad. The Black Forest is an integral part of the community. Its wood is used to build houses and furni-ture and bowls. And from spring until the first snow of winter, the forest's

23

dark moist ground is a glorious source of delicious wild mushrooms, which everyone in Chelm loves to eat. Besides, the Schvartzvald is not so big. You can see as much on the map. If you walk for an hour or two in any one direction, you're bound to come to a road.

There are only two roads in Chelm. The Smyrna Road goes north between Sunrise and Sunset, through the Schvartzvald, to Smyrna. The Great Circular Road is more mysterious. It heads east into the Schvartzvald, but it is such a long and twisted path that no one in Chelm is certain where it ultimately leads. Anyone who sets off on a journey down that road eventually gets disgusted with the endless forest scenery, turns around, and comes back. Everyone in Chelm knows that if you happen to be lost in the woods and come to a road, all you need to do is take a left and keep walking. Eventually you'll come back to the village. Jacob Schlemiel ought to have been able to find his way home by now.

While Jacob was missing, Rebecca Schlemiel showed her neighbors what a strong and determined woman could do. Not only was she feeding and caring for the boys; she had also taken charge of the rescue parties.

The searchers had looked everywhere. They had gone to the tops of Sunset and Sunrise. They had walked along the banks of the Uherka. They had even formed a human chain and arm in arm walked through the forests. If Jacob had been lying unconscious, as Rebecca had feared, they would have found him.

Rabbi Kibbitz sent word to Rabbi Sarnoff of Smyrna, and Reb Cantor inquired with his suppliers. Farmers talked to the cart drivers. Even the wandering peddlers were asked if they'd passed a lost carpenter. The world was not so big. Someone should have seen him. But no one had.

The gossips in Mrs. Chaipul's restaurant talked of nothing else.

"He's not dead," said Reb Gold, the cobbler.

"How do you know that?" asked Reb Stein, the baker.

"Because," answered the cobbler, "you don't hide yourself under a rock to die like a bug. Everyone I know who's dead, they died in their bed, walking to shul, or shoveling snow."

"That's the way most people go," agreed Reb Levitsky, the synagogue's caretaker.

"You think he was kidnapped?" asked Reb Shikker, the town drunk.

Everyone laughed. "What an idea!" "Ridiculous." "Who would want to kidnap a poor carpenter?"

"Who would want to kidnap anyone?" retorted Reb Shikker. "I'll tell you. In Gdansk a gang of thugs kidnapped ordinary men right off the streets and stole their livers!"

"Their livers?" Reb Stein raised a skeptical eye.

"Yes," Reb Shikker continued. "I suppose they had a taste for human chopped liver . . ."

"That is repulsive!" shouted Mrs. Chaipul. "I'll have no talk like that in my restaurant."

The men, still giggling, quietly apologized.

"It could happen," Reb Shikker insisted at a whisper.

"Shh," hissed Reb Gold. "Do you want to get us all banned from the only restaurant in Chelm?"

Reb Shikker glanced nervously at Mrs. Chaipul. "Can she do that?"

"Oh yes. Some idiot from Smyrna once claimed her corned beef was too dry and she chased him out with a frying pan."

"Besides," said Reb Levitsky, "we're ignoring the obvious. If Jacob Schlemiel is not lost, injured, or dead, only one thing's left."

"What's that?" Reb Stein asked.

"He's run off."

"Run off?" laughed Reb Gold. "Like a dog or a bird?"

"Birds don't run," said the baker. "They fly away."

"Whatever," answered the cobbler. "Jacob is a man, not an animal. He is married to a woman he loves, has a thriving business, and a beautiful new family. Why would such a man run off?"

"I'll give you two reasons," smiled Reb Stein. "Twins."

"What's the second reason?"

"Twins," Reb Stein said. "That's two reasons."

"Twins is only one reason," Reb Gold said. "Twins and something else, now that would be two."

"There are two boys," Reb Stein insisted. He held up his fingers. "Adam and Abraham."

"If you could tell them apart," said Reb Gold, "that would be two. But they look the same. So, I still say it's only one reason."

Reb Stein's face started to get red.

Reb Levitsky calmly raised his palms. "Friends. It doesn't matter. One reason, two reasons. What matters is that Jacob has not been himself since the boys were born. I am afraid he's had a change of heart."

Everyone nodded, except Reb Gold.

"What do you mean? A lovely wife and two healthy boys. Why would you run from that?"

"Joshua, you don't have any children."

"Not for lack of trying!"

Everyone laughed. The cobbler and his wife had only been married for six months.

"No! Children are a blessing. Esther wants five. I say ten. Twelve!"

"Have you lost your mind?" asked Reb Shikker, who had eight of his own. Reb Stein laughed and shook his head in agreement.

"He doesn't know," said Mrs. Chaipul from behind the counter.

"I don't know what?" said Reb Gold.

"Children change everything," said Reb Levitsky. "A blessing or a curse, wonderful or horrible, that's all a question of luck and how you look at it. What is indisputable, however, is that from the day your first child is born your life isn't the same. It is never yours alone again. And that's not an easy thing to accept."

"Especially," concluded Reb Stein, "with twins."

Meanwhile, not far from the restaurant, Rabbi Kibbitz had just broken the news to Jacob Schlemiel's seventy-two-year-old mother, Ruth, that her son was missing. He explained that he hadn't wanted to tell her sooner because he didn't want her to worry, but . . .

"Oy, that silly little boy," laughed Ruth Schlemiel. "I know just where he is."

"You do?"

"Yes." The old woman nodded. "And if he's not dead, I'll kill him myself."

A few minutes later, the old woman had teetered off, and Rabbi Kibbitz was eating a bowl of chicken soup and explaining the tale to everyone in Mrs. Chaipul's restaurant.

"She knows where he is?" Reb Shikker asked.

"So she says," the rabbi answered between slurps. "And no, she wouldn't tell me where. First she tells me she's going to kill him, and then she starts making him lunch. Seventy-two years old, she hops out of her chair like she's nineteen and begins cutting a salami."

"Ruth always was a good mother to Jacob," Mrs. Chaipul said.

"You think she really knows?" Reb Stein asked.

The rabbi shrugged. "I just hope she isn't deluding herself."

At that moment, Ruth Schlemiel was pushing open the door to her son's carpentry shop. "Jacob!" She shrieked. "Jaay-cob!"

In the tiny attic above the shop, Jacob Schlemiel's eyes popped open, and he sat up so suddenly that he smacked his head on a low rafter. "Ahh!" he yelped, muffling the sound by pressing his lips into his arm.

"I know you're up there!" his mother shouted.

He felt like he was ten again, cowering in fear from the old woman. Still, he kept quiet.

"Do you want me to come up there? I'm not so old I can't climb a ladder. Though my eyesight is not so good. I might miss a step and plunge to my death. Or even worse, I could lie on the dirty floor with a broken leg, screaming. But your shop is closed, so no one would hear me, so I would lie in sawdust and filth wondering if my every breath would be my last."

Jacob rolled his eyes but said nothing.

"The rabbi came to me today," Ruth Schlemiel said.

She set down her wicker basket and, after wiping off a section of the work table, took out a plate, the sandwich, and a slice of potato kugel. "He told me that my son hadn't been seen in three days."

As soon as the basket opened, Jacob began to smell the garlic of the salami and the sweet paprika scent of the still warm kugel. He'd been hiding in the attic for three days now and had long ago eaten up the few scraps of food he'd found littered around the workshop.

"I remembered that when my Jacob was just a boy, a cute little boy, whenever he was upset he would hide in the attic and pretend he was dead." She reached into the basket and found the jar of pickles she had packed at the bottom. "He was so quiet we never knew where he was until it was dinner time."

The sound of the pickle jar opening and the sour smell of the cucumbers in vinegar reminded Jacob of those days, so many years ago.

"Jacob," his mother said with a sigh, "am I going to have to come up there and look? Risk my life just to be certain that my little boy isn't dead?"

It was all too much.

"All right. I'm coming, I'm coming."

"Did I hear a mouse?" the old woman said. "Or could it be a rat nibbling on my son's bones?"

"I said I'm coming!" Jacob shouted. He yanked open the trap door, leaned out to repeat, "I'm coming!" and then fell six and a half feet onto a half-finished table, which collapsed with a crash.

"Are you all right?" his mother asked. "You fell."

"Ow!" he answered. She knew he was fine.

"Always with the dramatics," Ruth Schlemiel said, shaking her head but smiling inside. "Just this once you couldn't use the ladder?"

After Jacob had devoured the sandwich, the kugel, and the entire jar of pickles, he sighed and licked his lips.

"So?" his mother asked.

"Mama," Jacob answered.

"You still run away from your problems like when you were ten?"

The young man shook his head. "You don't know what it's like."

"I wasn't thirty-nine years old carrying a little baby named Jacob who screamed his head off for nineteen months with the colic?"

Jacob covered his face and rubbed his forehead. It was a story he had heard all his life. He was an unexpected child, born to a woman who had thought she would never have children. And he had been such a problem—crying, sickly—everyone thought he was going to die.

"I've got two, Mother," he said. "I know it was hard for you, but I've got two."

"You're only thirty-three. They're babies. They'll grow up. You can manage for a few years."

"It's not that," he said. Jacob grew silent. His mother opened her mouth and then decided to wait. She looked around the shop and thought about putting on her apron and taking a broom to the floor. No. For once, she told herself, sit still and be quiet. She waited.

At last, she could wait no longer. "So?"

"I'm afraid," Jacob said at last. His voice was soft in the dim afternoon light. "I'm a carpenter. I make things out of wood." He shrugged. "There isn't enough. When it was just Rebecca and myself, then I felt as if we could make do. But now I think about the boys . . . They're not eating much now, but in a few years it will be like living with voracious wolves. And what about school? And clothes. If you have two children in a row, then you can pass a jacket or shirt down from one to another, but we will need two of everything. And from what will the money come? Tables? Bookshelves? What can I make that everyone doesn't already have? How often does someone need a new table or a chair? Food. Clothes. Shelter. Those are things people need. If they have to, they'll sit on the floor or roll a rock inside."

"Jacob," his mother whispered. She put her hand on his shoulder.

He stood up and began pacing the room. "Already I hold the boys for eight hours, sleep for four, and work for twelve. Where can I get more money? And if I have that money, will I ever be able to rest? To catch a breath? To have a conversation with my wife?"

"So, you run away? You think that maybe you'll sneak out of your attic, go to Moscow, and forget about this family that you started?"

"I could go to America," Jacob retorted. "There is work there."

"Then you would never see your wife," Ruth said. "And you would miss the blessing of watching your two boys grow into manhood. You can run away if you want, but then you won't be able to see how good it is, enjoying the fine times and preparing for the difficult days to come. It's time for you to go back."

"Do I have to?"

"Yes."

"I know." Jacob nodded. "I know."

"Don't forget to say you're sorry. Then beg. If you're lucky, you'll only have to sleep under the table for a week."

Jacob smiled. "It wouldn't be any worse than sleeping in the attic." He wiped a tear from his mother's cheek and kissed her on the forehead. "Thank you, Mama."

Then he headed home.

Ruth Schlemiel smiled. Her seventy-two-year-old body felt warm and glowing. She looked around her son's shop and knew that, difficult though it might be, he would do well.

Then her eyes fell on the debris of his lunch and she clucked her tongue.

"Just once you couldn't clean up before you run off?"

The sun was setting into gloomy gray with the promise of a late overnight frost as Jacob arrived at the door to his house. His hand reached for the latch and stopped. What would he say to Rebecca? What could he say? For three days, he had vanished, hiding in the tiny crawl space of an attic above his carpentry shop. She must have been worried sick. How could he explain the panic that he'd felt and the thoughts he'd had during the long hours crouched in the dark?

He rehearsed his excuses . . . He'd been working on the oversized crib, planning to cut it in half and make two cribs! There was a piece of pretty burled wood in the attic that he would need to finish the project. He'd climbed the ladder and was searching for the hardwood when he'd felt tired. He'd only lain down for a nap, but the next thing he knew it was dark and he couldn't find the trap door without fear of falling down the ladder. Rather than risk certain injury, he'd decided to spend the night. It was so soothing to sleep uninterrupted by bawling and screaming. Late the next morning, he realized how comfortable he'd felt. The attic was cozy and quiet . . . So he'd just stayed there until his mother had come by to tell him it was time to go home. So, it was all very simple, straightforward, understandable even. But how do you explain that so your wife understands and forgives?

He stood, frozen on the doorstep of his own house, one hand reaching toward his family, but the rest of him inclined to run back to the attic. And he might have been there still if Rebecca hadn't opened the door and thrown a pail of dishwater and potato peels into his knees. (Chelm had no sewers; garbage was tossed into the street for the goats to eat.)

"Ahh!" Jacob yelped as the cold water soaked through his trousers.

"You!" Rebecca said, that one word both an expression of relief and a piercing accusation. She stared at him.

"I, uh . . ." Jacob's voice trailed off.

She wanted to scream at him. He wanted to hug her. They got to do neither because at that instant both boys began to cry.

Rebecca rushed to one, and Jacob to the other. They lifted the boys into their arms, held them tight, and together sang a lullaby, partly to soothe the babies, but mostly to try and drown out the twin's screams. It seemed to take forever, but eventually the tiny bedroom fell quiet as the boys dozed in their parents' arms.

Rebecca and Jacob stood beside each other. Tears ran down her cheeks.

"I'm sorry," he whispered. "I'm so sorry."

"I was so afraid," she said, her voice barely louder than her breath. "I thought that I had lost you. And that the boys had lost you. I've been frightened and sad and angry and outraged," she hissed. "And tired and alone. And finally I decided that if this was what God wished, then I would make the best of it. And then, as I planned our life without you, I found myself feeling stronger than I've ever felt in my life."

"I'm sorry."

"Shh." Rebecca scowled. "Don't be sorry for that. Tell me where you've been."

Jacob examined his boots for a moment, wondering if he could put down the boy and wipe them clean. Then he told her everything.

"Your Mamma sent you back here?" Rebecca said when he had finished. The scorn in her voice was so sharp he felt it bite into his chest.

"No," he said. "Yes. No. I was coming. I had already decided."

"Oh, so you decided now that you'd had enough of a vacation it was finally time to check in on your family?"

A dozen angry answers passed through Jacob's mind unsaid. Instead, he let his head drop and again whispered, "I'm sorry. I'm here now."

"Yes, I see that," Rebecca said. "The question is, do we want you?"

Jacob blinked.

"You see, we've been doing quite well without you," she continued. "The neighbors have been generous. I've even been offered a job by Reb Cantor, the merchant, when the boys are old enough to be on their own. Tell me, why should I allow you back into this house?"

In Chelm, there is a saying, "The wise man is silent when the fool is certain."

Jacob Schlemiel had no idea what this meant, but he knew that Rebecca needed an answer, and he had none. He would go back to his shop to live for a while, and then from there, who knew . . . perhaps to America?

"Who am I holding?" He looked at the babe in his arms. "Is this Adam or Abraham?"

"I don't know," Rebecca said, laughing a little. "I still can't tell them apart either. Why do you want to know?"

"Because if I am to leave, I want to tell him personally. I can't kiss the boy and say, 'Farewell, Abraham,' if it's Adam. Years from now, when he grows up, he would say, 'My father left me without even saying goodbye.'"

Rebecca looked at her husband, at the sorrow and remorse in his eyes. "Well then," she said. "I suppose you'll have to stay until we figure out which one is which."

"I suppose I shall," Jacob said. He kissed the sleeping boys on their foreheads. "Thank you, little ones."

Then he looked into the eyes of his wife, their lips inches apart.

"Can you forgive me?" he asked.

"No." She shook her head. "Not yet."

Jacob thought for a moment that his heart would crumble. This was his punishment. He knew men who lived without the love of their wives, but he'd never imagined that he would join their number. Perhaps some day she would look at him and know that it was love and devotion that had brought him back to their house. Until that day, he would have to make do.

"Please," he said, "let me know if you change your mind."

Rebecca felt angry. Did he really think that forgiveness came so easily? She could justifiably make him suffer for years. Who could blame her?

She shook her head and sighed. "All right. I'll forgive you."

"You will? Really?" Jacob was jolted with surprise. Then he asked, "When?"

"Now," she said, smiling just a little.

"Already? But I . . ."

"Shh." She leaned forward and kissed him—if only to quiet him and keep the boys asleep. "Some day, I'll ask you to do something for me to make you pay for this. No, I don't know what it is, but I'll think of something. Don't worry—it won't hurt. Now, set the boy down gently and let's get you out of those wet clothes . . ."

Jacob Schlemiel grinned with relief.

Of course, if he had known in advance the demand Rebecca was to make years later, he might have kept on his pants and run off to America that instant.

CHAPTER FIVE

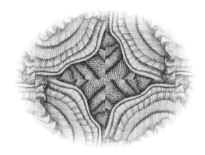

The Question Is Answered

So, when did Abraham and Adam Schlemiel begin to realize that they weren't the same person in two identical bodies? On the surface it seems like a foolish question (although in Chelm no question is considered too foolish to be asked), but from the time of their birth the twins themselves hadn't been too sure.

They were identical in every way. Their eyes, their lips, their ears, even the moles on their left elbows were in exactly the same place. They ate the same food, wore interchangeable clothes, and slept in the same crib because the moment their father tried to separate them they began to scream.

Not even their mother could tell them apart. When they were babies, she tried to keep Abraham on the left and Adam on the right. That might have worked, except Rebecca Schlemiel had an impossible time telling right from left. She'd set them down, turn around for a moment, and by the time she looked back, she felt certain that some impish demon must have switched the two boys.

When they were a year old, their grandmother Ruth suggested tying a piece of string around one boy's wrist. If only they'd thought of that sooner! It was decided that, as the oldest, Abraham would have the honor of wearing the bracelet. But have you ever tried to tie a string to a wriggling toddler? And five minutes after the string was secured, somehow it was gone. A new string was tied, but even in his sleep, Abraham managed to slip loose. That project was abandoned the morning that Jacob went to the crib and found both boys giggling happily with strings on all four wrists. This was but the first of many of the Schlemiel twins' pranks.

As they learned to walk they were inseparable. They stood up together, took three steps together, and fell down together. If one bumped his head, both howled. And they loved to climb. Everyone in Chelm got in the habit of saying, "Abraham, Adam, get down from that table . . . that chair . . . that book shelf!"

Every so often, Rabbi Kibbitz would pull one or the other aside and ask, "Are you Adam or Abraham?"

"Yes," the boy would smile. "I am."

It wasn't until the Passover after their fifth birthday that the boys themselves realized that they had something of a problem. You see, at the Passover seder it is traditional for the youngest child to recite the Four Questions. Abraham's and Adam's befuddled parents assumed that the boys would sing together. But everyone in Chelm, including the boys themselves, knew that Adam Schlemiel was twelve hours younger than Abraham—and therefore only he was entitled to ask the questions.

About a week before Passover, the arguments began.

"I think that I should say the Four Questions," said one boy.

"Me too," replied his brother.

"You think I should say them?" said the first. "Good!"

"No," answered the second. "I think I should say them."

"But I'm Adam!"

"I thought you were Abraham."

"You're Abraham."

"No, I'm Adam!"

It was the first time that they actually came to blows. Their mother hurried over to pull them apart.

"Abraham, Adam, stop that!" she said.

"I'm Adam!" both boys shouted simultaneously.

"You're Adam?" Rebecca asked the boy on her left. He nodded. "What about you?" she asked the other. "Are you Adam?" This boy nodded as well.

"Then where is Abraham?" Rebecca Schlemiel shouted in a panic. "I've lost my oldest child!"

Anywhere else such a reaction would have brought healing laughter into the room. In Chelm, however, such remarks are taken seriously. A search party was organized, and it was only after Adam and Adam had gone to bed that Jacob and Rebecca Schlemiel were relieved to count two sleeping boys instead of just one.

And the next morning, the search parties went out again as both boys denied being Abraham. This wasn't just malicious mischief. The truth was that neither boy was certain who he was.

On one level, they had always heard their names spoken together as "Abrahamandadam." On another level, they had sometimes answered to the individual names whimsically and indiscriminately. If Grandmother Esther offered Adam a treat, both shot forward, but if Grandfather Shmuel had a chore for Adam, neither responded. And sometimes, when neither punishment nor reward was offered, whichever boy was closest replied.

Even when they talked it was often simultaneous, both boys speaking like a Greek chorus, or with one finishing the other's sentence, as if they knew each other's thoughts completely.

It has often been asked, "When does identity begin? When does the child recognize that it is an individual and not an extension of its mother?" For the brothers Schlemiel, individuality came on the eve of that Passover seder.

The feast was held at Grandfather Shmuel's and Grandmother Esther's house. Only four of Rebecca's six sisters and their families were coming this year, so there was a little bit of elbow room at the table. Still, Rebecca and Jacob thought that it was best if the twins were separated on opposite sides of the table, to prevent kicks, elbows, and pinches from disrupting the service.

For his part, Jacob hoped that Rebecca's newest nephew, Moishe, who was by all reports a "remarkable and intelligent boy," would be able to recite the questions and thus avoid the impending conflict. Unfortunately, even if the boy was a one-year-old linguistic genius, Moishe was fast asleep in his mother's arms.

Rebecca was worried for a different reason. If both boys really thought that they were Adam, then might they not both grow up as Adam? Then what would happen to her oldest son, Abraham? Would he simply vanish as if he had never existed?

The early blessings and songs went smoothly. Hands were washed, wine was drunk, and the tale of the Exodus from Egypt began to unfold.

Grandfather Shmuel, as the leader of the service, was seriously considering skipping the Four Questions entirely. The last thing that he wanted was a long and drawn-out argument that made dinner come even later. He came to the page in the Haggadah and said, "Let's speed this up a bit and move along to . . . OUCH!"

Grandmother Esther had kicked him under the table. He looked at her, she stared him down, and he said, "All right. Fine. Who's going to read the Four Questions?"

All eyes turned to the twins.

"Maybe they both can read them together," said Grandmother Ruth.

"Or take turns," added Grandmother Esther.

"No!" both boys stood up. "Only one. The youngest reads the Four Questions."

Grandfather Shmuel rubbed his forehead and closed his eyes. Oy! He felt a headache coming on.

The room fell quiet. No one dared even to breathe. The two brothers looked at each other across the table, their faces carved in impassive stone. The candles flickered. The roast in the oven grew drier.

And then . . . without them saying a word to each other, it was decided.

Abraham sat down, and Adam remained standing.

They looked at each other again. A feeling of sadness filled their eyes with tears.

Abraham nodded at his brother, and in a voice sweet enough for two, Adam began to chant the Hebrew, "Mah nishtannah ha-lailah ha-zeh . . ."

In his seat, Abraham mouthed the words, but his voice was silent.

CHAPTER SIX

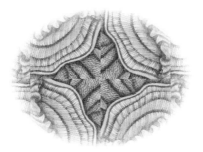

The Rom

Two years passed, and life in Chelm went on as usual until one evening . . .

They arrived after dark. No one saw them come. They quietly set up their camp in the village square. There were two wagons, three horses, and a mule.

The first person who noticed them was young Muddle, Reb Stein's nephew, whose job was to extinguish the gas lamp in front of the synagogue. He told Miriam, the egg lady, who told Deborah Shikker, who told her husband (the town drunk), and within an hour everyone in Chelm knew that an entire herd of wild elephants and lions had eaten Rabbi Kibbitz and was being subdued by Cossacks in the village square.

A crowd gathered.

"Where are the elephants?" asked young Avi Weiss.

"The Cossacks have gone," said Reb Cantor, the merchant. "Thank goodness."

"But what about the poor rabbi?" moaned Mrs. Chaipul.

Just then, a man's head peeked out the back of one of the wagons. He had short hair, tan-colored skin, and hooped earrings in one ear. He looked at the villagers, scowled, and withdrew. Everyone fell quiet.

Just then, Rabbi Kibbitz, still in his sleeping gown, arrived at a run. He had heard that the synagogue had been destroyed by a gigantic fire-breathing water buffalo. Naturally, the Chelmsfolk congratulated the rabbi on his daring escape, while he thanked them for quelling the inferno and rebuilding the synagogue so quickly. With order restored, the two painted wagons were soon forgotten and one by one people drifted home, to work, or to morning prayers.

Late in the afternoon, there was a knock on the door of Jacob Schlemiel's carpentry shop. The twins pushed into each other to answer.

"Are you the carpenters?" a little girl asked. She wore a bright red dress and had shiny brass earrings. Her head was covered by a beautiful silk scarf. Beside her stood a tall man with a long drooping moustache.

"We're not carpenters yet," said the young boys, who blushed and spoke together in one voice. "We're only seven years old. But we're learning."

"Who is it?" Jacob asked.

Both boys turned to their father. "A couple of Gypsies."

The man with the moustache hissed.

"Please." The girl said something to the man in a strange language. Then she said, "We are not Gypsies. We are the people of Rom. One of our wagons is broken, and we need some wood to fix it."

Jacob Schlemiel dusted himself off and came to the door. "There is plenty of wood in the forest."

"We need nails as well," said the girl. "And a hammer. And a saw."

"Reb Cantor's store sells those."

The girl did not answer.

"Papa," said the boys. "They need a carpenter."

"Ahh," Jacob Schlemiel said.

"No!" The man with the moustache barked. "The Kalderash need no one." He spun on his heels and departed.

The little girl looked uncomfortable. "Please. Come this evening to our camp. We have no money, but perhaps we can offer dinner at least." Then she turned around and ran after the man.

Jacob Schlemiel sighed.

"Will we go papa?" said one boy. "Can we?"

"Where are they from?" said the other. "Do you think he was her father or her uncle?"

"Abraham, Adam, shhh. Back to your chores."

For the rest of the day, nothing got done. The Schlemiels quit work early and went home to tell Rebecca the news. She immediately flew into a rage. She had spent all day preparing a delicious stew and now Jacob was telling her they were going out for dinner! He couldn't have told her sooner? Look at her clothes, what would she wear?

"You look beautiful, Mama," the boys said.

Rebecca patted their heads and then snapped at Jacob, "Do they even keep kosher?"

"I didn't have time to ask," Jacob said.

"How can we eat with them if we don't know?"

"It would be rude to refuse. Why don't you bring the stew along?"

"If I bring the dinner they promised you, then how will they pay for their work?"

"I don't know!" Jacob answered, exasperated. "How often do strangers come to Chelm, knock on the door of my shop, and ask for my help? We're not so poor we can't spare a piece of wood, some nails, and few hours of our company."

Rebecca smiled. "If I'd wanted fame, I would have married an actor. If I'd wanted riches, I would have married the merchant. Instead, I married you."

Jacob's face drooped. "Are you disappointed?"

She shook her head and kissed his cheek. "Not at all."

A half hour before sunset, the Schlemiels left their house. Jacob carried the stew pot, Rebecca carried the lantern, and the twins carried the wood and tools. When they arrived at the village square, they found that the quiet scene of two wagons, three horses, and a mule had transformed into a colorful camp, with three small fires, bustling men and women, laundry blowing in the breeze, and a dozen or more barefoot children running after two yapping dogs and a pig.

Rebecca saw the pig and nudged Jacob.

"So?" he said. "It's alive. At least we know we're not eating that one for dinner."

They were met at the edge of the camp by the little girl, who introduced herself as Rosa. As she led them toward her wagon, she apologized for her father. He was the duke of Kalderash, she explained, a proud man.

"What of your mother?" Rebecca Schlemiel asked.

"She is with God."

"I'm sorry," Rebecca said.

"Oh, don't be," Rosa answered. "I talked with her last week and she said that she is very happy there. Heaven is a wonderful place, and she said that she'll welcome me herself when it is my time."

"Ahh," Rebecca nodded. She didn't say another word.

It was an awkward meal. Rosa's grandmother had prepared a huge feast of bread and cheese and vegetables. The stew pot sat to the side, untouched. (Rebecca had decided that it would be insulting to mention it.) While Abraham and Adam were delighted at the way the Kalderash family tore off pieces of thin bread and used it to pick up their food, Rebecca was horrified.

"Ask if they have a fork," she whispered to Jacob.

"Hush," he said. His eyes widened as the duke pulled a large curved knife from his belt, which he stabbed into a hunk of cheese before handing it, hilt-first, to Rebecca.

No one said much of anything after that. The sun set, and they ate a sweet baked dessert in the flickering firelight and dim glow from the street lamp.

The boys wandered off to play with Rosa, and Jacob took his tools and the lantern and vanished into the back of the wagon with the duke to examine the damage.

Rebecca found herself left alone by the fire with the old woman.

"That," Rebecca said, talking loudly and slowly, "was delicious." She patted her tummy and smiled.

"I understand your language." Rosa's grandmother answered. "Give me your hand."

"Why?" Rebecca hesitated.

"I shall tell your fortune."

Rebecca Schlemiel extended her right hand. The old woman took it roughly. She peered at it in the dim firelight, examining first the palm, then the back.

"Give me the other one," she said. Her voice had the ragged rasp of a life-long smoker.

"Maybe I shouldn't," Rebecca said. She ran her fingers over the back of the hand the old woman had touched, as if checking to be sure everything was still there.

"Are you afraid?"

She hadn't been, but now she was. What good was knowing the future? If all was to be well, then that would be revealed in time. As would evil.

How could knowing the future be of any use? It would only cause worry and anxiety.

"No," Rebecca said. "I'm not afraid, I just . . . I don't believe in fortunes."

"The seventh daughter of a seventh daughter does not believe in fortunes?"

"How did you know that?"

"What sort of a soothsayer would I be if I could not recognize a fellow seeker of sooth?" The old woman smiled. Remarkably, she had all her teeth, though most were stained yellow and chipped.

Rebecca felt her heart beating rapidly.

"I see you doubt me even now." The old woman's eyes narrowed. "Tell me, when your husband vanished for a time so many years ago, were you worried?"

"Of course I was."

"But not for long. Because you saw. You saw that all would be well."

"I didn't know where he was. It was terrifying."

"Of course it was." The woman chuckled. "Fate must jar us from time to time. How else would we learn who we are? Do you think your coming here is an accident? There are no accidents."

"My husband came to fix your wagon."

Rebecca glanced over the old woman's shoulder. The door to the covered caravan was closed. Jacob had been in there for quite some time, and she hadn't heard the sound of his hammer or saw. The boys had been playing nearby with the old woman's granddaughter, Rosa, but Rebecca could not see them. Instead, she only heard the sounds of the fire and a man at another campfire playing a sorrowful tune on a strange stringed instrument.

All at once, the space surrounding the camp seemed to close in upon her. Was she really still in Chelm? Could this all be happening in the village square, within shouting distance of the synagogue? To escape she needed only to stand and run. It was but a few hundred yards to Reb Cantor's house and only a short distance beyond that to her cozy home.

She did not move. Nor did the old woman.

At last, Rebecca extended her left hand. Once again the woman seized it. She squinted at it, back and front, only a glance really. Then she held it firmly and stared into Rebecca's eyes.

"You have two boys," the woman began. "They are the same. And yet they are different."

Oy, Rebecca thought, she's telling me the obvious. This is what I was afraid of? She rolled her eyes.

The old woman squeezed her hand harder.

"They look the same. They are the same. And yet they are of different countries. They have different lives. Different futures."

For a number of years, Rebecca had known that the twins, born twelve hours apart, did not share the same nationality. Abraham was Polish and Adam was Russian. It was a quirk of fate that the title to Chelm had been transferred to Russia from Poland at that exact moment. How did the old woman know?

But she went on. "One will be a cook, the other a carpenter. One will travel, one will stay. There is a woman. One will run. Vanish. One will live on in Chelm, the other will go."

"What do you mean?" Rebecca asked.

The woman shook her head and droned on. "The older is not one but two. The younger . . . one day here, the next gone."

"Now, you're scaring me," Rebecca said. "Stop it."

But the old woman would not let go. "And yet from one comes two. The years have passed. The lost son returns, but the son who has vanished has never left. They come together. One becomes two—different, and yet the same."

"You're babbling," Rebecca said. She yanked her hand away, and the old woman let go. "You're just saying things to sound important. I'm sorry that I came. I enjoyed your dinner, and as soon as my husband is done repairing your wagon, we will have to go."

"You know what the strangest thing is?" The old woman looked puzzled.

"No," Rebecca snapped. She stood up and brushed off her dress. "And I don't want to know."

"Suit yourself," said the old woman. She leaned forward and poked a stick into the fire.

Now that she was standing, Rebecca saw the twins playing tag with Rosa near Chelm's sole street lamp. They were handsome boys, seven years old. So innocent, so gorgeous. How could the witch try and scare her like that? Yes, from time to time Rebecca, like any mother, had wondered and worried about the day that her boys would leave her. But to hear of it so suddenly and with such mystery . . . She would put it out of her mind.

She paced back and forth. The sounds of Jacob's hammer from inside the wagon reassured her.

The old woman picked her teeth with a fingernail.

Rebecca looked away. Nonsense. It was all nonsense. She should just forget about it. And yet . . .

"What," Rebecca asked at last, "is the strange thing?"

"Are you sure you want to know?"

Rebecca snorted. The old woman laughed.

"The woman," she began softly. "The wife. She both comes between them and draws them together again."

"What nonsense!"

"Her name. Would you like to know? It is Rebecca."

"Phooey!" Rebecca spat. "That is my name."

"I know," said the old woman. She laughed louder and louder. "That's what's so strange!"

Rebecca Schlemiel spun around, wanting to strike the old woman, to silence her, but the sudden movement made her feel dizzy. She sat down for a moment and rubbed her forehead.

The next thing she knew it was morning and she was in her own bed.

"What happened?" She sat up suddenly. "Where are the Gypsies?"

"The Rom?" Jacob answered from the kitchen. "They left this morning. You were very tired last night."

"That old woman," Rebecca said, the words nearly a curse. "She told my fortune."

"The queen?" Abraham and Adam said simultaneously.

"What?"

"She was the queen," they said. "The queen of the Rom."

"What did she say?" Jacob asked.

"Nonsense," Rebecca said. "Utter nonsense."

Still, she gathered her two boys up and hugged them close until at last they wriggled away.

"Nonsense."

CHAPTER SEVEN

Growing Pains

Eight-year-olds can be such trouble makers. Although the twins knew who they were, Abraham and Adam Schlemiel did their best to keep everyone else guessing. For example, they made a habit of never going into a room at the same time. Abraham would enter - first, and then Adam, or the other way around. Then Abraham would duck out a window or another door and come in again. They could keep this up for an hour or more, until everyone else's head was spinning.

Now, in any other city, this sort of nonsense would never be tolerated. Unfortunately, the villagers of Chelm had notoriously short memories, something that the brothers played upon mercilessly. And as they got older they got better

On Friday mornings, for example, Rebecca Schlemiel would send the boys to the bakery for the Shabbos loaf of challah and two sweet rolls for them to share. Abraham would enter the store and Adam would lag behind, lingering beneath a beech tree.

"Good morning," Reb Stein would say. Then he would playfully scratch his head. "Are you Abraham?"

"No," the boy would fib. "I'm Adam."

"You're not tricking me, are you?" Reb Stein would shrug. "One day I will find you out! "The usual?"

A nod. "The usual."

Then, the baker would reach for a challah for the mother and two sweet rolls for the boys. Abraham would gather up the bundle and trundle off.

A few moments later, Adam would enter the store.

"Good morning," Reb Stein would say. "You must be Abraham!"

"No," the boy would say. "I'm Adam. I need to pick up our order."

"Weren't you just in here?"

"No. Every week I come for our bread. Maybe you're thinking of my brother."

"Ahh well." Reb Stein would shrug. "One day I will find you out! The usual?"

A nod. "The usual."

Again, Reb Stein would reach for a challah for the mother and two sweet rolls for the boys. This time, Adam would gather up the bundle and trundle off.

The boys would stuff themselves with sweet rolls and bring two challahs home to their mother. Rebecca, who was embarrassed by Reb Stein's charity, always gave the second challah to a pauper or some tradesman to whom money was owed.

Thus, everyone was happy—even Reb Stein, who knew that no matter how many challahs he had baked, one was always mysteriously taken up to heaven as an offering.

The twins were also masters at avoiding chores.

As in most households, the everyday work that no one really wanted to do was divided up among all of the members of the family. Early on, Rebecca and Jacob agreed that the boys needed to work in order to help things run smoothly and to learn responsibility.

Abraham was given the task of making the beds and sweeping the kitchen. Adam was given the jobs of throwing the garbage into the streets for the goats to eat and watering the garden. Both boys were responsible for cleaning their own chamber pots and fetching water from the well.

Emptying a chamber pot is a difficult thing to forget to do, but making a bed or watering the garden are the sorts of tasks that can slip anybody's mind. Whenever Rebecca was angry at the boys for neglecting their chores her brow would knit into a frown and the color in her face would grow as red as a ripe cherry. As soon as they spotted her coming in a rage, one of the boys would duck under the bed or hide behind the pickle barrel.

"Abraham!" Rebecca would roar. "Why didn't you sweep the kitchen?"

"I'm Adam," the boy on the bed would answer, regardless of the truth.

Rebecca would spin around in a rage. "Where is your brother?"

Usually, the other boy was right under her nose muffling his snickers with a hand across his mouth.

Then, Rebecca would turn on the sole visible son.

"All right, Adam," she would say, trying to be patient. "There is garbage from yesterday in the kitchen and the garden is as dry as a desert."

"Why are you telling me this?" The imp sitting on the bed would look puzzled. "I'm Abraham." Under the bed the other one would be holding his side, barely suppressing his guffaws.

Rebecca's eyes would go wild. She would sputter and puff. "Fine!" she'd shout. "I'll do it all myself!" Then she would turn on her heels and vanish in a fury.

If only her anger had diminished a little sooner, her head would have been clear enough to hear the chorus of gleeful laughter behind her. But by the time she realized anything was amiss, the boys had slipped out and she was once again left alone to tend to all the household tasks.

Now, you shouldn't think too badly of these boys. They didn't mean to be wicked or dishonest. They were youngsters and it is as much the job of a child to escape duty and learn the boundaries of rules by breaking them as it is the work of a parent to establish limits and lay down the law. The villagers of Chelm were kind, understanding, forgiving, and often completely ignorant that they were being made fools of. As a result, though the twins suspected that they were pulling stunts and engaging in trouble that was not quite kosher, no one ever managed to pin them down and clearly explain the difference between right and wrong.

But, you think, they surely must have learned that it is a sin to tell a lie. And when Abraham said he was Adam or Adam said he was Abraham, the boy making the claim must have known he was not telling the truth. You would think. But if that were so, then the story of the brothers Schlemiel would be far shorter and much less interesting than it really is. Besides, although they had chosen their identities on that Passover evening so many years earlier, both Abraham and Adam knew that on some level the decision had been somewhat arbitrary. So, with the logic and precision worthy of the greatest legal minds, the boys assumed whatever identity was most convenient for them at that particular moment. They were happy and everyone else was confused and more than a little frustrated.

It wasn't until the arrival of the new schoolteacher that the boys found their inventiveness severely tested . . .

A New Teacher ... The Plot ...
The Demon Is Banished

Rumors had it that the new schoolteacher was nine feet tall and as thin as a fence rail. They said his hair was as red as a blacksmith's fire and that his beard was striped, red and white, like a barber's pole. They said his smile was a snarl, his laugh a cackle, and his sneeze like opening a door into a raging thunderstorm.

The children of Chelm knew all of this without having met him. And they were all terrified at the prospect that this half-human half-demon was about to become their new schoolteacher.

"Why can't we study with Rabbi Kibbitz the way that you and Grandfather did?" Abraham and Adam Schlemiel asked their father.

For a moment, Jacob Schlemiel smiled faintly at the memory of the doddering chief rabbi of Chelm trying in vain to control a room full of rowdy, screaming, laughing, shouting youngsters. Then it occurred to him that he was a parent now, and that kind of chaos was exactly the sort of behavior he didn't want from his children. "Rabbi Kibbitz is too old," Jacob said. "Rabbi Abrahms will be a fine teacher."

"But the new teacher is an ogre," said Abraham.

"A monster," added Adam.

"A lunatic madman!" they said as a chorus.

"Stop!" Their father raised his hands. "How dare you speak ill of a stranger. After all, it is because of you that Rabbi Abrahms has moved to Chelm."

Both boys looked at their boots in shame. It was true.

Newly ordained, Rabbi Yohon Abrahms had been scouring the newspaper's help wanted ads in search of a position when he learned that the village of Chelm was in urgent need of a *mohel*'s services. He immediately pawned all his possessions and spent his last kopek to catch the fastest train to Chelm. Of course, it is a rare train that comes anywhere near Chelm, so after arriving in Minsk, Rabbi Abrahms was forced to travel by goat cart through Pinsk to Smyrna, and from there walk. Or rather run. After all, in Jewish tradition, the circumcision must be performed on the eighth day following a birth, and it had already taken Rabbi Abrahms seven days just to reach Smyrna!

At last, exhausted, hungry, and broke, he arrived at the synagogue, knocked on the door, and breathlessly told Reb Levitsky, the synagogue's caretaker, that he hoped he wasn't too late to circumcise the twins. Naturally, this troubled Reb Levitsky, since at eight years old the Schlemiel twins were already more than half way to bar mitzvah age. It wasn't until Rabbi Kibbitz arrived and Rabbi Abrahms showed them the tattered clipping that they began to understand.

It was such a typical misunderstanding. Rabbi Kibbitz had simply forgotten to tell the newspaper when the advertisement was to expire, so it had been running every day for eight years.

"Ah." Rabbi Abrahms looked dumbstruck. The poor young man was shattered. "Then it's all a mistake? I don't belong here. I'll go. I'm sorry for bothering you."

With that, Rabbi Kibbitz and Reb Levitsky broke into broad grins, clapped the young rabbi on the back, and shook his hand firmly. "Welcome to Chelm!"

Rabbi Abrahms looked confused, so Rabbi Kibbitz explained.

"Anyone who comes to Chelm on purpose we assume is lost," Rabbi Kibbitz said. "Only those fortunate few who arrive by accident are welcome to stay and make their homes here. After all, is it not written that 'the lost are found and the found are lost?'"

"Is it?" Rabbi Abrahms asked. "Where? I don't remember."

"It must be written somewhere," Rabbi Kibbitz answered, offhandedly. "Nearly everything is."

"Ahh!" Rabbi Yohon Abrahms's face broadened into a wide grin. All his life he had searched for a wise teacher to study with, and now purely by chance he had found him!

So, over a nice chopped liver sandwich at Mrs. Chaipul's restaurant it was settled. Rabbi Abrahms would take over all the duties that Rabbi Kibbitz was getting too old for. He would teach all the children at the yeshivah; he would lead the early morning services when there was snow on the ground; he would become the new *mashgiach* (making sure that all the meat served in Chelm was kosher); and since they had promised it in the advertisement, he would become the village's new *mohel.*

"Unfortunately, you're a little late," Reb Levitsky whispered while Rabbi Kibbitz settled the restaurant bill. "The last boy Rabbi Kibbitz performed a circumcision on is a double amputee."

Rabbi Abrahms looked horrified.

"I'm kidding!" Reb Levitsky burst out laughing. "Welcome to Chelm. We have the biggest sense of humor in all of Russia."

"I thought this was Poland," Rabbi Abrahms said.

"Poland, Russia, Austria, Russia, Poland, China, who can keep track? We pay our taxes, they leave us alone." Reb Levitsky knocked three times on the wooden table.

Now, all of this had occurred at the end of the growing season when the harvest was beginning, and naturally school was not in session. Rabbi Abrahms found himself busy building a house to live in and tramping around the countryside from farm to farm examining the cattle, chicken, ducks, and goats for impurities.

All of this activity was debilitating. Yohon Abrahms had been born and raised in a city. What little he knew of farming and house building could have been written on the back of his left hand in chalk and then washed away. So, instead of rising with the sun and greeting the morning with prayers, he slept. And on Saturdays, when most of the village was in the synagogue welcoming the Sabbath with prayers, he slept.

And so it happened that at the end of the summer, when it came time for school to begin again, the children of Chelm realized that none of them had ever actually seen their new schoolteacher. Was it possible? How could anyone living in a village as small as Chelm escape their notice? Did he even exist? Perhaps he was a demon, hiding during the day, coming out only at night, and biding his time. Yes, that was it. He was a demon, waiting for the right moment when he would devour an entire schoolchild whole!

"Father, you must understand," Abraham said. "Since it is our fault that

Rabbi Abrahms is here, it is up to us to make things right."

With a serious face, Jacob Schlemiel listened to his boys' fears.

"Don't worry," he said, stroking his beard thoughtfully. "There are two of you. If he is a demon and he eats one, the other is bound to escape."

Their young eyes widened in terror. Jacob Schlemiel winked, but his sons were too afraid to understand that the wink meant he was kidding. This was not the first time that the famous Chelm sense of humor resulted in unexpected consequences, but it was one of the more dramatic. Because, it was right then and there that Adam and Abraham Schlemiel decided that, since no one else was going to, they needed to take care of the demonic schoolteacher themselves—if only to save the village.

In every couple there is a leader and a follower. One has the idea, and the other reluctantly agrees. One is more cautious, the other impulsive. So it was with the twins, Abraham and Adam Schlemiel. Adam made all the trouble, and Abraham (who as the older brother felt it was his duty to be responsible) took all the blame. Or so it seemed most of the time.

After their long conversation with their father, Adam wondered aloud what would happen if the tea kettle's spout was plugged with a potato. What, you may wonder, does this have to do with the heroic plot Adam devised to rid the schoolchildren of Chelm of their demonic teacher? Well, Adam convinced Abraham to steal a potato from the root cellar. They waited until their mother went to the market, and then they pressed the potato onto the kettle and blew on the coals. The kettle first hummed, then vibrated, and finally shook like a goat gone mad. The two giggling boys ducked underneath the kitchen table. Then there was an awesome explosion. The potato shot out of the kettle and blew a hole in the roof.

"Oy!" Adam shouted with glee. "Did you see that?"

"See that?" Abraham said. "There's rain pouring into the kitchen."

"I know, but it was like a gun."

Just then, Rebecca Schlemiel returned home. She was already dripping wet and had been looking forward to sitting down for a nice hot cup of tea in front of a warm fire. She saw the pool of water forming on the kitchen floor and began screaming.

"Who did this? Who is responsible?"

Silence. There was nothing but the steady dripping from the roof on the damp wooden floor.

"You want to tell me, or do you both want to suffer?"

Glumly, Abraham stepped forward and received a long and heartfelt tongue-lashing. He was responsible for cleaning the floor, emptying the buckets, and patching the roof. He would also, his mother said, move his bed underneath the leak so that he would learn the value of sleeping under a roof at night. Abraham nodded, lips tightly pressed together, and agreed. Adam stood silent, a few steps behind his brother, and wondered if he shouldn't have taken the blame instead.

It is well known in mystical circles and even in the scientific community that some phenomena cannot be explained. So, although Abraham took the responsibility, Adam only appeared to escape the suffering. The truth was that even though they lived in two different bodies, the twins shared their discomfort equally. And not just punishment. Both pain and pleasure were, from time to time, transferred from one of their bodies to the other. When Abraham tripped over a log, Adam felt the bruise grow on his knee. If Rivka Cantor pulled Adam's hair, Abraham winced and felt his head jerk sideways. Once, when Adam had stolen a blueberry strudel and eaten the whole thing himself, Abraham (who was working in their father's carpentry shop at the time) had found himself grinning a blueberry smile, which was unfortunately followed by a severe stomachache. This wasn't something they had ever discussed. Why should they? At the age of eight, they simply assumed that everyone shared pleasure and pain evenly.

So, although Abraham went without dinner that evening, he felt nourished every time Adam took a bite. And, while Abraham slept soundly in the puddles, Adam, whose bed was as dry as the bottom of Red Sea when Moses and the Israelites fled from the Egyptians, somehow felt that his hair was soaking wet and his skin felt cold and damp.

Unable to sleep, Adam stayed awake thinking. The idea came three hours before dawn.

"Abraham."

"Glug."

"Take your head out of the puddle."

"What?"

"We can't kill him, right?"

"Huh? Kill who?"

"The schoolteacher," Adam reasoned. "He's a demon. You can't kill demons."

"That's true, but they say he's only half a demon. We could kill half."

"No," Adam shook his head. "Chickens run around after their heads have been cut off. I don't want to think about what a demon might do."

"So," Abraham said, wiping rain from his eyes, "when school begins, he'll eat us one by one and eventually Chelm will become a village with no children."

"But I know what we can do!" Adam said. "What do demons fear most of all?"

"The master of the universe," answered Abraham with certainty.

"Yes, that's true," Adam agreed. "But I was thinking more of humiliation. Think about it. In every story I've heard about demons, the only way that the people win is by making a fool of the demon. So, that is what we have to do."

"Is that all?" Abraham asked.

"Yes."

"Can I go back to sleep?"

"No! We have to make more plans. School starts next week. We have to drive the demon out of Chelm, or else we'll all be doomed!"

"Uh huh.

"Doomed!"

Abraham rolled over. Even his blankets were sopping. "I heard you the first time. But, in all the stories, the demons are fighting with grown-ups. We're just boys. How can we possibly outwit a demon?"

"You forget that we live in Chelm, the center of wisdom in all of Poland."

"In all of Russia," Abraham countered.

"If the demon was from Chelm, we'd be in trouble. But isn't it said that the youngest baby in Chelm is as wise as the oldest sage in Warsaw? We are going to be nine years old next spring. Surely we can outsmart one feeble demon."

"Yes!" Abraham agreed. He was beginning to feel excited by the prospect. "I think you're right. So, what shall we do?"

"What is the most humiliating thing you can think of?" Adam asked.

"Playing tag with Rachel Cohen when she wins."

"Good one," Adam said. "More humiliating."

Abraham thought for a moment. "The time I had an accident in my pants in synagogue and had to stand there for two hours knowing that everybody was watching."

"Yes," Adam said. "Closer. Now, think of something that would be even worse."

"That was pretty bad," Abraham shuddered. "I can't think of anything worse."

"It's when people laugh at you. When everybody laughs at you."

"Sure," Abraham nodded.

"Naked."

"Naked?"

"No clothes. Not a stitch. Maybe a yarmulke."

"Wait a moment," Abraham said. "You're suggesting that we get the entire village of Chelm to laugh at the demonic schoolteacher naked?"

"Exactly!"

Abraham shuddered. "I don't think I want to look at Rabbi Kibbitz or Mrs. Chaipul without their clothes on."

"Not the villagers," Adam said. "The schoolteacher. Just the schoolteacher would be naked."

"Oh. That's all right." Abraham nodded. "But how are we going to do that?"

"I don't know, yet." Adam shrugged and then shivered. Although his nightshirt was dry, it still felt wet . . .

"Wait," both brothers said it together. "I know!"

And they laughed and plotted until dawn.

Getting the schoolteacher naked turned out to be easy. Their plan worked perfectly. On the very first day of school, Abraham stood on a chair while Adam sat on his shoulders to balance the bucket filled with water on the partially opened classroom door. Then, Adam tied a short rope from the bucket's handle to a nail above the door. The other schoolchildren giggled with barely suppressed glee.

The schoolteacher would open the door and the bucket would fall and drench him, but not bash him on the skull. Humiliating a half-demon was one thing, cracking its head open was another. They wanted to embarrass the monster into running away from Chelm, not enrage it enough to destroy the village.

Their major concern was that the new teacher might be wearing his broad-brimmed hat as he opened the door. In that case, most of the water would be diverted onto the floor.

"One of us will have to wait outside," Adam said.

"But then he'll know," Abraham argued.

"By then, it'll be too late. He'll vanish in a puff of smoke."

"We hope." Abraham knocked three times on the wooden door.

"Careful!" The bucket wobbled but did not fall.

"Is everyone else in the village coming?" asked Rachel Cohen, the first girl who had ever been admitted into the formerly all-male school.

"They'll be here." Adam nodded. "Everything is timed out to the last moment."

"Hsst! He's coming!" hissed Rachel's brother, Yakov.

Abraham looked at Adam and then sighed. "You know, as long as I'm going to get blamed, I might as well do the deed." Adam nodded. They shook hands solemnly. Then, Abraham squeezed out a window and ran around to the front of the synagogue, just barely catching up to the new schoolteacher.

As he got closer, Abraham started to feel puzzled. Rabbi Abrahms looked rather normal and harmless, like a skinny young man. Ahh, Abraham realized. It's a perfect disguise.

"Good morning, Rebbe."

The schoolteacher looked surprised. "Good morning, ahh . . ."

"Adam," Abraham lied, smiling. "Adam Schlemiel."

"Ahh," Yohon Abrahms said. "So, you're one of the boys who brought me to Chelm. I trust your *bris* went well."

Abraham blushed. He couldn't think of anything to say, so he just nodded and kept walking. But at least now he was certain the "rabbi" was actually a demon. After all, what kind of a man would ask a boy such a thing?

Abraham looked over his shoulder to see if the villagers were gathering to watch the spectacle. But the village square was still empty. Where was everyone?

Not far away, the breakfasters in Mrs. Chaipul's restaurant were in heated discussion about a note Mrs. Chaipul had found that morning nailed to the door of her restaurant.

"A demon?" Reb Cohen, the tailor, scratched his head.

Reb Gold, the cobbler, shrugged. "That's what the note says. 'The demon will be driven from the synagogue at nine o'clock sharp.'"

"Nonsense," said Reb Cantor, the merchant. "There hasn't been a demon in Chelm for generations."

"How would you know?" Mrs. Chaipul asked. "Is there a regulation that visiting demons must receive your approval?"

Reb Levitsky laughed a sip of warm tea through his nose and then promptly began a sneezing fit.

"No." Reb Cantor looked hurt. "But wouldn't the demon seek to corrupt the richest man first?"

"Or the poorest," said the cobbler, glumly.

"Why not the wisest?" said Reb Cohen. "After all, why should a demon visit Chelm but to destroy the wisest of the wise?"

Mrs. Chaipul looked worried. "Do you think Rabbi Kibbitz is in danger?"

The restaurant grew quiet and serious.

"Perhaps," said Reb Cantor at last, "we ought to go and find him."

Throughout the small village, dozens of notes were being found, variations on this conversation repeated, and similar conclusions drawn. Coats were thrown on, bootlaces tied, and all at once, the citizens of Chelm converged on the village square.

Just outside the synagogue, in front of the booby-trapped door that led into the school, Yohon Abrahms stopped suddenly. He barely noticed as Abraham Schlemiel bumped into his leg.

The young rabbi shivered. Me, a schoolteacher?, he thought. He had never felt so nervous in all his life. It was a cold autumn day. He rubbed his hands together and blew into them to get warm. He told himself, if I am to become a wise and respected schoolteacher, then I must make a strong and powerful first impression. I must not be afraid. He drew a deep breath and stepped forward.

"Rebbe!" Abraham said. "Your hat . . ."

"Thank you, Adam." Just as he reached the door, Rabbi Yohon Abrahms removed his broad-brimmed hat and then stepped inside.

The first part of the plan was going perfectly. The door opened, the bucket tipped, the icy water spilled, and the schoolteacher was soaked!

"The demon!" one of the excited children shouted.

Yohon Abrahms, the new schoolteacher of Chelm, was stunned.

"Quick! Out of those wet clothes," said Adam Schlemiel, trying to sound just like his mother. "Hurry, hurry, before you catch your death of cold."

Without thinking, the poor young rabbi obeyed, shedding his clothes even as his teeth began to chatter.

"The demon, the demon!" the chorus of schoolchildren chanted.

Slowly the words began to penetrate the rabbi's frozen brain. A demon? In his school. Where? Even as he poured the water from his boots and slid his wet trousers off, hopping first on one foot and then the other, he scanned the room. He saw nothing aside from a gaggle of frightened and shocked schoolchildren.

Using his most commanding schoolmaster tone, he bellowed, "Where is this demon?"

"Outside!" Abraham and Adam Schlemiel replied. "Outside!"

So, without a stitch of clothing, the brave rabbi turned and rushed back out into the square.

There he came face to face with the entire assembled village of Chelm. There was a gasp.

"Have you seen the demon?" Rabbi Abrahms shouted.

"No!" they answered as one.

"What demon?" someone asked.

"I didn't see a demon."

"It's gone!" someone else said.

"Then it's gone," Rabbi Abrahms said. "It must have flown away."

Inside the classroom, Abraham and Adam Schlemiel were jumping up and down with joy.

The villagers began to cheer. "The demon is gone! It has fled. Rabbi Abrahms the pure has chased the evil demon away!"

An instant later, amid cheers and song, the stark naked schoolteacher was lifted off his feet and paraded through the village as a hero.

All the other children ran after the crowd, leaving behind a worried Abraham and a confused Adam.

"What happened?" Adam asked.

"I don't know," Abraham answered. "But we'd better clean up."

Just then Rabbi Kibbitz walked in the door. He looked at the bucket dangling on its rope and at the pile of damp clothes on the floor.

The Demon is Gone

"I see that there was at least one demon in Chelm this morning." His ancient voice creaked. "Maybe two."

The Schlemiel brothers stood as still as statues, their faces as white as marble.

"I trust those demons have been banished," the old man continued, "and that they will give Rabbi Abrahms no more trouble?"

Adam and Abraham nodded their heads. "Yes, Rebbe."

"Good," said the rabbi. "And in honor of your new teacher, Rabbi Abrahms, and his accomplishment in facing such a terrifying ordeal naked, I believe that you both will happily volunteer to clean the classroom every day this year."

Abraham and Adam nodded their heads again.

"Good," said the rabbi. "Very good."

So, much to their mother's surprise, every day after school Abraham and Adam Schlemiel could be found clapping out the erasers, washing the blackboards, emptying the garbage, and scrubbing the floors. And, after his defeat of the demon, Rabbi Yohon Abrahm's position as the second wisest man in Chelm was secured forever.

CHAPTER NINE

Separation Time . . . Adam Alone . . . In the Black Forest

Jacob Schlemiel yawned. "It's getting late."

Late? Abraham and Adam Schlemiel exchanged looks. The sun had barely risen in the sky, and they had only been in their father's carpentry shop for a few minutes. As always, it had still been dark when their father had wakened them with three short knuckle raps on the forehead. ("To knock the knotholes out," he always joked.) They had dressed, done their chores for the day, eaten breakfast, stumbled out of the house, and opened up the shop all before dawn. How late could it be?

As if on cue, Mordechai Blott, the village timekeeper, bellowed the hour, "Three o'clock in the afternoon!"

"You see," their father said. "Before we know, it will be dark again."

Adam and Abraham rolled their eyes. Outside, the ground was still moist from the dew, and their more well-to-do classmates in Chelm's small school would only just be getting out of bed.

It is said that time is money. Money was always a problem in Chelm, so was time. Wealthy towns like Smyrna could afford to indulge in fanciful construction projects, like a railroad depot and a central clock tower. Such expenses were unthinkable in Chelm, where brainpower was in greater supply than gold.

For centuries the villagers had relied on hourglasses. At sunrise, the head of the house would turn the glass over and the day would officially begin. If you said to someone, "I'll meet you five hours after sunrise," you'd bring a book and read a few chapters until he arrived. It was a pleasant and relaxing system, unless your meeting was outside and it was raining or snowing.

When word reached Chelm about the invention of the minute and then the second, life in Chelm was transformed. All of a sudden, these new increments added precious moments to every day. It was one thing to nap for an hour, but to spend sixty minutes dozing seemed so frivolous. And if you broke that into seconds—thirty-six hundred seconds—think of the waste!

The villages became obsessed with time. Everyone wanted a clock, but timepieces were too expensive. So, Jacob Schlemiel's grandfather Adam had seized the opportunity. "Tick tock, tick tock," he'd said. "A couple of gears, a few wheels, a ratchet or two, how hard could it be?" And, with no plans whatsoever, he began construction.

His first clock was the size of a small barn. Not only did it count the seconds, it shouted them out in four languages—Hebrew, Yiddish, Russian, and Polish—simultaneously. Tourists traveled for miles to listen to the din and watch the twelve-foot-long second hand spin around and around at unbelievable speed. Day and night the clock bellowed the exact time, so that everyone in Chelm lying in their beds awake knew exactly how much sleep they were missing. No one, including the inventor, was particularly upset when the thing inexplicably burst into flames and burned to the ground.

Having learned from his mistakes, the next clock Jacob's grandfather built was a masterpiece of simplicity. It was a small device, about the size of a musk melon, had no moving parts, and made no sound. In fact, the second hand didn't even move because it was painted onto the clock's face. The odds of this clock keeping anyone awake or bursting into flames were minimal.

"But does it tell time?" the villagers asked.

"Pff," answered the master clockmaker. "Clocks never tell time. People tell time."

"Ahh," the villagers nodded. "Then what time is it?"

"It's now," Abraham Schlemiel said wisely.

This new system worked perfectly for more than a generation. No one in Chelm spoke of tomorrow or yesterday or even lunchtime. There was only now. They ate now, they slept now. They worked now. It was amazing how much got done, and at the same time how little got done.

Then one day, the present Reb Cantor's father returned from Moscow with a cartload of clocks.

"They were factory seconds," he explained. "Such a deal I got." And he sold them for a small profit to every household in Chelm. Now everyone had a clock of his own, but none of them kept the same time.

Smyrna had solved this problem by building a huge clock tower in the center of town. The villagers of Chelm knew that it would only be a matter of time before this building would burst into flames and explode, so rather than waste their money on construction they devised another plan.

They pooled their resources and hired Mordechai Blott to become the village timekeeper. His job was to count the seconds, add up the minutes, and call out the hours. If Reb Blott called out two o'clock and your clock said it was seventeen minutes past two, then you knew you were running fast.

Reb Blott was zealously dedicated to his job. He bragged that he never missed a second. Every night, he made a specific point of remembering the exact second at which he fell asleep, and every morning he picked right up at the next second the moment he woke up.

It might have been unsettling to see the sun rise at ten-thirty one day and four in the afternoon the next, but no one had the heart to fire Reb Blott. As long as they ignored their clocks everyone kept more or less the same time, and within a few years, they got used to the situation. After all, given enough time people can get used to just about anything.

All of this is a very roundabout way of explaining why Jacob Schlemiel was certain that it was getting late, while Adam and Abraham Schlemiel were equally certain that since it was not even midday there was plenty of time left before dark. So, as children often do when their parents say or do something that is patently absurd, they laughed to themselves, shrugged, and went back to work.

They were nearing the completion of a fine oak chest that Reb Cantor had commissioned Jacob to build as a gift for the new provincial governor. It was a beautiful piece of furniture—seven-sided and with ten legs. "It should be unique," Reb Cantor had ordered. And so it was. Jacob had even specified that it should be finely polished on the inside, while the outside remained rough and splintery. "You keep valuables inside a chest like this," he planned to tell Reb Cantor, "not on the outside."

Then, all of a sudden, Jacob smacked his head. "Adam!"

"I didn't do it!" Adam said quickly.

"Do what?" Jacob asked, his eyes narrowing.

"Nothing. Nothing."

"Good," Jacob said slowly. "Adam, I need you to go to Smyrna. Go to the coppersmith's shop and pick up the brass clasp that I ordered last month. It's a good thing I remembered it. What good is a chest for valuables if you can't lock it shut?"

Brightening at the thought of a nice walk on a pleasant spring day, Adam and Abraham set down their hammers and reached for their coats.

"Not you, Abraham. Just Adam."

Abraham looked puzzled. "But, Father, we always go together."

"You heard me," Jacob said. "Adam will go by himself. I need someone to go to Smyrna and bring back the clasp, and I need someone to stay here and help me."

"But," Abraham said, "we've never been so far apart."

Jacob smiled and nodded. "Then it is time you were."

Adam, his heart filling with pride at the thought of being sent on such an important mission, grinned widely, crinkled his nose at his brother, and was out the door before another word could be said.

Abraham jumped as the door slammed shut. Through the window, he watched as his brother dance up the road and out of sight.

"Come on," Jacob said, putting a hand on his older son's shoulder. "Let's go back to work. It's getting late."

Abraham nodded quietly. He didn't know what he felt, and he wasn't sure he could explain it, perhaps because it was the first time in his life he had felt frightened and alone.

Two farmers stood on the outskirts of Chelm, leaning against their rye rakes in the late morning sun.

"There go the Schlemiel brothers on the Smyrna Road," said one. "Running as usual."

"What brothers?" said the other. "I only see one."

"It's a trick of the light," said the first farmer. "If you squint, you can see them both."

The second farmer squinted. "Ahh yes. In fact I see three!"

"Hmm," said the first farmer. "I wonder if their mother knows."

Completely alone perhaps for the first time in his life, Adam Schlemiel found himself enjoying this newfound sense of freedom. He ran, he jumped, he twirled in mid-air. Then, he caught his foot on a rock and stumbled head first in the dirt. But nobody saw. When he got up and looked around, the laughing, mocking face of his twin brother Abraham was nowhere to be seen. His mouth opened into a wide grin and he howled at the clear blue sky like a wild animal.

"Yip Yip Yip! Yooooh!!"

"What are you yelling about?" Jacob Schlemiel barked angrily at Abraham. "When I'm about to saw a board the last thing I need is for you to howl like a wild animal so I lose maybe a finger or three."

Abraham was just as surprised as his father at the strange yapping noise that had emerged from his mouth. Not only that, but the palms of both his hands smarted.

"Nothing, Papa," Abraham said. "I was just thinking of Adam."

"Well, stop thinking of him and go back to your sanding and polishing. Some day you'll inherit this business and you need to pay attention to the details."

"Yes, Papa," Abraham said, glumly.

It isn't far from Chelm to Smyrna, maybe ten miles by road. Still, it is not a journey that is taken on a whim, since the road twists and winds through the heart of the Black Forest. During the daytime, the Schvartzvald wasn't so bad. Just a lot of trees and leaves and the occasional chipmunk.

But after dark, the stories said that the woods were transformed into the kind of nightmarish place where wolves howl, bears prowl, and woodcutters abandon their poor defenseless children to wicked witches in gingerbread houses.* Not only that, there were thieves, brigands, robbers, and cutthroats who lurked in the shadows ready to leap out at the least provocation. In

---

*Actually, the villagers of Chelm originally had a different story. In the Chelm version, two wicked children, Haimy and Gittel, ate a house that their grandmother had made out of mandlebread, and they got stomachaches. The Brothers Grimm heard the Chelm tale, changed the names, and made the grandmother into a witch. The revised story was so scary that the villagers promptly believed it and never made mandlebread houses again.

other words, even if you knew your way around, it wasn't the kind of place you wanted to spend the night.

Adam Schlemiel should have been home in plenty of time. Even though he left his father's shop at three in the afternoon Chelm time, he managed to reach Smyrna shortly before lunch. He went straight to the coppersmith's shop and bought the brass clasp that his father had said would be waiting for him.

His errand accomplished, Adam then did what any normal boy will do when left to his own devices—he went looking for food. The marketplace was nearby, and he had a wonderful time wandering up and down the crowded streets, nibbling first on a loaf of bread, then a chunk of cheese, an early apple, an orange all the way from Spain, a piece of halvah, a chunk of Turkish candy, a bowl of chicken soup with matzah balls, half a chicken roasted with garlic and herbs, a baked potato with fresh black pepper and salt, and some more Turkish candy followed by a gallon of water drunk from the town well. With the sun still high in the sky, Adam smiled, patted his belly, and lay down on the side of a grassy hill just outside the marketplace for a nap.

"Abraham, wake up!" Jacob Schlemiel yelled, shaking his son by the shoulder. How was it possible for a nine-year-old boy to doze off in the middle of hammering? One moment he was banging away, and the next moment the hammer had fallen to the ground and the child was snoring like an elephant. "What's the matter with you? Wake up! Hey! Hey!"

"I don't feel well," Abraham mumbled, clutching his stomach.

"It can't be food poisoning," his father said, "because you didn't eat a thing your mother made you for dinner. Come on, get up. Walk around a little."

But despite Jacob's prodding, the boy would not be moved. His eyes closed, his chin fell against his chest, and he was out cold once again.

Jacob put his hand on his son's forehead but felt no fever. Then he shook his head, picked up the hammer, and began whacking away. Eventually the noise would rouse the boy.

The sun was just going down when the sound of a woodpecker roused Adam from his slumber. The marketplace was already shut up. The streets of Smyrna were nearly empty. It was time to hurry home. With luck, he would get back to the shop just as his father was closing up for dinner.

He jumped up, patted his pocket, which held the brass clasp, and started walking. But which way should he go? Smyrna looked so different in the twilight. Even worse, all the roads looked the same. From Chelm there were only two roads, the Smyrna Road and the Great Circular Road. But Smyrna was a big city. There were at least six roads leading away from the marketplace.

That was when Adam Schlemiel realized that he was lost. And it was getting dark. And cold. And he had spent all of his money on the brass clasp and the food that he had eaten for lunch without saving even a crust of bread for dinner.

"Don't panic," he said to himself. "Just ask Abraham what to do . . ."

But Abraham was in Chelm, now lying safely in bed with the stomachache he had gotten from Adam's lunch.

At first, Adam tried to stay calm. He didn't panic. He ran back and forth, up and down the streets of Smyrna, trying to find a landmark, something that would point him in the direction he needed to go to get home.

Every passerby on the street he asked, "Excuse me, can you tell me where the Smyrna Road is?"

But no one knew. It was as if the people of Smyrna had never heard of the Smyrna Road.

"Where are you from?" one kind woman had asked.

"I'm from Chelm," Adam answered.

"Oh," the woman smiled. "You want the Chelm Road."

"No, thank you," Adam said. "There's no Chelm Road in Chelm. Only the Smyrna Road and the Great Circular Road."

"Silly boy," the woman began. "From Chelm, the road is called the Smyrna Road, but from Smyrna it is called the Chelm Road."

Adam ran away from her, certain that she was a witch trying to trick him into her gingerbread house. Finally, exhausted and frightened, he threw himself down on the hillside where he had napped and began to cry. He sobbed and he sobbed until at last he felt a soft and gentle hand on his shoulder.

"Adam, are you all right?"

Adam looked up and saw the face of a young girl.

"Rosa?"

"I don't know what's the matter with the boy." Jacob Schlemiel had been watching Abraham carefully. "One moment his stomach hurts, the next it's fine. One moment he's crying like a baby, and the next he's got a smile on his face like he's met a long-lost friend."

"Why didn't you send both of them to Smyrna?" Rebecca whispered angrily.

"They're nine years old. Old enough to go their own ways for once. I thought I might get some work done. It was a mistake."

Rebecca Schlemiel nodded as she and her husband stared out the window into the darkness.

"Tag!" Rosa said. "You're it." And then she took off at a run.

Adam Schlemiel grinned as he chased after her through the woods. Never mind that the Schvartzvald was quiet and creepy. Never mind that it was after dark and a full moon was rising in the sky. Even when thin branches whipped by his cheeks, and he heard the howl of a wolf in the distance, his smile never faltered.

He trusted Rosa. She said that she knew a shortcut, a secret way through the Black Forest that would have him home in time for dinner. And she was a Gypsy princess, so she should know such things.

Just ahead of him, Rosa laughed and dodged around a large boulder. Adam hurried to catch up. She was fast and clearly knew her way through the woods after dark. But Adam was as fit and fleet as a hunting dog in its prime. Even though he stumbled and tripped, slowed by the shadows and the underbrush, he knew he would catch her at any moment. His smile grew broader with the anticipation.

But the next instant Rosa was gone. Vanished—as if whisked from the face of the earth. Where was she? Adam continued to run, peering ahead. Had she hidden herself behind a tree or fallen over a cliff? Maybe this was a trap. Now he remembered the rumors he'd heard about Gypsies, that they were witches and did magic. Rosa hadn't seemed evil. She was just a young girl, around his age. But perhaps this wasn't really Rosa but a demon luring him deep into the woods to eat him. Had she led him somewhere to kill him? Adam slowed as he felt the panic begin to rise in his stomach.

Then something soft wrapped around his foot. Adam stumbled and fell, sprawling head first into a pile of soft leaves and moss. He jerked his leg free and was about to shout when a thin hand clamped over his mouth.

"Shhh," Rosa whispered. Her face was close to his.

"Brrfrum," Adam said, his words muffled by her palm.

"Shhhhh," she insisted.

Something urgent in her shushing told him to stop for a moment, catch his breath, and wait. If he needed to, he could always fight her. If nothing else, he could peel her fingers away and scream.

"Shh." Rosa took her hand away and held her finger to her lips. Then she pointed to her ears. Listen.

So he listened. That's when he heard them. Footsteps. Hooves.

There was something out there—and not far ahead. Adam squinted and saw three men leading their horses through the woods. Two of them were cursing the third loudly.

"He's heard of a shortcut," said one. "A quicker way to Chelm. 'We'll be there in no time,' he said. 'We'll steal everything in town and be gone before dawn.' Of course Alex Krabot, the great criminal mastermind, has no sense of direction, so here we are lost in the woods . . ."

A second robber giggled.

"Shut up, Dimitri," said the third thief. "Do you hear something?"

All three men stopped. Their horses began to graze at the leaves. Adam and Rosa held their breaths. A horse whinnied.

"Alex, you think it's a werewolf?" said the second thief, clearly terrified.

"Bertie, there are no such things as werewolves," said the first one. "Now, vampires, ghosts, and demons, maybe . . ."

"Shut up!" hissed the third, and he slapped both of the others across their cheeks.

Adam winced at the sound. Then his heart began to pound. That was why Rosa had stopped him. These men were bandits, maybe murderers. They planned on sneaking into Chelm and robbing everyone of everything! If they heard him, they would surely kill him.

"Who's there?" shouted the third thief, who was clearly the leader. "Who's out there?"

Rosa made a hoot like an owl.

The leader's head spun, listening.

The first robber said, "Alex, it's just a bird."

"Oww," said the second. "That hurt."

The leader waited another moment, nodded, and then the three men and their horses continued along their way.

Rosa and Adam lay very still for a long time after the men had gone.

Then Adam leaped to his feet. "They're going to rob Chelm!"

"I know," Rosa said. "I'm trying to think."

"But there's nothing in Chelm to steal!"

"I know," Rosa said. "And when they find that out, they're going to be angry. And angry men do stupid things."

Chelm was a peaceful village. Three men with guns and swords could hold the entire town hostage—or worse.

"What are we going to do?" Adam asked.

"We need help," Rosa said.

"What about your family?" Adam asked. "Are they nearby?" It was funny, he thought, only a few minutes earlier he had been afraid that Rosa was leading him to her family's stew pots. Now he hoped that the Gypsies might be close enough to offer assistance.

"No." Rosa shook her head. "They are in Minsk."

"Your family is in Minsk and you're here? You're just a girl."

"In my family, when you reach a certain age you must spend some time alone. It's a long story."

Adam sat down on a rock. "Then my village is doomed."

Rosa put her hand on his shoulder. "Don't give up. Not yet."

"What can we do? It's a long way back to Smyrna. We're so not far from Chelm, but the bandits are between us and the village. Even if we could get home in time, the only weapons my people have are rakes and shovels and scissors." Adam felt despair rising in his heart. When he had thought himself lost in Smyrna he had been afraid, but that was only fear for himself. Now he worried for the people of his village.

"You still have a brother?" Rosa asked. "Abraham?"

"Yes, of course."

"You are twins?"

"Yes," Adam snapped. "What about it?"

"Do you ever talk to him without talking?"

"What do you mean?" Adam began, but then he fell quiet. He couldn't believe he had forgotten! He pursed his lips and then told Rosa, "Yes, sometimes Abraham and I talk without talking. Or at least we used to. How did you know?"

"Among my people," Rosa nodded, "twins are often very close. Can you call him now?"

"I don't know," Adam said. "When we were very little, it seemed as if we were the same person. But now . . . This is the first time we've ever really been apart. I don't know . . . It's so far."

"You must try." Rosa took Adam's hand. "Close your eyes. Think of your brother. Call to him."

"All right. Quiet, please."

Abraham! he thought. *Abraham! Can you hear me?*

"It's not working. I can't hear him."

"Shh," Rosa said. "Be patient. Close your eyes. Don't hold your breath. Listen for Abraham. Picture him. Feel his breath."

Adam sighed. He shut his eyes and took a deep breath.

Abraham . . . Abraham . . .

Less than three miles from where Adam and Rosa sat, Abraham Schlemiel sat at the dinner table; his eyes were closed as he prayed for his missing brother's safe return.

Adam . . . Adam . . .

Then his eyes snapped open.

"Mother, Father," Abraham said, his voice firm. "Trouble is coming."

CHAPTER TEN

Thieves, Caught

The robbers arrived at dawn. Alex Krabot, Bertie Zanuk, and Dimitri Dimitriovich, known from Yalta to Yaktusk as three of the deadliest bandits in Eastern Europe, had planned to appear in Chelm just after sunset the day before. Unfortunately, they had been delayed in the woods. First they were lost. Then there were the mysterious sounds. Then a shower of acorns, as if the squirrels themselves were defending their territory. So, instead of three terrifying figures on horseback riding mysteriously out of the dusk, the three men stumbled into the small village in the early morning, tugging on the reins of their exhausted nags, and cursing.

"Alex, where is everyone?" asked Bertie. "You think the spirits of the forest told them we were coming?"

The streets were deserted. The farms they had passed were empty. They had peered into several windows and had seen no one.

"Maybe they're in church," Alex Krabot said. "You know these Jews, always celebrating or mourning something."

"I think they call it a synagogue," said Dimitri.

Alex shot him a murderous stare, and the bandits continued to search the village for signs of life.

Meanwhile, in the synagogue's social hall, the entire village of Chelm had gathered to argue about Abraham Schlemiel's strange warning. For what seemed like the thousandth time, his father, Jacob Schlemiel, explained what had happened.

"Aren't you listening?" Jacob said. "Just after dinner, Abraham went all stiff. He said, 'Trouble is coming.' I said, 'What kind of trouble?' He said, 'Robbers.' I said, 'So, Mr. Smart Guy, how do you know this?' He said, 'Because Adam told me.'"

"But Adam wasn't there," said Reb Gold, the cobbler.

Jacob nodded. "I pointed this out to him. The boy says he heard Adam's voice in his head."

"But you said he was acting strange all evening," Reb Gold insisted.

"Yes!" Rebecca Schlemiel snapped. "Yes, yes, yes. For a hundred times, yes!"

Jacob patted his wife's shoulder. "She's had a long day."

"A long day?" Rebecca hissed. "A long day? Yes, I've had a long day. You send one son off by himself on an errand to Smyrna and he doesn't return. And the other one is acting like a diseased lunatic. Yes, it's been a long day!"

Jacob stood still, a smile frozen on his face. Rebecca buried her head in her hands. Abraham sat next to her, still in a daze, nodding his head and talking to himself. He paused for a moment, smiled, and patted his mother's knee.

Whispers filled the social hall. No one in Chelm knew what to make of Abraham's strange warnings. Were his warnings true or had the boy lost his mind in grief over the disappearance of his twin brother? Everyone had an opinion, and they had been arguing for hours. There were even two farmers who swore that the boy who had gone to Smyrna was not Adam, but Abraham.

Then, the doors at the back of the social hall opened and three men, filthy with dust from the road, walked in.

"What's going on?" Alex Krabot barked.

"We're waiting for the robbers," said Reb Shikker, the town drunk.

"You see, Alex," Dimitri said. "They knew we were coming."

"Oh, you're them?" Reb Shikker smiled. "We've been expecting you. Hey, they're here! The robbers are here!"

The three wicked thieves stood with their legs planted firmly on the ground and their meanest grimaces fixed on their faces. Usually the announcement of their arrival to a crowd was good for a shriek, a scream or two, and at least a couple of faintings. Then someone, usually a young man, stepped forward and tried to stop them. He was usually killed quickly, as an example. After that, everyone else was much more cooperative. Instead, much to the thieves' chagrin, the villagers began to applaud.

"Hooray! The thieves are here"

"At last!"

"It's about time!"

"Can I go home now?"

With a flourish of pride, Reb Shikker escorted the three dazed bandits to the stage at the front of the hall. There they were introduced to the rabbi, the merchant, and the caterer.

At last, Rabbi Kibbitz held up his hands. "Shh, shh." The crowd fell silent.

"So," Rabbi Kibbitz said, "you're here to rob us?"

Again, the villagers cheered, clapped, and stomped their feet until they were silenced by a wave from the rabbi.

By now, the bandits were completely confused. "Yes, we are here to rob you," Alex Krabot snarled, stifling any cheers before they could begin. "Bring us all your wealth."

All of a sudden, there was a noise like a donkey with hiccoughs. "Ha HAW! Ha HAW!"

Everyone turned and stared at Reb Shikker, who was doubled over with laughter, his face as red as a boiled tomato.

"You!" Alex shouted. "What's so funny?"

The other two thieves dragged the helpless Reb Shikker onto the stage. "Who is this man?"

"He's the town drunk," said Reb Gold.

"Oh," said Dimitri, about to punch Reb Shikker in the face.

"And our bookkeeper," Reb Gold quickly added. "He keeps all our accounts."

The bandit leader stared at Reb Gold. "You let the town drunk keep the books?"

Reb Gold shrugged. "He's got a gift."

"Enough!" Krabot shouted. "Bring all your gold here."

"Gold?" Everyone laughed now. "HA HAW!"

"Stop it!" Alex Krabot fired a gun into the ceiling and didn't even flinch as plaster and chunks of wood fell at his feet. Then he handed the gun to one of his men to reload and said, "Who is the wealthiest man in Chelm?"

"Ahh, that would be me. Reb Cantor, the merchant." He performed a low bow. "At your service."

"You, bring me your money."

"Excuse me," Reb Cantor said. "May I have a word with you?"

Alex threw his hands up. "Why not?"

They both stepped to one side of the stage.

"Let me be blunt," Reb Cantor whispered. "I don't have any money."

"What? You're the richest man in Chelm, and yet you say you're penniless? What kind of a fool do you take me for?"

"None at all," Reb Cantor said quickly. "I buy and I sell. Right now, I'm arranging one of the largest shipments of caviar to Egypt! So, all my money is in caviar."

"Bring me the caviar," Alex Krabot said through tight lips.

"Well, the caviar is in the sturgeon. The sturgeon is in the Caspian Sea. The sea is in Russia. The governor of the province, who is Russian, needs to sign the papers. He needs a bribe. I have no money, so I'm having a chest built. A beautiful thing . . ."

"Shut up!" Alex Krabot spat. "Bring me the chest!"

"Well, it's not quite finished."

The bandit leader spun around. "I'm going to kill someone!"

Just then, a boy of nine years stood up and said, "Kill me!"

"Sit down, Abraham!" Rebecca grabbed at his hand but missed as he jumped onto the stage. "Are you crazy?"

"No. Take me outside and kill me," Abraham Schlemiel said. "I'll volunteer."

"Abraham, no!"

"Shh, Mama. I know what I'm doing. Look, Mr. Tough-Guy Robber, kill me."

"Abraham?" Rebecca stood up. "You come back here at once. If anybody is going to die, it should be me."

Jacob Schlemiel fidgeted uncomfortably in his chair. It was just about then that he felt he really ought to be jumping up and volunteering himself to be killed, but the truth was that he really didn't want to die.

"This is a very strange town," Alex muttered. "Take the boy outside."

"No, not him!" Rebecca shouted.

Krabot held up his gun. "Lady, sit down or I'll kill you both. Take the boy."

"Can I do it?" Bertie asked. "I'll do it!"

"No, me," Dimitri said. "Bertie got to do the last one. Please."

Alex Krabot shook his head in disgust. "Why don't you both do it? Take the boy outside."

"Both?" Abraham's eyes widened in fear. "Don't you think that one of them should stay inside to protect you from this crowd?"

"From this crowd?" Krabot chuckled. "No, you're right. Caution is prudent. Fine. Dimitri Dimitriovich you go. Bertie Zanuk, don't say a word. He's right, you did the last one."

Dimitri stuck his tongue out at Bertie and dragged Abraham off the stage, through the crowd, and out the front doors.

"My boy," Rebecca moaned. She collapsed into her chair. Jacob put his arm around her, wondering if he should have done more, and if so, what, and if it would have made any difference.

Everyone fell quiet. Alex grinned. At last there would be fear.

The villagers of Chelm had watched with sinking hearts as the notorious thief dragged Abraham Schlemiel from the synagogue's social hall.

A few moments later, everyone in the synagogue heard a bloodcurdling scream. It was a long and mournful howl of agony, abruptly cut short, "YaaaH-OoooWWWWW-rp!"

When they heard his cry, they felt despair. Rebecca Schlemiel screamed and then fainted. Jacob Schlemiel burst into tears. My boy, he thought. My poor boy.

"Now," Alex Krabot said firmly. "Bring me all your silver, all your gold. Everything you have of value."

Outside, however, it was a different story.

Squinting as he had emerged into the sunlight, Dimitri had been trying to decide whether to waste a bullet on the boy or just cut his throat with a knife. The bullet was less bloody, but the blade was less expensive. He had just about settled on the knife when he heard a voice behind him.

"Let me go!" the voice had said.

He spun around and saw something that made him blink.

The boy he was about to kill was standing behind him.

He turned again. No, the boy was still there in front. Dimitri was still holding him by his shirt. For a moment, he thought he was seeing double. Then, Dimitri actually heard double.

Seeing Double

"Whatever you do," two voices echoed in both Bertie's ears, "don't look up!"

Naturally, Dimitri looked up. At that exact moment, Adam pulled the rope, and Dimitri was just in time to watch as hundreds of potatoes fell out of the sky smacking him right between the eyes. Then everything went black.

"I meant you should drop an empty sack of potatoes over his head," Abraham Schlemiel said. "I wanted to tie him up."

"Now you tell me." Adam said. "Abraham, are you all right?"

For the first time since he had learned that three thieves were going to rob Chelm, Abraham Schlemiel smiled. "Yes, I'm fine. Where have you been?" Abraham asked his twin. "He almost killed me."

"Sorry," Adam said. "I got here as quickly as possible. Rosa went to Smyrna for help. She told me to tell you that you were very brave risking your life like that."

Abraham blushed. "Thank you. Still, we don't have much time. In a few minutes, the other thieves will begin to wonder what happened to this one."

"Yes," Adam said. "And that was too quiet. He was supposed to make some noise."

He reached over and pinched Abraham hard, right under the armpit.

"YaaaH-OoooWWWWW-rp!!" Abraham wailed until Adam slapped his hand over his mouth.

"All right, all right," Adam whispered. "That's enough."

Abraham slapped Adam's hand away. "That hurt!" he hissed.

"Sorry," Adam grinned. "Abraham, how many guns do they have?"

"I don't know," Abraham said, rubbing his armpit. "There are three robbers. They each have at least one gun, maybe more."

Adam got up and began searching the felled thief. "This one only has one gun," he said as he spotted a pistol butt sticking out of the unconscious man's pocket. He pulled it free.

"It's too bad we don't know how to shoot," Abraham said.

Adam shrugged, "I think maybe it's time to learn. I know that if you pull the trigger it goes off, but as for hitting something . . ."

Abraham shook his head. "Mama says that guns are dangerous, and I tend to agree with her."

"Abraham, if you won't," Adam said, "I will . . ."

"No. You can't," Abraham said. "There are too many people inside to take the chance."

"Well, I'm going to keep this thing just in case," Adam said, examining the heavy pistol. "We don't have much time. We need to do something."

"I know, I know." Abraham paced back and forth.

Adam sighted down the barrel of the gun and said, "Bang." Then he slipped the gun into his pocket.

"I've got it!" Abraham said at last.

"What?" Adam asked. Then he nodded. "Oh. That's a pretty good plan."

"Thank you," Abraham agreed.

The brothers shook hands and grinned at each other.

"Let's go," they said as one.

On the social hall's stage, Alex Krabot, the bandit leader, listened impatiently as the villagers begged and pleaded.

"We don't have any gold."

"We have nothing of value. Our silver candlesticks are made of tin."

"The *kiddush* cup from the Holy Land? It's brass."

"What about my mother's diamond wedding ring?"

"Sarah, I'm telling you for the last time, it's not a diamond, it's a piece of glass!"

"You know, I should invest in diamonds," Reb Cantor muttered, "they're easy to hide."

Krabot wanted to kill them all, but he knew that if he let them complain and moan and deny that they had any money eventually they would wear themselves out and reveal all their secret hiding places. If not, then as soon as Dimitri got back from killing the boy, he'd have another one taken out and killed.

But where was Dimitri? What was taking him so long? He'd told the fool to kill the boy, not bury him.

Just as he was about to send Bertie out, the doors to the social hall opened. In ran the boy. His hands were covered with blood, screaming, "Murder! Murder!"

Of course there was a murder, Alex Krabot found himself thinking. Only you're supposed to be the dead one.

And then the boy vanished into the crowd of people.

"Alex, what was that?" Bertie asked in a quiet whisper.

"I don't know," Krabot said. "Go and find him."

And then, again the boy appeared. This time he was at the door at the front of the room, near the stage. His hands and face were red with blood, and he was shrieking "Murder! Murder!"

"How did he get there, Alex?" Bertie asked nervously. "You said that the forest wasn't haunted."

"Idiot, we're not in the forest," Krabot said. "He ran. Boys are fast."

But just then the boy appeared in two places!

"I'm dead!" the boy on the floor yelled

"I'm dead!" the boy near the stage yelled.

Bertie's face was as white as a sheet. "A ghost. We killed a ghost!"

"You can't kill a ghost," Krabot said. But it was too late. Bertie Zanuk's eyes rolled back in his head and he collapsed in a terrified faint. Alex Krabot sighed. Good help was so hard to find these days.

"I'm dead!" the two bloody boys were yelling. "A ghost!"

A cry rippled through the crowd. "They're dead. The twins are dead."

"Twins?" Alex said. "Twins?"

"Oh, yes," said Reb Shikker. "Abraham and Adam Schlemiel are twins. It's impossible to tell them apart. They're quite the troublemakers. Still, it's a shame that they've been murdered."

Alex smacked his forehead. Twins. Somehow they had overpowered Dimitri and then scared Bertie half to death by covering their hands and faces with wine and screaming like castrated pigs.

"Enough!" Alex bellowed. "Shut up! Everyone!"

He grabbed the woman nearest to him, the one who had tried to prevent Bertie from taking the boy in the first place.

"Stop it!" he shouted. "Or I will kill your mother."

The room fell quiet. The two boys stood still.

Alex Krabot stuck his pistol in Rebecca Schlemiel's ear. "You, Merchant, get your wealth. Get everything of value in this godforsaken village. Put it in that chest you were having made for the governor and bring it here. Now! You have one hour, and then I'll blow her head off."

The whole village gasped.

"You," Rebecca Schlemiel winced as she said to the thief, "are not a very nice man."

"No," the thief said. "I'm not."

Then, Alex Krabot, one of the blood-thirstiest cutthroats in all of Eastern Europe, threw his head back and laughed.

CHAPTER ELEVEN

The Robber's Story

It was hot in the social hall. After the robber leader sent Reb Cantor and Reb Gold out to gather up the wealth of Chelm, he had the twins brought up on the stage, where he could keep an eye on them. Bertie and Dimitri were still laid out cold. Alex wondered if he'd ever manage to find good help. Still, one thief with a gun was more than a match for an entire village of fools. He huddled everyone else into one corner, far away from both doors. Some of the villagers gossiped, some prayed, some complained, others napped. A quartet of yeshivah students was playing pinochle.

"Come here, boy." Alex Krabot beckoned with his gun.

Abraham came closer.

"What's your name?"

Abraham told him.

"Abraham, you were very brave earlier," Krabot said. "Like when I was a boy. Feisty."

Abraham nodded. He glanced over at his mother, who looked scared. "Why are you doing this?" he asked at last.

Krabot laughed. Adam, who had been dozing, was startled awake and briefly thought about pulling out the gun he'd taken from the other robber. No, it was still too dangerous.

"You mean aside from the money?" Krabot scratched his beard. "Excitement maybe. Like a cowboy in America, you ride into town and everyone is watching you. They treat you with respect, and then they give you all their money. Then you go somewhere else and you drink and play cards and meet ladies. Everyone treats you like a big shot, at least until the money runs out. Then you find a new village, ride into town, and start all over again. It sure beats killing pigs for a living. Abraham, you're what, nine years old?"

Abraham nodded.

"When I was your age, I had already killed my first man. He was a Pole, a real hard case. He deserved it." Krabot's voice trailed off.

After a while, Abraham asked, "Why?"

"What's that?"

"Why did he deserve it? The Sixth Commandment is 'Thou shall not kill.' You put yourself in God's place when you killed that man. I was wondering why."

Krabot's eyes narrowed. For a moment, he thought about backhanding the boy. Instead, he coughed, spat, and said, "No one else has been stupid enough to talk to me like that since I was a child. They've all been afraid. Aren't you afraid of me?"

"Yes," Abraham nodded. "I'm sorry. I shouldn't have . . ."

"No, no," Krabot said. "You should know. You live in this nice village. Your parents and your brother love you. Other people don't have it so good.

"I was born in a Russian village on the border of Poland. My father worked at a slaughterhouse. Everyone in the village worked at the slaughter-house. He killed pigs all day, and when he came home he was drunk and he beat me and he beat my mother. That would have been my life, too. It was the way things were.

"One day, he didn't come home. It was payday. And on paydays, like most days, he went to the tavern. But it was getting late. My mother was afraid that he would drink all his pay. So, she took me and we went to the tavern. I was eight years old.

"Well, we arrived and found the tavern filled with song and cheer. My father was playing cards and laughing. I don't think I'd ever seen him so happy. I didn't know why my mother was so anxious. That tavern didn't seem like such a bad place.

"But then this Polish man grabbed my mother, and he started to kiss her. If my father saw it, he ignored it. I ran to him and he told me not to worry, that it would do her good. She was screaming. So, I killed the man. I grabbed my father's sharp butcher's knife and stuck it in the man's gut. It was awful.

The blood went everywhere. The tavern fell silent. My mother was in tears. 'Run boy,' my father said. 'Before the police come. Run.' And so I ran. I left my village, I left my parents, and I never saw them again. Once I went back. About ten years after that, and everything was gone. The whole village, as if it never existed.

"And that, Abraham, is why I am who I am today. What do you think?"

Abraham whispered, "Am I supposed to be sympathetic?"

Krabot laughed. "You're either a hero or a fool. I've killed men for less."

"Violence again," Abraham said. "Where has it gotten you? No home, no family. You come to my village and you threaten my mother. You've turned into the man you killed."

"Shut your mouth, boy," Krabot said, his lips tight with rage. "What do you know about violence? I'll teach you about violence." He stood up and drew a knife from his belt. "You see this knife? This was my father's knife. He used it to slit the throats of the pigs. You keep kosher, boy, don't you? This is not a kosher knife."

Abraham's eyes were wide. Adam was reaching for his gun. The social hall was as silent as a graveyard at midnight.

Just then the front doors burst open and in came Reb Cantor and Reb Gold dragging the beautiful seven-sided chest that Jacob Schlemiel had been making for the provincial governor. They tugged the chest up the center aisle and brought it to the edge of the stage.

"Just in time, boy," Alex Krabot said, putting his knife back in its sheath. "Open it."

Reb Gold looked at Reb Cantor, who nodded. Together they pulled back the lid.

It was filled to the brim with books.

"Books?" Alex Krabot roared. All the sleeping villagers awoke with a start. "Books? I don't want books. I want gold. I want silver. I want jewelry."

"We told you," Reb Cantor said. "We don't have any of that. You wanted our wealth? This is our wealth. You've got the Torah, you've got the Mishnah, that's part of the Talmud . . . you've got the collected stories of Sholem Aleichem. This is pretty good stuff!"

Reb Shikker moaned. "No! You can't give him my accounting books. I won't know where to begin!"

Alex Krabot was dumbfounded. Was the entire village insane?

"Empty it," Krabot ordered, waving his guns at the men. "Pile the books in the corner and burn them."

"Burn our books?" Rabbi Kibbitz said. "We have little enough already, you would take them away?"

"Burn them!"

Moving quietly, the villagers formed a line. One by one, they gently removed the books from the oak chest and began passing them down the rows into a pile in the middle of the hall. Occasionally, someone would stop to brush away a tear or sigh at the memory of a particular volume.

At last, the chest was empty. Krabot stood at the edge of the stage, grinning. "Set that pile of books on fire," he said. "I'll burn the whole building!"

Adam leaned next to Abraham and whispered, "Ready?"

Abraham looked at the thief and nodded.

Adam drew his gun and shouted, "No!"

Krabot turned and saw the boy with the gun. "Are you going to shoot me? I don't think you will." He turned his back on the boy. "You. The rabbi. Light the match."

Adam's face grew white as a sheet. His hands were trembling. "Now, Abraham," he said. "Now!"

Abraham took one step closer to the robber and gave him a push. Alex Krabot, gun in hand, toppled forward off the stage and landed in the seven-sided oak chest with a thud. In an instant, Reb Gold, Reb Cantor, and Reb Shikker slammed the lid shut and jumped on top. There was a gunshot, and a small hole exploded out of the chest not two inches from Reb Shikker's bottom.

"Oy gevalt!" Reb Shikker shrieked. The box shook with angry pounding from the inside.

"Adam, the latch," Jacob Schlemiel shouted.

Quickly, Adam ran down from the stage, reached into his pocket, and removed the small brass latch he had purchased in Smyrna. Jacob took the gun from his son's hand, spilled the single bullet on the floor, and used the gun's butt as a hammer to attach the latch to the chest, locking it securely.

"Done!" Jacob shouted. A cheer erupted from the villagers. Jacob and Rebecca Schlemiel hugged their boys close.

At exactly that moment, the doors to the social hall opened once again, and in strode five provincial constables, followed closely behind by an exhausted Rosa Kalderash, who had run all the way back to Smyrna to fetch help and had ridden back with the police.

"Where's the trouble?" one constable asked.

Reb Cantor stepped forward. "No trouble at all. Only two unconscious robbers, the one on the stage and the other one you passed on the way in. And this other one in this box, which by the way is a gift from me to the governor. Please give him my regards."

In the end, the puzzled looking constables had nothing to do but haul away the criminals while the villagers of Chelm raised their voices in a song of joy and relief.

CHAPTER TWELVE

Trouble

Avi Weiss ran into the classroom, went right up to the front of the room, and handed Rabbi Yohon Abrahms a note. Then he sauntered to his seat, whispering to Abraham and Adam Schlemiel as he passed, "You're in trouble . . ."

The twins, who had been mind-talking with each other, plotting a daring egg-bombing raid on Rabbi Abrahms's house, looked up with a start.

The schoolteacher glanced at the note and said with a sigh, "Abraham, Adam, go and see the rebbe."

They stood, glared at Avi, and left the classroom. They dawdled in the synagogue's cellar until Reb Levitsky, the janitor, caught their arms and dragged them into the chief rabbi's office.

"Adam, Abraham," said Rabbi Kibbitz. "Sit down. Sit down." He gestured to the chairs in front of his table.

Puzzled, the boys sat. Usually, when they were in trouble, the grown-ups made them stand at attention for hours while they were lectured and scolded. Rabbi Kibbitz was smiling.

We're in for it now, Adam's voice echoed in Abraham's mind. *What did you do?*

It wasn't me, Abraham mentally whispered back. *What did you do?*

Then both pointed at the other and shouted aloud, "He did it!"

Rabbi Kibbitz jumped with a start. "Did what?"

"He put the congealed chicken fat in Rabbi Abrahms's shoes."

"Well, he put the book paste in the shoes so that the rabbi couldn't take them off!"

Rabbi Kibbitz covered his mouth, gave the boys a stern look, and giggled behind his hand. His poor young colleague had been trapped in his boots for

84

six weeks, and the rancid smell was beginning to cause the elders to recon-
sider his contract.

"What did you say?" Rabbi Kibbitz said. "I'm deaf in one ear. I didn't quite
hear you . . ."

"Umm," both boys said. "Nothing. Nothing."

"All right . . ." the rabbi said slowly. "Well, I wanted to talk with you about
the robbery."

Two heads perked up with smiles. Less than a month had passed since
the Schlemiel boys had apprehended Alex Krabot and his henchmen, and no
one in Chelm, let alone the heroes, had tired of retelling the story. Two boys
and one girl capturing three of the most notorious thieves in Europe was
something impressive.

"Rosa and I were in the forest," Adam began.

"Wait, wait," the rabbi said. "I already know more or less what happened,
but I do have some questions. May I?"

Adam nodded his head.

"Tell me, Adam, why didn't you and Rosa go straight to Smyrna for help?
I am told that you followed the bandits through the Schvartzvald for several
hours. And your plan? Ghosts?" The rabbi raised his eyebrows as though he
didn't think much of the idea. "Thank goodness your friend Rosa was able to
run all the way to Smyrna and return with the constables."

Adam's brow creased. He had never really thought about it, but the rabbi
was right. If he and Rosa had turned around and hurried back to Smyrna,
they could have gotten the police and been back in Chelm almost before the
robbers arrived. Adam's mouth opened and closed.

"He was lost," Abraham said, coming to his brother's rescue. "And he was
tired and scared. He's only nine years old."

Rabbi Kibbitz nodded. "Tell me, Abraham, how did you know the robbers
were coming?"

Abraham's eyes widened. The twins exchanged glances. How could they
explain it? The fact was they weren't sure themselves. Rosa had told them
that twins often had such a bond. Still, it was something that the boys had
instinctively kept quiet. Should they tell the rabbi?

What harm will it do to tell him? Abraham thought-spoke to Adam.

He might think we're demons and kill us, Adam answered.

But we're not demons.

Maybe we are.

Abraham had never considered that, and it stumped him.

During the long pause, Rabbi Kibbitz looked from one boy to the other. At last he said, "It wasn't the Gypsy girl, was it? She didn't do anything to you? Cast a spell?"

"No," they said. It would have been easy for Adam and Abraham to blame it all on Rosa. That would have handled their problems in an instant, but despite their propensity for troublemaking the twins were relatively honest. "She didn't. It wasn't her."

"Then what?" the rabbi asked.

"I can hear his voice in my head," Abraham said at last.

The rabbi looked startled. "Whose voice? The Almighty's?"

"No," Abraham said. "Adam's voice. I heard him speaking to me when he was in the forest."

"We don't know how we do it," Adam said. "It's just like talking to each other, but without moving our lips."

"Oh," Rabbi Kibbitz said, relieved. Historically, whenever somebody thought he or she personally heard the voice of the Creator of the Universe, it meant that that person and everyone else who lived nearby were in big trouble. If the two boys thought they were talking to each other, well, that was a little strange but not such a major problem. "Okay. So, one more question."

It didn't seem to bother him, Adam thought.

I don't think he believed us, Abraham answered in his brother's mind.

"Are you boys doing it now?" Rabbi Kibbitz said. "If you are, please stop. It's a little rude, like whispering."

"Sorry, Rabbi."

"All right." The rabbi waved his hand. "This question is harder to ask. I want you to think before you answer."

The boys fidgeted uncomfortably.

"Adam," Rabbi Kibbitz said at last, "how did you feel when you were holding that gun? Were you going to kill that man?"

Instantly, in their minds both boys were back in the moment in time at the edge of the stage when Adam had pointed his pistol at Alex Krabot and the thief had laughed. The gun was loaded and aimed. Then Abraham had pushed Krabot into the trunk and it was all over.

Adam stared at his feet. He felt sick to his stomach. "I . . ."

"He didn't shoot him, did he?" Abraham said.

"Shh," Rabbi Kibbitz said. "Abraham, you're a good boy, but this is important for Adam. You thought about it, didn't you? Here was this man, he had threatened your parents. He held everyone hostage. He was going to rob the village. And then burn our shul and all our books. You held the gun. It was aimed at him. Pulling the trigger would have been very easy, wouldn't it?"

Deeply ashamed, Adam nodded his head, and began to cry.

"But he didn't do it!" Abraham shouted.

Rabbi Kibbitz winced and rubbed his good ear. "No, he didn't. And in some ways that was the most heroic deed I have ever witnessed. To hold another person's life in your hands and then to save it is a blessing. But to hold a wicked man's life in your hands and let him live . . . That is most dangerous and very courageous."

"What?" Abraham said, not certain he had heard the rabbi correctly. "You mean it was okay?"

"Who knows," Rabbi Kibbitz said. "It's difficult to say this, because I applaud what you both did. But, I just received a letter from the provincial governor inviting me to accompany the two boys who captured Krabot and his men to Minsk, where the men will stand trial. It's an order, really. It means that the governor wants you to testify. One of two things will happen. Either the men will be convicted or they will be released. Either way, these bandits are likely to want to kill you. Can you imagine the humiliation they must feel at having been defeated by two boys? Although you spared Alex Krabot's life at great risk to your own, men of violence rarely see that as a blessing."

"So, I should have killed him?" Adam asked quietly.

"I don't believe so," the rabbi said. "On one hand, it would have been easier, but not very nice. On the other hand, if you had killed him, this all would be over and done with. I think you made the right choice, but it does create a problem. On the other hand, what is life without a few problems? How many hands is that? Never mind. We'll leave tomorrow."

The two boys were quiet.

"Don't look so glum!" the rabbi said, heartily. "We'll figure something out. After all, what chance does a thief stand against the accumulated wisdom of Chelm?"

Somehow, neither Adam nor Abraham felt reassured.

CHAPTER THIRTEEN

The Man Who Complained Himself to Death . . . Training

"All the way to Minsk?" Rebecca Schlemiel said. "They're only nine years old!"

"Shh!" her husband, Jacob, said. "Rebecca, they're sleeping. Yes, all the way to Minsk. You've only said it a million times. But the rebbe is going with them. And it's not as if you can ignore a request from the provincial governor to meet the heroes who captured the Krabot gang."

The boys, however, were not asleep. Abraham and Adam Schlemiel lay in their bed, wide awake.

Abraham whispered. "We're going to go to Minsk!"

"All the way to Minsk," Adam said. And both boys convulsed with muffled laughter.

Three days later, trudging through a barren field, the twins already wished they were back home. So far, their great adventure had consisted of a waterlogged schlep to Smyrna in the rain and then hours standing in the mud beside the railroad tracks in what passed for a railroad station.

The rabbi had asked when the train would come, but the villagers of Smyrna had just shrugged. "Sometimes it comes. Sometimes it doesn't come. When it does come, sometimes it stops, sometimes it doesn't stop."

Rather than stay still, the rabbi had decided that they should start walking. So they did. Two days they had spent trudging through the mud alongside the railroad tracks.

88

The twins were quietly miserable. Ordinarily, they might have complained, but they were too tired and uncomfortable even to moan. This was just as well because struggling along beside them, Rabbi Kibbitz was complaining enough for an entire army.

"Oy, my feet are soaked," he was saying. "You could fill the ocean from my boots. There's enough mud in my socks to plant a garden in. I think my hat has turned into a sponge, and I think that water is leaking into my brain through my ear!"

At any other time, the boys would have laughed.

"It's so dark, I can't tell if it's day or night," the rabbi said. "I'd look up at the sky, but then my eyes would be flooded by a bucket of rain. If this keeps up, maybe we can swim to Minsk. Of course, I can't swim, so I'd drown. What a way to go, to drown in the middle of a field. All we need now is lightning."

As if on cue, a thunderbolt cracked and the three travelers watched in amazement as a lightning bolt split a nearby elm tree in two.

"Oy!" Rabbi Kibbitz said. He closed his eyes in prayer for a moment. When he had finished, he removed his gigantic backpack and brought out a large cloth tent. "Let's make camp."

It took an hour, and they lost half the tent spikes, but at last the twins and the rabbi were inside the tent, cozy and dry wearing nothing but their underwear.

"Look at me," the rabbi said. (The boys did their best not to look.) "I'm nearly Moses' age. I've got corns on my feet the size of apples. And my boots are soaked. At least the Almighty was merciful and let Moses walk through the Red Sea dry shod." He heaved a big sigh. "You two are very quiet."

Abraham and Adam nodded.

"No complaints?" the rabbi asked.

They shook their heads.

"Why not?" the rabbi said. "It's rotten outside and not that much better inside. I wouldn't be surprised if the tent sprung a leak or was full of spiders."

Both boys squirmed.

"Our mother says we shouldn't complain," Abraham said. "She says we're very fortunate."

The rabbi looked thoughtful. "It's true, we are all very fortunate. But complaining is one of the greatest pleasures in life. Why, without complaints, my wife (may she rest in peace) and I would have had nothing to say to each other."

"Our father says that complaints are a waste of breath," Adam said.

"Nothing is a waste of breath so long as you enjoy it," Rabbi Kibbitz said. "Let me tell you the story of the man who complained himself to death."

Once upon a time, not so long ago, there was a kvetch. This man was known far and wide as the greatest complainer the world has ever known. You could give him a silver piece and he would complain it wasn't gold. You could remove a splinter from his toe and he would say that by mistake you'd pulled out a bone.

He lived in a house that was too small on a farm that was barren. He had a skinny cow, a flea-ridden dog, and a wife who was deaf, which was fortunate for her because she couldn't hear his constant litany of woe.

From morning until night he whined, he cried, he kvetched. The sun was too early, it was too bright, it was too hot, and then it was dark already. Why bother planting a seed? It would just encourage the weeds. Every day he ate a rotten breakfast that gave him indigestion, and then he sat on his porch until lunchtime, wondering aloud what horrible misfortune would come his way.

His neighbors avoided him like the plague. Not only did the kvetch's moaning make them miserable, but so did his smell. The man refused to bathe for fear of catching pneumonia, so he stank like a moldy dead skunk smeared with Limburger cheese.

One day a giant arrived and declared himself the ruler of the land. This giant was a cannibal who demanded to be fed. In an instant, the neighbors decided that the kvetch would be the first to go. They sent a committee to the farm to inform the kvetch of their decision.

He nodded glumly and said, "Of course. Just my luck." Then off he trundled to the giant's palace.

When he got there, the door was open, so he walked inside. Then he heard a voice, a big booming loud voice. "Fee Fie Foe Fum, I smell . . . GAAAH! What's that horrible smell? Ugh!"

The kvetch lifted his arm, sniffed underneath, and gagged himself. "It's me," he said, at last. "Something's growing under my arm."

The giant held his nose and peered down at the thin pitiful man. "Why don't you take a bath?"

The kvetch explained at great length about pneumonia, the number of people who drown in bathtubs every year, and the possibility of leeches.

"Shut up!" the giant said at last. "Stop complaining or I'll cut off your head!"

For a moment, the kvetch looked thoughtful. Then he shrugged. "Why bother?" he said. "If I were going to live forever in paradise, then maybe I could keep my tongue. As it is, I'm starving, I'm miserable, everyone hates me, and you're going to eat me anyway . . ."

The Giant's Deadly Dinner

With that, the giant drew out his great knife and with one stroke cut off the kvetch's head.

Amazingly enough, that's not the end of the story, because with his last breath, even as his head was flying across the room, the kvetch managed to groan, "Oy! My neck!"

This so infuriated the giant that he picked up the kvetch's body and swallowed it in one bite, without even chewing. A moment later, the giant's face turned blue, he coughed, gagged, sputtered, and died on the spot.

The giant was dead, and when the kvetch's neighbors found the poor man's head, they were surprised to see that he had a big fat smile on his face. Everyone knew that he had died complaining.

By now, the two boys were nearly asleep. Abraham, however, managed to open his eyes just enough to ask, "Rabbi, what's the moral of that story?"

"Moral shmoral," Rabbi Kibbitz laughed. "Does every story have to have a moral?"

In the morning, the rain stopped, the sun came out, and chirping birds dove through the field beside the railroad tracks. Abraham and Adam Schlemiel rubbed their eyes and poked their heads out of the tent. It was a beautiful day. The grass glistened wet and twinkling, and mist rose from every puddle.

"It's so different from Chelm," Abraham said.

"What's so different?" Adam answered. "Same birds, same grass, same sun."

"It's peaceful and quiet," Abraham said. "And there is no one around who we know."

Just then, from inside the tent, Rabbi Kibbitz let loose an earth-shaking snore. Both boys giggled. Then, in the distance they heard another sound that was even louder than the rabbi's snore. The train was coming.

"Rebbe, Rebbe, the train!" the boys shouted.

Startled from fond dreams, Rabbi Kibbitz leaped to his feet, which was unfortunate because his head tore a hole in the top of the tent. He blinked twice, and then felt the wind blowing across his bald skull.

"You two are going to kill me," he said, snatching his *kippah* from the roof of the mangled tent. "Quick. We'd better get packing unless you want to walk all the way to Minsk."

The boys leaped into action without another word, and by the time the train puffed into sight, they were all dressed and the tent was folded (more or less) and stuffed into the rabbi's huge backpack. Abraham and Adam stood by the side of the tracks, waving handkerchiefs and jumping up and down.

"Do you think it will stop?" Adam asked.

"Oh, it will stop," the learned sage answered with certainty. "The question is, 'Will it stop for us?'"

It didn't.

If the rabbi and twins had been Cossacks, the train would have stopped in an instant. If one of them had been the czar, it would have expelled all the other passengers to make room. As it was, the engineer had just enough compassion to slow the train down barely enough to give them a slim chance of running alongside and then jumping onboard.

Betting among the passengers was fierce. The conductor gave the boys even odds. The rabbi started at ten to one, but as his breath began to falter the odds skyrocketed to fifty kopeks to a zloty. If a sly merchant from Moscow hadn't dashed up front and bribed the engineer with a percentage of his profits, the rabbi would have been left standing alone in the field, with his young charges lost in the distance.

As it was, he was pulled aboard at the last moment to a chorus of cheers from the winners and boos from the losers. New wagers were immediately placed about how quickly he would keel over and die of a heart attack.

Fortunately for himself, the twins, and the entire village of Chelm, Rabbi Kibbitz eventually caught his breath and at last gasped, "Oy . . . vey . . ."

Everyone laughed, and more money changed hands.

CHAPTER FOURTEEN

The Governor's Palace—in Pinsk

By the time the train approached the city, Rabbi Kibbitz was fully recovered. The merchant, who had made a small fortune betting on the rabbi's survival, had shared a goat cheese pie with the travelers from Chelm.

The train blew a long and loud whistle.

" . . . insk!" the conductor shouted. "Last stop! Everyone off!"

All the travelers clapped and stamped their feet with joy that the long cramped ride was about to end.

"Such a din!" Rabbi Kibbitz said, although no one could hear him. The crowd surged toward the doors. "Stay near me boys."

They were, of course, immediately separated. Adam went this way, Abraham went that way, and Rabbi Kibbitz, with his gigantic backpack, was lucky to get off the train at all.

The station was a whirl of people, animals, machinery, and smoke. Using their mind-speech, Adam and Abraham agreed to meet at the far end of the station, near the ticket seller's booth. They picked the right spot because as the station slowly emptied out, Rabbi Kibbitz tottered toward them, his face white with fear and exhaustion.

"Yes, you boys are definitely trying to kill me," he said with relief. "Since it is because of you that we have to look for the Governor's Palace, then you two should carry this." He dropped his backpack onto the ground with a thud.

"Of course, rabbi," the boys said. They each took a hold of one strap and lifted. The pack didn't budge an inch. "What's in this?" Abraham asked.

"Besides the tent and a week's worth of clothes?" Rabbi Kibbitz said.

"Food of course. I have some blintzes, two kugels, and fifty dehydrated matzah balls for an emergency. Then there are the books. I couldn't leave Chelm without something to read. There's the Torah, a haggadah, and twenty-six other books I've been meaning to read."

The boys looked at each other dumbfounded.

"Maybe it's time we hire a cart," the rabbi said. "You boys wait here."

A moment later, Adam saw Rabbi Kibbitz waving him to bring their bags outside. Just in front of the train station, Rabbi Kibbitz stood, haggling with a man. Grunting with effort, Abraham and Adam threw their bags in the back of the small cart. They wondered if the man's old donkey would be able to pull such a heavy load.

"Where to?" the carriage driver asked.

"The Governor's Palace," Rabbi Kibbitz said.

The carriage driver laughed. "The Governor's Palace? The three of you?"

"I'll have you know that I am Rabbi Kibbitz of Chelm, and these boys are the Schlemiels who defeated the famous Krabot gang."

"Oh, really?" the driver smirked. "And I'm the lover of Catherine the Great."

"Shh!" Rabbi Kibbitz said. "A man oughtn't to say such things in public. Especially in front of young boys."

The driver shook his head. "Are you sure that you don't mean the Governor's Palace in Minsk?"

"Isn't that what I said?" Rabbi Kibbitz asked.

"You said you wanted to go to the Governor's Palace. That means something quite different in Pinsk than it does in Minsk. And this is Pinsk, not Minsk."

"Pinsk, Minsk, Sminsk," Rabbi Kibbitz said. "How can the Governor's Palace be anything other than the Governor's Palace? I have heard that people in the big city sometimes like to play jokes on those of us from small villages. Take care, because I am on to your tricks. Now, please, take us to the Governor's Palace."

"All right," the driver said. "But don't say I didn't warn you." With that, he cracked his whip, and the donkey grunted in momentary agony before the cart began to roll.

"Rabbi Kibbitz," Abraham said, "aren't we supposed to be in Minsk, not Pinsk?"

The rabbi smiled, and patted the boy's arm. "Minsk and Pinsk are hundreds of miles apart. We started our journey on the train to Minsk. When we got off the train, could this be Pinsk?"

"But it might have been a different train," Adam said.

Rabbi Kibbitz didn't seem to hear. He had opened his pack, removed a book, and was reading intently.

"What are we going to do?" Adam asked his brother.

"Minsk or Pinsk, we're here now," Abraham said. "We'll go to the Governor's Palace. How different could it be?"

"This is not what I pictured."

Abraham had to agree.

They'd imagined the Governor's Palace as a splendid castle, high on a hill, overlooking fertile green fields, lovely gardens, and well-tended woods filled with deer. Instead, the carriage was rumbling down a rutted road through a part of Pinsk with open sewers, broken-down hovels, and the unmistakable stench of a glue factory. At every intersection, a dozen children swarmed out into the street begging for kopeks until the cart driver chased them away with his whip. When Abraham reached into his pocket to throw one of the more pitiful little girls a copper, the cart driver hissed that it would only encourage them. Even the sun seemed to go into hiding in this neighborhood. It was hardly a regal landscape.

"The wise ruler does not set himself apart from the people he governs," Rabbi Kibbitz explained when Abraham asked. "For, if he lived apart, how would he know their problems or understand their troubles?"

"This governor must be really wise," Adam said wryly.

"Perhaps the wisest," the rabbi agreed.

The cart driver snorted and then announced with a grand sweep of his hand, "The Governor's Palace!"

The visitors from Chelm turned their heads and stared.

"It's a tavern," Adam said.

The building was two and a half stories tall and not quite as broken down as the rest of the neighborhood. The windows were intact, although covered with soot, and the roof looked as if it should have been replaced ten or twenty year earlier. Above the door was a sign of crossed scepters over a mug of ale.

"Are you sure you took us to the right place?" Abraham asked. "You're not trying to cheat us?"

"I tried to explain this to you," the cart driver began. "In Pinsk, this is the Governor's Palace."

"It's perfect," Rabbi Kibbitz said, jumping to his feet and hoisting his backpack, his energy quite refreshed after the long cart ride. "What better place for a wise man to rule from than a tavern? It is a gathering place, a meeting house. A center both of social and political life. I can hardly wait to meet this governor!"

"And I can't wait to see this," chuckled the cart driver. He tied his mule to a pole and followed the trio up the three broken steps to the front door. Rabbi Kibbitz led the way, Abraham stayed close behind, and Adam kept his eyes open for robbers and thieves.

Inside, the tavern was dark, almost pitch black. It wasn't even noon, and already it was filled with smoke and the stink of stale spilled beer that was never completely washed away. Several heads turned when the rabbi, two boys, and the carriage driver entered, but most of the two dozen denizens of the Governor's Palace ignored them.

As Rabbi Kibbitz's eyes adjusted to the light, he began to look for the governor and immediately spotted him—an elderly and distinguished man with a long flowing beard sitting on a stool at one end of a long table. With a broad smile, Rabbi Kibbitz rushed over to the governor, took his hand, and began shaking it vigorously.

"Your Excellence," he said. "We came as soon as we could. It isn't easy to travel from Chelm to Minsk. Or to Pinsk for that matter, especially with two young boys."

The rabbi paused to take a breath, and the old man whose hand he was still holding tottered, wobbled, and fell to the floor with a thud.

"Yi! I killed the governor!" the rabbi gasped, his eyes growing wide. He let go of the governor's limp hand in horror.

The room filled with laughter. Rabbi Kibbitz burst into tears. He began chanting the prayer for the dead. Abraham and Adam were terrified. Having killed the governor, the three of them would probably be executed on the spot.

Just then, a hefty woman with the shoulders of a mule and the face of a weather-beaten Madonna climbed out of a trap door in the floor. She took the scene in with a single glance and then shouted, "Quiet!" The room fell

The Governor of Pinsk

silent, save for the rabbi's chanting.

The woman strode over to the fallen man and gave him a soft kick. The man moaned.

"He's not dead," she scowled. "Just drunk."

Rabbi Kibbitz opened his eyes. "The governor is drunk?" he said. "How can that be? How is it possible that a governor so wise would fuddle his mind with drink, especially before lunchtime?"

"He's not the governor," the woman said, squinting at the rabbi.

"Ahh." Rabbi Kibbitz sighed with relief. "You see the governor asked me to bring these boys to see him, so . . . Um, where, may I ask, is the governor?"

The woman stared at him. Then she looked at Adam and Abraham. The boys flinched under her gaze and stepped behind their rabbi's long black coat.

"Who brought these idiots here?" she bellowed suddenly.

The cart driver's hand shot into the air. "I did. They asked me to take them to the Governor's Palace. What was I supposed to do? They're from Chelm."

Again, the dark room filled with laughter until the woman silenced it with a stare.

"It's important," said Rabbi Kibbitz. He paused as the drunken man, who he'd thought was the dead governor, began crawling across the floor toward the door. When the man crawled outside, the rabbi continued, "It's important that we see the governor immediately, if not sooner."

"And who exactly are you?" the woman asked, her polite words undercut by contempt and exasperation.

"I am Rabbi Kibbitz of Chelm," said the rabbi proudly. "And these are Abraham and Adam Schlemiel, the two youngsters responsible for the defeat and capture of the notorious Krabot gang."

Another roar of laughter was cut short as the woman held up her hand.

"You're kidding?" she asked. "Alex Krabot and Dimitri Dimitriovich finally got captured?"

"And Bertie Zanuk as well," Adam added.

"Hush, little one," Rabbi Kibbitz said. "Let us save your heroic story for the governor, whom I am certain would like to hear it in person."

"You really did it, didn't you?" the woman asked quietly. "I'd heard rumors, but I assumed that they were lies . . ."

"Yes, we did," Abraham said.

A startled murmur rippled through the room as all eyes turned to the boys. Adam and Abraham felt like running, but they bravely stood and weathered the unwanted attention.

"So, you see it is important," Rabbi Kibbitz said, "that we speak to the governor as soon as possible. The boys need to give evidence at the Krabot gang's trial. Then, I would like to get back to Chelm before Shabbos. If we can catch the evening train to Smyrna, then by tomorrow afternoon . . ."

"Excuse me," the woman interrupted.

"Yes?" said the rabbi.

"You wanted to speak to the governor, so shut up and speak already."

The rabbi looked confused.

The woman rolled her eyes. "My name is Babushka Krabot," she said, a wicked smile cutting across her wrinkled face. "And I am the governor."

"But . . . but you're a woman," Rabbi Kibbitz sputtered. "I'm sorry, but I don't remember the governor being a woman." He reached into his pocket and withdrew the sheet of parchment that had summoned the Schlemiel boys. He reread the paper and showed it to the large old woman who owned the inn. "No. I didn't think so. It doesn't say that here. This isn't the real Governor's Palace, is it? I mean the official governor."

Babushka Krabot took the paper from the rabbi, glanced over it, and said, "No. And this isn't Minsk. This is Pinsk."

"Minsk Pinsk Shminsk!" said Rabbi Kibbitz cheerfully. "Mrs. Krabot, it's clear that we've made a mistake. We won't trouble you any more. If we can just find our driver, we'll hop back on the cart, go to the train station, and . . ."

"Wait," Babushka Krabot bellowed.

Rabbi Kibbitz fell silent. Adam wondered if this might be a good time to bolt for the front door. Abraham put an arm on his brother's shoulder and whispered, "Wait."

Babushka Krabot frowned, her face a road map of displeasure. "You come into the Governor's Palace and ask to see the governor. You tell an incredible story about how these two boys have captured my son, Alex, and then you want to just leave?"

"Your son?" Rabbi Kibbitz said. "Krabot? Oh, I see. Yes. It's clear we have made a mistake. A big one. Oy vey. Well, Madam, it has been a pleasure, but we really ought to get to Minsk. The governor, you see, he is expecting us."

The crowd closed in around the three fellows from Chelm.

"What shall we do with them?" a one-eyed man hissed.

"String them up?" said a man with a wart on the tip of his nose.

"I'm hungry," said a girl wearing what looked like a wolf's head for a hat.

(Or maybe, Abraham thought, it was a wolf wearing a girl's head as a neck-lace . . .)

"Shut up!" Babushka Krabot roared. "You're all giving me a headache."

"Let's put them on trial," said the one-eyed man. "Give them a taste of their own medicine."

"Well, first, we're not sick," said Rabbi Kibbitz, "so we won't need any medicine. And second, these boys were supposed to testify *at* the trial, not be *on* trial. The distinction is small but nevertheless important."

"Just kill them" said Wart-Nose. He drew out a long sharp knife.

"Then eat them!" giggled the girl.

"A trial," said Babushka Krabot, smiling. "All right, a trial. Set the room up. Enough of you good for nothings have been dragged into court to know what it looks like. Get moving!"

Immediately, two dozen men and women began hurrying about to transform the Governor's Palace from a dark and dingy barroom into a dark and dingy courtroom. All the chairs were arranged in rows. Tables were set for the prosecution and the defense. A platform was constructed from old vodka crates, and the judge's bench appeared tall and threatening.

During the chaos, Abraham, Adam, and Rabbi Kibbitz began edging their way toward the door. They might have made it, too, if Abraham hadn't accidentally stepped on Wart-Nose's cat, which hissed and snarled.

"Bailiff," shouted Babushka Krabot, as she hoisted her huge body into the judge's chair, "grab those prisoners and bring them to me!"

"Clumsy" Adam whispered.

"Shh," Abraham said. "I'm beginning to have a plan."

"Don't worry, boys," Rabbi Kibbitz said. "This is a court of justice. We are innocent. I have no doubt that the truth will set us free."

Abraham and Adam exchanged looks. They were now more concerned than ever.

The rabbi was shoved into a chair. Abraham and Adam were brought before the governor.

"Mr. Prosecutor," Babushka Krabot said. "What case have you brought before me?"

"Your immenseness," One-Eye began, "these two boys claim that they are responsible for the imprisonment and imminent demise of your one and only son, Alex."

"Objection!" said Rabbi Kibbitz, rising to his feet. "Your son is not dead."

"Not yet," hissed One-Eye, "but when he is found guilty of attempted armed robbery, he will surely be sentenced to the gallows."

"Objection! Who is to say that he will be found guilty?"

"Rabbi," Abraham said, "Krabot and his gang tried to rob Chelm. Remember?"

"Oh," Rabbi Kibbitz said, nodding. "Well, he was definitely guilty of that."

"Abraham!" Adam looked aghast. "What are you doing?"

"The witnesses have admitted their own guilt," One-Eye said. "The prosecution rests. We demand the death penalty."

The spectators in the gallery cheered and stamped their feet. The wolf-girl hurried behind the bar, brought out two bottles of vodka, and began filling glasses for a toast.

"Death to the righteous!" Wart-Nose said, raising his glass and tossing down the clear liquid in a single burning gulp.

"Death to the righteous!" everyone echoed—except for the Schlemiel brothers and Rabbi Kibbitz.

"Oy," Rabbi Kibbitz said, rubbing his forehead. "Oy."

Abraham, if you have a plan, Adam said into his brother's mind, *this would be a good time . . .*

You're the one with all the ideas.

Not today. I'm sorry.

All right, I'll try something . . .

"Your giganticness," Abraham said. "May I speak in our defense?"

Babushka Krabot's eyes narrowed, but she banged her glass on the podium for silence. "Speak."

"Your son, Alex, spoke kindly of you," Abraham said. "He told me that you tried to save him from a wicked world."

"Objection!" One-Eye stood. "The guilty party is clearly trying to influence the judge with a pack of patently false lies."

"If they're false lies," Rabbi Kibbitz said, "then they must be true!"

"What did Alex say about me?" Babushka Krabot asked.

Abraham tried to remember exactly what Alex Krabot had said about his mother. "He said that the last time he saw you, he was trying to protect you. That he killed a man and hadn't been home since. I think he misses you."

"You think?" One-Eye said. "Pure speculation!"

"Go on," Babushka Krabot said.

"He said that you told him to run from the police," Abraham said. "You thought he would get away safely. And he did. He has been on the run, living in danger for years. And he might still be free if only he hadn't tried to rob Chelm at gunpoint and threatened everyone, including my mother."

"You see," One-Eye smiled. "A full confession!"

"He did that?" Babushka Krabot said. "Alex did that?"

Abraham nodded sadly. "Yes. He held a gun to my mother's head and told my father and our village to give him all we had. It was only by luck that she still lives, that our village was not burned to the ground like the one that you and your son once lived in."

Babushka Krabot frowned. She stared at her fingernails, which were black with grime.

"It has been fifteen years since he ran away," she said. "And never a day passes that I wish I hadn't told him to run. Perhaps if he had stayed he would have been found innocent. At least by now he would have served his prison term. Instead, I hear my son is a big shot robber. Sometimes I think he is doing well for himself, but other times I wish I could bring him here to my palace, give him a good dinner, and tuck him into bed. I miss him."

"Your hugeness," the prosecutor began. "Don't be swayed by this obvious ploy. Your son is going to die because of these two. The people demand revenge!"

"Fydor, shut up. The game is over. We've had our fun. We scared them, and that is enough."

"So, are we free to go?" Rabbi Kibbitz asked, jumping to his feet with surprising agility for a man so old.

Adam grinned and slapped Abraham on the back. Abraham smiled.

"Wait." Babushka Krabot looked at One-Eye. "Tell me what will happen to my son if these boys do not appear at the Governor's Palace in Minsk to testify at his trial."

One-Eye stood and thought for a minute. "If there are no witnesses at Alex's trial, the court will have to let him go," he said.

Babushka Krabot waited for him to sit back down before she continued, addressing the three visitors. "You are sentenced to return to Chelm with your sacred promise never to leave that village. You will not be able to testify at my son's trial. He will be released. And then perhaps he will at last come home."

"Babushka," One-Eye said. "You can't be serious."

"You mean that they just shouldn't leave Chelm to testify at the trial?" Rabbi Kibbitz asked. "Or are you talking about something broader than that?"

"Forever," she said. "My son may be a thief and worse, but he is still my son. Will you abide by my judgment, or should I leave you to them?"

Abraham and Adam stared out at the leering crowd in the derelict palace. Then they slowly nodded. "We promise," they said, their voices barely a whisper.

The weary woman banged her empty vodka glass on the podium, sealing her judgment. She climbed down from the bench and without another word vanished through a door behind the bar.

The stunned crowd remained silent as Abraham and Adam Schlemiel and Rabbi Kibbitz gathered their belongings and made their way outside into the gray and rainy afternoon. They paused for a moment, greeting the fresh damp air with a blessing of relief. Then they climbed into the donkey cart and set on their way back to the train station.

"You see?" Rabbi Kibbitz said. "All is well."

Adam frowned and stared blankly ahead. Rabbi Kibbitz patted him on the shoulder.

Abraham looked back at the tavern and wondered how many more years Babushka Krabot would have to cry before her lost son came home.

CHAPTER FIFTEEN

Let's Not Talk about It . . .

Babushka Krabot's sentence hung over Abraham's and Adam's heads like a millstone. It weighed them down and made them weary. By unspoken agreement, neither they nor Rabbi Kibbitz mentioned the mistaken trip to Pinsk to anyone in Chelm.

When they first returned to yet another hero's welcome, Mrs. Chaipul asked Rabbi Kibbitz, "So, how did the trip go?"

There was a long pause, as every ear in the room strained to hear.

"Well . . ." Rabbi Kibbitz began. He nodded. He pursed his lips. He nodded again.

Everyone waited.

Rabbi Kibbitz took a sip of water. He nodded a third time, and then he rubbed his beard.

"What did he say?" asked Oma Levitsky, who was eighty years old, hard of hearing, and had assumed that she'd missed something.

"Shh, Mamma," said Reb Levitsky, the janitor.

"And the governor," asked Reb Cantor, the merchant. "Did he like my gift. What did you think of him?"

"Him?" Rabbi Kibbitz frowned. He raised an eyebrow and smiled in an awkward way. "Well . . ."

"What?" asked Oma Levitsky. "What?"

"Shhh."

"And the trial?" Jacob Schlemiel asked his boys. "That went well, too?"

Abraham looked at Adam. Adam looked back. They both looked to the rabbi, who smiled and shrugged. "Well enough."

"What?" the old woman asked. "What?"

"Well, Mamma, well," her son replied.

"Well?" Oma Levitsky looked puzzled. "Well what?"

"Well enough!" Abraham shouted with frustration. This the old woman could hear.

"Well enough!" Oma Levitsky repeated, grinning from ear to ear.

Well enough. Such a wise man Rabbi Kibbitz was. So succinct. What more could anyone ask for?

Glasses were lifted and a cheer was raised to "Well enough!" Everyone went home happy. Everything went back to normal—or as normal as it gets in a village such as Chelm.

But for Abraham and Adam, the world had changed very much. It had grown smaller, confining. They had given their promises, and now they were in prison instead of Krabot. It was true that their prison was as large as a village, but it was a prison nevertheless.

"What if I want to travel?" Adam grumbled one day as they hauled water from the well.

"You can't," Abraham said.

Another day, their father ordered them into the Black Forest to help him cut down trees. They hesitated. Where did Chelm end and the rest of the world begin? The forest, they decided, mind-talking back and forth, could be considered within the realm of Chelm, but not Smyrna, which was another village entirely. So, while they were free to cut trees or pick mushrooms in the forest, they weren't free to go to Smyrna. The next time Jacob asked the boys to go there for brass tacks they refused.

"I don't know what's wrong with them," Jacob said to Rebecca that evening. "They used to jump at the chance to go to a big city like Smyrna."

"They're frightened," Rebecca soothed her husband. "They're young. Give them time."

"They're nearly ten years old. It wasn't as if I was going to ask one of them to go off by himself . . . When I was ten years old I was sent off to be an apprentice by myself."

"Times change," Rebecca said. "Children today don't understand."

But years passed and still Abraham and Adam Schlemiel would not set foot beyond the bounds of the Schvartzvald. Once, after a particularly prosperous winter, their father suggested a family trip to see Warsaw and visit distant relatives. A look of such sheer panic filled the boys faces that he never again mentioned such a thing.

It was sad how much such a small promise had changed their lives. To all appearances their lives went on as might be expected. In addition to their schooling with Rabbi Abrahms, they took on new chores around the house and began to learn Jacob's trade. They learned how to saw, plane, hammer, sand, and polish wood. They learned that if a chair's legs were too skinny it would break, but that if they were too thick the chair would be as ugly as a stone.

Months passed, And then years. They had a birthday, and then another.

Now they were eleven years old and their days seemed long and exhausting. Summer mornings were filled with chores and work in the shop. Then it was time to go to *heder* to learn to read and write and understand the ways of the world. Rabbi Abrahms couldn't open the windows because then everyone would look outside, so the classroom grew hot and stifling. Dozing was not allowed, and whenever a head began to nod, Rabbi Abrahms brought his ruler down on the offender's desk with a loud WHACK!

In the old days, the other children had looked to Abraham and Adam for comic relief and retribution, but now they were disappointed to find the boys too worn out to play the sorts of tricks they had played in the past. No longer were Rabbi Abrahms's feet glued into his shoes, nor was the seat of his chair covered with grease so that every time he sat down he slid to the floor with a thud.

These were sad times for the children of Chelm, tired times. But it was summer, and summers were always this way. Days were long, and the growing season was short. Everyone had to work their hardest to store enough food and firewood to last the long cold winter.

So, after school, it was back to more chores—cleaning the shop, sweeping the kitchen, peeling the potatoes, weeding the garden. It never ended!

One morning, in this long summer following their eleventh birthday, Adam said to Abraham, "Well enough? I've had enough. We need a break."

They were dragging a load of water back from the well, and Abraham sighed. "Adam, it's Tuesday. We'll have a break on the Sabbath."

"No." Adam shook his head. "On the Sabbath we'll spend half the day in shul and the other half studying with Rabbi Kibbitz. Today is going to be hot, the sun is already high, and I need a break now."

"Stop talking such foolishness," Abraham said. "There is work to be done."

At the door to their house they stopped to wipe their feet and made sure they didn't spill a drop of water on their mother's carefully polished floor.

Adam gave him a look. "There is always work to be done. There always will be work to do. You sound like Father. What happened to my carefree brother, who once managed to tie the schoolteacher's bootlaces to a billy goat's beard?"

Several months before the Krabot disaster, Rabbi Abrahms had taken the class to a farm to observe his work as a *mashgiach,* and while the rabbi had been inspecting a goat's kid Abraham had sneaked up behind the teacher . . . The billy goat had butted the poor rabbi in the *tuchas* fifteen times before the laces finally snapped. For a week afterward, the sore man had sat on a pillow.

It had been brilliant. For once Abraham had even managed to escape punishment because no one had seen him do it, and the goat had eaten both the shoelaces and the rabbi's shoes.

"All right," Abraham grinned. "What do you propose?"

Adam's smile grew broad.

Before he could answer, they heard their father's voice from behind the house. "Boys! Come on already. Give me some help with the wagon."

Even if they hadn't been able to read each other's minds, they would have known what to do. They looked at each other, nodded . . . and ran.

CHAPTER SIXTEEN

Summer Day

Their father's shouts quickly faded in the distance. Abraham and Adam kept running anyway, running for the sheer joy of running. Out of the village proper, off the road, across the farm fields, and into the edge of the Schvartzvald where at last they collapsed, laughing with exhaustion.

They lay on the ground of the dark forest for a long time, clutching their sides and giggling. Just as one boy began to settle down and breathe calmly, the other would snort or guffaw, and they'd be off again laughing like two maniacs.

"Oww!" Abraham said at last.

"Ow-wow!" Adam agreed.

They each took a deep breath and held it. One, two, three. And slowly they let their breaths out. Adam felt his stomach jump, and Abraham nearly giggled, but at last they had managed to contain themselves.

Now they rested, enjoying the soft crinkle of the fallen elm leaves, the smell of moss and dirt, the light breeze, and the rustle of the trees. It felt good to be away, out of town. It felt even better to finally relax and be themselves once again.

Something had changed since their trip to Pinsk with the rabbi. Everyone had treated them as if they had somehow improved, and without realizing it they had found themselves doing exactly what was expected of them. What was needed was some fun.

They both knew that they would be in big trouble when they got back. But for now the air was cool in the forest, the birds were chirruping, and their father's carpentry shop with all their chores and work to be done was far away.

"So, shall we go swimming?" Adam said.

Abraham thought for a moment and nodded. "Maybe we can catch a fish and bring it home for dinner."

"There are no fish in the Uherka," Adam said. "You know that. Why do you always have to try and do something nice? Why can't we just go for a swim?"

"Fine," Abraham said. "Fine. We'll swim."

The Uherka River was cold and refreshing. Actually, it was quite cold, so cold that the twins were soon shivering. Their lips turned blue and their fingers and toes went numb. Abraham liked swimming down to the bottom and tugging on Adam's leg as if he were a monster from the deep. Adam liked waiting until just after his brother surfaced to splash a handful of water into his open and gasping mouth. All in all, it was just about as much fun as two brothers could possibly have together. At last, they climbed out, half frozen, and found a grassy spot high on the banks of the river to warm themselves in the sunshine.

"We should have brought towels," Abraham said.

"We should be hard at work in Father's carpentry shop," Adam said. "I think we can live without towels."

Abraham nodded. His eyes were closed and he felt the warm orange glow on his face. "Do you ever worry that Alex Krabot might come and kill us?"

Adam sighed. "I didn't until just now."

"It scares me some times," Abraham said. "I'm not even sure that we should be outside of Chelm. We did give our promise to the governor."

"Abraham, stop it. We've discussed it over and over," Adam said. "She wasn't the governor, she was his mother. And the whole point was to prevent us from testifying at her son's trial so he'd be set free. That was almost two years ago. He must be free by now. As far as I can tell, it worked and we kept our end of the bargain. Even if we hadn't, I don't think Alex Krabot would care if we sneaked out to go for a swim. He might kill us, but I doubt he'd blame us."

"I suppose so," Abraham said glumly.

"Why can't you just relax and enjoy yourself?" Adam asked.

"I'm hungry. And we're probably going to get sent to our room without dinner tonight."

"Stop." Adam swatted at Abraham. "Enough of that. If you could have anything you wanted, what would it be?"

"Brisket," Abraham said without hesitation, "and *kasha varnishkes* with plenty of gravy."

Adam nodded. "But no kale. It doesn't matter what Mama does to it, I hate kale."

"I kind of like it. Especially when she cooks it with garlic and onions and vinegar."

"Eccch!" Adam shuddered. "Eruwaaagh!"

Abraham laughed.

They lay silently for a while. The grass was cool and tickled their naked backs. Every so often, a cloud would slip in front of the sun, enveloping them in shadow until it blew away. Nearby they heard the sounds of two squirrels fighting over a nut and a tree filled with birds cawing at the sky.

At last, Abraham said, "What do you want to do?"

Adam thought for a moment. "I want to marry Rosa and live in a house as big as Reb Cantor's. Maybe bigger. I want to have plenty of money and never have to work. I want to be respected in the shul, but not be the kind of person who they talk about when he doesn't show up. I want to have a garden. And I'd like to visit Moscow. And maybe Arizona, too. What about you?"

Abraham had propped himself up on one elbow. He stared at his brother in amazement. "Actually," he said, "I was just wondering what you wanted to do now. This afternoon."

"Oh," Adam said. "I want to take a nap." Adam's eyes were closed, and even though he was hungry he felt happy and safe.

"Are you asleep?" Abraham asked.

"Yes. Definitely."

Abraham poked him.

"What?" Adam said.

"You really want to marry Rosa?"

"Sure," Adam shrugged. "There's nobody in the village that I'd want to marry. Can you see me married to Rachel Cohen? She would talk my head off. Or Rivka Cantor? She's so mean to me."

"I think that means she likes you," Abraham said.

"That kind of liking I can do without."

"But you can't marry Rosa. She's not Jewish."

Adam sighed. "I know. Maybe she'll convert. Or I could become a Gypsy."

"I don't think you can become one of them. And if you did, then you couldn't own a house. They're travelers."

Adam opened his eyes. He realized that Abraham wasn't going to let him nap. "So, what's your perfect plan, Mr. Smart Guy?"

Abraham smiled. "That's easy. I thought I'd marry someone like Mother, take over Father's shop from him, and live happily ever after in Chelm."

"Boring," Adam said.

Abraham shrugged. "After facing the Krabot gang and traveling to Pinsk, I don't care if I never have another adventure."

"It wasn't so bad," Adam said.

Abraham snorted. "You complained the whole time."

"Well, so did you," Adam said. "Most of the time I was scared or wet. Or both. And now we're heroes? People as far away as Pinsk know that the Schlemiel brothers are not to be trifled with. Ha!"

"Are you sure they do?" Abraham said. "I think you have an overinflated sense of our reputation."

"So? When you're old and fat and still living in Chelm, I'll send you a letter from Arizona."

They both laughed. At the bottom of the hill, the Uherka River gurgled along. If either of them had opened their eyes, they might have seen a family of deer nibbling at the wild flowers on the edge of the clearing.

"Do you really think we'll ever live apart?" Adam asked.

Abraham didn't answer with words. Instead, he spoke directly into Adam's mind. *Don't worry, little brother. No matter where we live, I'll always be close by.*

They reached out and held hands in a comforting squeeze.

And then, since they were normal eleven-year-old boys, the handshake turned into a tug of war, which turned into a tussle, and in two minutes they were rolling together head over heels back down the hill and into the river.

Splash! The cold water startled them apart. They opened their eyes and saw that the sun was almost below the tops of the trees.

"Father and Mother are going to kill us," Abraham said as he stumbled to shore.

"Yes," Adam said. "But it was worth it. We'd better hurry, though. Abraham, where are our clothes? What did you do with them?"

"What do you mean?" Abraham asked. "Aren't they right there?"

They looked at the log where they'd put their clothes.

"Adam, what did you do?" Abraham said. "While I was asleep you swam across the river and hid the clothes, didn't you?"

Adam shook his head. "No. I was going to ask you the same thing. Do you think Alex Krabot stole our clothes?"

"No," Abraham said. "He would have killed us. Maybe one of the boys from the village did it."

"We would have heard them. They probably would have thrown mud at us and woken us up. It must be a tramp. What are we going to do?"

There wasn't much to do. Clutching twigs covered with leaves, Abraham and Adam sneaked their way back to Chelm, hiding behind bushes and rocks. When they reached the edge of the village, the going was trickier. They ran in short bursts from the edge of one house to the next, hoping that no one would see them scurrying around naked.

At last, their house was in sight.

"We'll go in through the bedroom window," Abraham whispered to Adam. They were hidden behind a stable near their house. "I'll go first. We'll get dressed quickly and then afterward worry about what Mother and Father will do."

Adam nodded. Together they stood up, ready for the last dash home.

"Well, hello there!" said Rabbi Yohon Abrahms, the schoolteacher. Beside him stood every schoolchild in Chelm, laughing and pointing. "We were just coming out to watch the sunset. It's been such a lovely day, hasn't it. You two weren't in school today. I suppose missing class is one thing, but missing your clothing is something else entirely . . ."

Adam and Abraham turned as red as the sunset and ran. They didn't stop to think that their window might be shut; they just dove inside. Fortunately, the window was open. There, on the bed, neatly laid out, were their missing clothes.

"Abraham," Mother called from the kitchen. "Adam. After you're dressed, come out. It's nearly dinner time."

Adam looked at Abraham. "Do you smell *kasha*?" he said.

"She's torturing us," Abraham said, terrified.

A few minutes later, they sat down at the table, surprised to see that portions of brisket and *kasha* were laid out in front of their seats as well.

"I missed you today," their father said softly. "But I'm glad to see that you've come back safe and sound. Next time you run off, make sure you tell somebody. Something horrible might happen to you and we'd never know."

Jacob Schlemiel winked at his wife, who patted his shoulder and shook her head. Abraham and Adam stared at their shoes and mumbled apologies.

"Eat up," their mother said, "before it gets cold." Her face was stern, but her eyes twinkled with a barely suppressed smile.

CHAPTER SEVENTEEN

A Girl

Rebecca Schlemiel always smiled. It was who she was. She was a mother, and she always smiled. She had smiled as she had watched her babies grow into boys, and she smiled as she watched her boys growing into men. Sometimes, of course, she wanted cry—when she was tired or frustrated, but even then the feeling didn't last.

Once, a few years earlier, Adam had told her that he felt as if everyone liked Abraham better than him. Rebecca had felt the tears of sympathy welling up inside her. What a beautiful and wonderful boy he was. And that made her smile. She held Adam close, hiding her smile so he wouldn't think she was laughing at him, and told him how much she loved him.

"If you ever run out of smiles," the saying in Chelm went, "visit Rebecca Schlemiel. She's got so many, she'll be happy to give away one or two."

Rebecca, you see, had learned a secret that many people know in their brains, but only a few know in their hearts. She knew that her life was good and perfect in all ways. No, she didn't have much money. Yes, there were times that she coughed so hard it turned her cheeks almost purple. True, Abraham and especially Adam were always getting themselves in trouble of one kind or another. Still, it was a perfect world, and she would not change a thing.

Well . . . maybe one thing.

More than anything else, Rebecca Schlemiel wanted a daughter. The boys were wonderful, and her husband was fine, but there were days when she longed for the company of women. She wanted to teach someone how to bake, how to sew, how to look at a field of wild flowers and know exactly which seven to pick to make a perfect bouquet. She wanted a baby to tickle, but not one who would grow up to make even more trouble. She wanted a little girl who would stay at home and help her fix dinner instead of going to the shop with her father. She wanted a young woman who would tell her of problems with boys and whose hair she could help pin up on her wedding day. A daughter wasn't so much to ask for, was it?

So far, though, nothing. Jacob and Rebecca had tried. And tried. No luck. Jacob had even gone to Rabbi Kibbitz and asked his advice. He'd told Rebecca later that the old man's face had turned so red that his beard looked as if it were going to catch on fire. After the rabbi had caught his breath, he'd gone to his bookshelf and found an old book with strange letters and pictures of men and women with slanted eyes. Those pictures! Rebecca had no idea that human beings could be so inventive. But the magic book hadn't worked either, even though they'd gone through it from cover to cover twice. Rebecca smiled fondly as she remembered the last time the boys had gone to bed early . . .

Now, however, it was time to try something else. After Jacob and the boys went to the shop, she put on her shawl and hurried across town to Mrs. Chaipul's restaurant.

It wasn't often that a woman went alone to Mrs. Chaipul's restaurant. Mostly the women of Chelm were too busy to sit around a table and drink endless cups of tea, as some of the men did. And they were also frugal. Why buy a meal when you could make it at home, especially if you were a better cook? It wasn't that Mrs. Chaipul was a bad cook, but . . .

When Rebecca opened the door to the restaurant, Mrs. Chaipul looked up from behind the counter with surprise, as did her three usual customers—Reb Cantor, the merchant, Reb Cohen, the tailor, and Reb Gold, the cobbler. Rebecca smiled at them, and they all nodded back. Then she sat at the counter, and they all looked at her nervously.

"Are you going to the market?" Mrs. Chaipul asked.

"Not today," Rebecca Schlemiel said. "I wanted to talk with you." Her voice dropped. "You see, I have a bit of a problem . . ."

At their table, the three men pretended to talk among themselves while their ears grew eager to hear what that problem was.

"You think you have a problem?" Mrs. Chaipul said. "I have customers who sit here all day, drink one cup of tea for hours at a time, and then wonder why their businesses make no money."

A silence fell over the restaurant. The three men shifted uncomfortably in their seats for a moment, then Reb Cantor rose and paid the bill, and with another set of nods they all left.

"Good customers," Mrs. Chaipul said. "So, what is it? You've got a cold? I noticed you coughing the other day. Some of my chicken soup with *knaidels* will cure that in a minute."

"No!" Rebecca raised her hands perhaps too quickly. Mrs. Chaipul's soup dumplings were famous for being as heavy as lead and tasting nearly as good. "What I meant to say is, thank you, but the cough comes and goes. What I want is a girl."

"I completely understand," Mrs. Chaipul said. She poured them both tea and sat down next to Rebecca at the counter. "I want one too."

Rebecca looked at Mrs. Chaipul in amazement. The woman was a widow, in her sixties at least, and she wanted a girl?

"Girls are so wonderful," Mrs. Chaipul continued. "They cook, they clean, they do laundry."

Rebecca laughed. "But not right away."

"Oh, no," Mrs. Chaipul agreed. "It takes a day or two to train them. They need to learn what goes in which cabinet, how many cloves of garlic to put in the soup, and so forth."

"Only two days? Boys take forever. I had no idea girls learned so quickly."

"Girls these days are very smart. That's why they're so hard to come by."

"Ahh," Rebecca nodded. That explained a lot. "Why do you suppose it takes so much longer with boys?"

"Boys are impossible," Mrs. Chaipul said. "It's a girl you want. Shoshona Cantor, she just got a girl last week. She was telling me about it. Now she has so much more free time."

"Mrs. Cantor? The merchant's wife? Isn't she a little old?"

"Exactly. But now, the girl even does the shopping for her. Cooking, cleaning, shopping, the girl does it all. Shoshona hardly knows what to do with her days. I told her to come in here, have breakfast with her husband, and talk with the men, but she just laughed."

Rebecca smiled. "I had no idea she was even pregnant. I'll have to get a gift."

"Pregnant?" Mrs. Chaipul laughed. "No, she hired a maid."

"A maid?"

"Yes, a servant girl. To live in. They have such a big house, with empty rooms and . . ." Mrs. Chaipul's voice trailed off. "You thought I meant . . . you thought that I wanted a baby?"

Rebecca Schlemiel looked at her teacup and nodded.

"Ha!" Mrs. Chaipul cackled. "That's a good one! I wouldn't have another baby if you paid me all the gold in the czar's money locker. Let the children have the babies. I'll visit them. Hee hee hee. Me having another baby, who could imagine such a thing?"

Embarrassed though she was, Rebecca managed a smile.

That was when Mrs. Chaipul noticed that she was laughing alone. She giggled a moment longer and then calmed herself down.

"Oh, I see," Mrs. Chaipul said at last. "You meant that you want a baby girl. Not a servant."

Rebecca nodded.

"Okay. All right." Mrs. Chaipul rubbed her chin. "Let's see what we can do . . ."

CHAPTER EIGHTEEN

Breaking the Good News

It only took two months and then suddenly she knew.

"Jacob! I have good news!" Rebecca Schlemiel was calling. "Have you seen Adam and Abraham?"

"No. I think they're in their room," Jacob answered.

"Could you go get them?" Rebecca Schlemiel asked. "I want to have a talk with everyone."

Abraham and Adam were not quite in their room, though. They had been in Reb Cantor's apple orchard, filling their bellies with not-quite-ripe fruit. Now they were trying to sneak back in their house. Adam was climbing up onto the water barrel.

"Come on! Hurry," Abraham whispered.

Adam heard his father's footsteps approaching their bedroom door. He jumped over to the kitchen window ledge. From there it was only a short dive through the bedroom window and onto Abraham's bed. He was just about ready to leap when he heard the door to their room open, and their father said, "Abraham? Adam? They're not in here."

"Where else could they be?" Rebecca asked. "Did you look under the bed?"

Adam didn't dare move. He heard his father's footsteps, imagined him crouching down and looking under the boys' bed. "No. Not there."

"Is their bedroom window open?" Rebecca asked.

"What difference would that make?" Jacob Schlemiel asked.

"Oy," Rebecca said. She shook her head. "Maybe they're outside."

Adam dove. He landed perfectly and got out of the way so that Abraham, who had already hoisted himself up onto the pickle barrel, could make his move.

"Abraham!" their mother shouted from the front door. "Adam! Come here. I want to talk with you."

"I'm right here, Mama," Adam called, coming out of the room and nearly running into his startled father.

"I thought I checked your room," Jacob said. "Where's Abraham?"

"Oh, he's coming," Adam said, just as Abraham made his leap.

It was almost perfect, and if he hadn't rushed he would have been fine. Unfortunately, his foot slipped on the kitchen window ledge, and just as he was shooting through the window, Abraham saw the back of his father's head and panicked. His leg swung around and banged against the stick that held the twins' bedroom window open. The stick shot out of the house, and the window slammed down on Abraham's leg.

He tried not to scream, but couldn't quite manage it. He kept his mouth shut while he yanked his foot out of the window and then howled like a wolf with its foot caught in a trap.

"Abraham," Rebecca called out, turning around and shaking her head. "How many times have I told you not to yell like a wild man. Always with the theatrics."

Adam and Jacob rushed into the bedroom.

"What happened?" Jacob said.

Abraham rose, took one look at his twisted left leg, and said, "I don't think I can walk." His face turned white, and he started to collapse. Adam caught Abraham as he fell, and panic rose in his eyes. "Mama, help!" Rebecca's heart froze. She didn't remember hurrying to the boys' room. Jacob and Adam carried Abraham to his bed while Rebecca ran for Mrs. Chaipul, who came scurrying with her carpetbag.

"What happened?" Mrs. Chaipul asked. It was clear that Abraham's leg was broken.

"I don't know," Abraham said. "I guess I slept wrong."

Mrs. Chaipul looked at the strange way the leg was bent, clucked to herself three times, and then (without any warning) snapped the bone back into place. Abraham now howled like a dying wolf. Adam felt a sudden blast in his mind like a thunderbolt. He fell backward into the bedroom wall.

Rebecca Schlemiel fainted, and even Jacob looked stunned.

Mrs. Chaipul shrugged. "You think it would have felt any better if I told you what was coming?" She splinted the leg and then bound it firmly with lengths of white plaster-dipped cloth.

For the next week Mrs. Chaipul came by every day to check on her patient. And once the initial shock wore off and the plaster dried, Abraham found that he could actually walk, albeit stiffly.

"No running around like a wild animal for six weeks," Mrs. Chaipul warned. "Two months if you want to be sure, but you're a boy, so . . . six weeks. Okay?"

"Okay." Abraham looked ashamed.

Life in the Schlemiel household slowly got back to its normal everyday drudgery. Abraham spent his days and nights in bed while Adam did both of their chores and all of the work helping their father in the shop.

Nearly four weeks sped by before Rebecca Schlemiel finally remembered the important thing that she had meant to tell her family. She gathered everyone together in the boys' room. Abraham lay in bed, Adam sat next to him, and Jacob stood near the door.

"I can't believe I forgot!" Rebecca said. "I have such good news!"

"You mean," Adam said, "Mrs. Chaipul doesn't have to amputate Abraham's leg?"

"You mean," Abraham retorted, "Mrs. Chaipul is finally going to cut that unsightly bump from on top of Adam's shoulders?"

"What bump?" Adam asked.

"The one that starts at your neck and ends with your *kippah.*"

"Boys," Jacob warned. "Your mother is being serious. Go on."

"It's wonderful news, actually," Rebecca said.

"You mean he's adopted?" the boys said, simultaneously pointing at each other. They grinned until their father gave them a look that could have stripped paint off a canvas.

"No," their mother said patiently. "This is something very, very special. I want you to know that we're having . . ."

"A pot roast for dinner on Friday night?" Adam interrupted.

"With roasted potatoes and gravy?" Abraham continued.

"And an apple strudel for dessert?" Jacob said, his mouth salivating at the thought.

Both the boys and Rebecca were staring at him. "Sorry. It sounded good."

"You think it's funny?" Rebecca said quietly. Her head was nodding now, up and down like a fishing bob that had just hooked a snapping turtle. "You think that my good news is nothing but jokes and food? You think I'm just talking for no reason. Maybe I like to listen to you make fun of me?"

"No, Mama," Abraham said.

"We like your food," Adam said.

"Please, Rebecca," Jacob said. "Nothing was meant by it. Go on."

"I don't know if I should tell you now." She scowled. "And if I didn't have to tell you, I wouldn't. I'd just keep quiet about it."

Then, much to her family's surprise, Rebecca Schlemiel burst into tears.

"Mama!" Abraham said.

"We didn't mean to hurt you," Adam said.

"My sweetness." Jacob tried to put his arm around Rebecca, but she shrugged it off and stepped away.

"I try to tell you something so beautiful," she sobbed, "so special, but you have to ruin it. Men. You're all boys. Like children. Why do I want more children. Already I have too many!"

"No, no," Jacob soothed, patting her back. "It's not ruined. Merely delayed. Please. Please. We're listening now. Go on. Sit. Adam, get a chair for your mother."

Adam hurried into the kitchen and brought back a chair. At last Rebecca sat and daubed at her tears with a handkerchief.

"We're going to have an addition," she said, still crying. "An addition!"

"What?" Jacob said. "This is good news? You want me to build another room on the house? Rebecca, I've got work to do. Ever since Reb Cantor commissioned me to do more pieces for the governor, I've been very, very busy.

"Besides," he continued. "What do we need another addition for? We have our room, the boys have their room. There's the kitchen, where we also eat. How many rooms does a house need? You want maybe a library? We don't have so many books. And where would we put it? We can't build into the road. You've got your vegetable garden on the south side of the house. The outhouse is on the west, and the Lieberman's house is very close on the east . . . What? What?"

Abraham and Adam were giggling. Even Rebecca, who had been half an inch from losing her temper, was now shaking her head with amazed amusement.

"No, don't you all start laughing at me now," Jacob said, which just made things worse. "What? Am I completely out of line here when I say that adding a room to this house is not something that this family needs at this time? What? WHAT?"

Adam and his mother were rolling on the floor while Abraham rolled around on the bed, slapping the pillows with his hands.

Their laughter was so loud and so infectious that it was heard throughout Chelm. Across town in the restaurant, Rabbi Kibbitz looked up from his chicken soup and grinned at Mrs. Chaipul.

"Fine," Jacob scowled. "You want an addition. You want another room? You boys are going to help with the work. It's labor we're talking about. Hard labor. Do you boys even know what labor is?"

By this time, the twins and their mother were gasping for air. "Stop! Stop!" the boys begged.

"No," Jacob said, shaking his head firmly. "No. You can't just stop something like this. Once an idea like this is conceived it must be planned, it must be nurtured . . ."

At last, Jacob stopped. His family wasn't listening to him. He threw up his hands in exasperation. "What is so funny?"

"Papa," Abraham sputtered at last. "We're not *building* a new addition, we're *having* a new addition."

"Oh," Jacob said. "You think there's a difference? Building, having. Life doesn't come so easily . . ." Jacob broke off. "Having an addition? You mean having a new addition?"

Rebecca nodded, smiling at her husband.

Jacob Schlemiel grinned in amazement, ran over, picked up his wife, and twirled her around three times before setting her down gently.

"An addition?" he asked.

"And it's a girl. I think."

"Well then," Jacob shrugged, "I suppose we will need to build a new room for the new addition."

And now their laughter could be heard all the way to Smyrna.

CHAPTER NINETEEN

The Eighth Light

Hanukah was early, and Rebecca Schlemiel's baby was late. The sky was clear, and there were only ten inches of snow on the ground, crusted over by a thin layer of ice. The conversation in Chelm was a mixture of excitement for the coming festival of lights and anxiety because the czar of Russia was threatening the king of Poland over something or another.

On the first night of Hanukkah, as was their custom, the Schlemiel family gathered in the kitchen. Everyone knew his or her job. Jacob grated the potatoes while Rebecca mixed the recipe and cooked the pancakes. The smell of frying potatoes filled the warm air. Abraham (whose broken leg was completely healed except for the occasional throb) held the *shammes,* and Adam lit it with a match.

Rebecca sighed. "We are truly blessed."

Jacob nodded. "Truer words were never spoken."

"Come on," Adam said. "I'm getting hungry."

But Abraham would not be hurried. He knew enough to savor the delicious moment before the candles were lit.

"It's time," his mother said.

"Yes, Abraham," Jacob agreed. "It's time. Before the *shammes* melts."

"No," Rebecca said softly. "I mean it's time. Now. I'm going to have the baby."

Jacob blinked. "Right now?"

"Yes!"

Adam grinned and said the blessing as fast as he could. Abraham quickly lit the first candle.

Everyone sighed. Then Rebecca rolled her eyes and moaned.

"Go," Jacob sputtered at last. "Get Mrs. Chaipul."

"I'll go!" both boys said together. And in the next moment they were off, running without coats through the snow-covered streets, slipping and sliding on every patch of ice before scrambling to their feet and dashing off again.

Even though everyone in Chelm knew that Rebecca Schlemiel was over-due, the furious banging at her door startled Mrs. Chaipul. The old woman peeked down through her curtains and grabbed her black bag as soon as she saw the twins. She pulled on her coat and ran downstairs. The three of them rushed back to the Schlemiels' house.

"Shh." Jacob met them at the door with his finger to his lips. "Shhh," he repeated. "She's asleep."

"Are we too late?" Adam asked.

"Did we miss it?" Abraham said.

"No," Jacob whispered. To Mrs. Chaipul he said, "Rebecca said that the pains stopped and she was tired."

Mrs. Chaipul plopped herself down in a chair next to the fire and set her feet on the hearth to warm. "False labor," she said. "It happens. You two, wrap yourselves in blankets and sit next to the fire."

Teeth chattering, the two boys hurried to obey the old wise woman. While their mother slept in peace, the four others spun dreidels and ate latkes until late in the night.

The next day the temperature dropped and a new snow began to fall, but the baby still did not come. At last, night fell and the Schlemiels gath-ered around the kitchen table to light the menorah. This time the grins and laughter had a different flavor because they all expected that tonight would surely be the night. Jacob grated the potatoes and Rebecca cooked them. Adam held the *shammes* and Abraham set it afire with a match.

"Well?" Adam looked at his mother. "Is it time?"

"Go on, light the candles," she said, swatting at him with the wooden spatula. "Oof."

"Careful," Jacob warned.

"It's time," Rebecca whispered.

"Really?" Jacob said. "Are you sure?"

"It's TIME!"

In an instant the boys were off and running without their coats. Again Mrs. Chaipul nearly leaped out of her skin when they bashed on her door. And again, Rebecca was asleep before they arrived back.

"She said she was sorry for causing all this trouble," Jacob apologized.

"Nonsense," Mrs. Chaipul said shivering. "Maybe you boys should wear your coats inside tomorrow night."

The next three days were almost exact repeats of the first two, only the snow was deeper and the winds were colder. Each day Rebecca felt wonderful and fine right up until the moment before the first candle of the evening was about to be lit. Then the pains started like a sudden landslide and the boys were off and running.

By the fifth night of Hanukkah, Mrs. Chaipul had decided that it would be smarter to sleep at the Schlemiels' house. She also thought it would be prudent to send for the doctor. Reb Cantor had business in Smyrna and promised to see (and pay for) the doctor as soon as he got there. One or two days of false labor the old midwife knew about, but this repeated threat of imminent birth frightened her. She could see that even though Rebecca Schlemiel got up every morning with a smile on her face, the mother-to-be was growing weaker.

Even worse, no sooner did the merchant set out on the road than the blizzard began in earnest. With all the snow, it would take him at least a day to travel to the neighboring village, and it would take the doctor another day to arrive back in Chelm.

The snow did not stop.

Once a long time ago the villagers of Chelm hired porters to carry them so that their footsteps wouldn't ruin the beautiful carpet of snow. That would have been nice. This year the winter snows were so deep that the villagers were forced to dig tunnels just to go to their outhouses. Rabbi Kibbitz was forced to cancel the annual Hanukkah party, not because he wanted to but because he was afraid someone would freeze on the way home. And even though in every house candles were set in the windows, not a flicker could be seen in the snow-covered valley.

All of the Schlemiels were cranky by now. For seven days they'd eaten nothing but latkes. Abraham and Adam slept crowded on one mattress that they'd dragged onto the kitchen floor while Mrs. Chaipul rested warm and comfortable in the other bed in their room. It was impossible to sleep because whenever they did manage to doze off they'd be awakened by one of their mother's moans or groans.

On the eighth and last night of Hanukkah everyone was on edge. Jacob grumbled as he grated potatoes. Rebecca scowled as she cooked the pancakes. Abraham and Adam argued over whose turn it was to hold the *shammes*. Mrs. Chaipul kept looking out the window into the great wall of snow and wondering whether the doctor would arrive and if he would be too late.

At last, Rebecca Schlemiel slammed down her spatula and shouted, "Enough! Both of you hold the *shammes*. Jacob light it. I'll say the blessings and let's get this over with!"

The room fell silent.

"But Mama," Abraham said, "that's not how we . . ."

"NOW!"

Jacob's hand shook as he touched the match to the *shammes*. Rebecca said the blessings so quickly you couldn't have sneezed twice before they were done. Because they couldn't take their eyes off their mother, Abraham and Adam nearly set Mrs. Chaipul's hair on fire. At last all eight lights were burning brightly.

"There," Rebecca Schlemiel sighed. "I'm going to go to bed now."

After she had gone, Jacob turned to Mrs. Chaipul. "Is she all right?"

"I'll go check," the old woman said.

"Come boys," their father said. "One more game of dreidel. This time we'll play for latkes."

Abraham and Adam groaned but joined their father at the kitchen table. A few moments later, they heard a cry from their parents' bedroom, and all three were standing at the door when Mrs. Chaipul opened it, her eyes filled with tears of joy.

"It's a girl!"

Abraham and Adam stared open-mouthed at the tiny baby cradled in Mrs. Chaipul's arms while Jacob rushed to his wife's side.

"How is she? Her hand is cold."

"She's tired," Mrs. Chaipul said.

Rebecca opened her eyes and managed a weak smile. "Shmeenie," she whispered. "We'll name her Shmeenie."

CHAPTER TWENTY

Drudgery

After eight days of labor, Rebecca Schlemiel found it almost impossible to get out of bed. Her daughter was beautiful and perfect. Still, every bone in her body ached, and she was constantly exhausted. Opening her eyes, she had just enough strength to smile at Shmeenie and kiss her little one's nearly bald head before dozing off again.

First one week and then another and another went by and still Rebecca could not stand for more than the few minutes it took to go to the outhouse and back.

Food was brought in from Mrs. Chaipul's restaurant. Mrs. Cantor sent her cleaning helper over once a week to change the sheets and sweep. Rebecca smiled and tried to protest that she was all right, that everyone should just give her a moment and she'd get right to it. Then she'd doze off and forget by the time the girl was gone.

Jacob was starting to get worried, but he tried not to show it to the boys. One evening while they were doing laundry, he brought up an idea he was working on.

"Abraham, Adam," he said, "while your mother is resting, we're all going to have to pitch in and do more around the house. We can't keep eating Mrs. Chaipul's food, and sooner or later the Cantors are going to be upset that we can't keep our own house clean."

"Babies are revolting," Adam complained. He wrinkled his nose as he took a long stick, lifted one of Shmeenie's soiled linens, and dropped it into a vat of boiling water. Immediately a sickly stench filled the kitchen.

"Adam," Abraham yelled, "you're supposed to scrape the cloth and rinse it before you drop it into the pot!"

"You do it your way, I'll do it mine," Adam hissed back.

"Boys, boys," Jacob said, covering his nose with a towel. "I don't like this any more than you, but keep your voices down."

Just then, a feeble voice came from one of the bedrooms. "What's going on out there?"

"Nothing, sweetness," Jacob said. "We're making soup."

Both boys started giggling.

"Soup?" Rebecca said. "Let me get up to help you."

"No, Mama!" Abraham said. "We're doing fine. You rest."

"All right," Rebecca said. "I'll be up in a day or so. But I think you need to use a little less garlic."

By now, both Adam and Abraham were laughing loudly, and Jacob was doing everything he could to maintain his stern face. "Shh," he said. "Quiet."

Lying in bed, Rebecca winced and then rolled her eyes. Boys . . . Men . . . They were all the same.

At last, when they were sure she had gone back to sleep, Jacob resumed the discussion. "What it comes down to is this," he said. "I don't need both of your help in the shop all the time. We need to divide the chores around the house."

While his father was talking, Abraham took a heavy towel, picked up the diaper vat, lugged it out the front door, and poured the polluted water in the snow. "I'm already having a hard time doing all my chores, plus all of our school work," Adam moaned. "If I have to do one more thing around the house, I think I'll burst."

Jacob shook his head. "You boys shouldn't complain. We live very fortunate lives. We have a roof over our heads and enough food to eat."

Abraham packed fresh snow into the diaper vat and brought it back inside. "You could try smiling," he suggested. "That would make your work go easier."

Adam sneered. "Saint Abraham, the cheerful martyr."

"Hush," Jacob said. "Don't say things like that."

"I'm just trying to do my best," Abraham defended himself.

"You like it," Adam said. "You like cooking. You like cleaning. You probably even like changing Shmeenie."

Abraham smiled. "She giggles."

"You see? My point exactly. She doesn't giggle, she dribbles. You're completely hopeless."

"Oh? And what should I do, sulk and mope about and then do the job so badly that somebody else will have to come and do it over?"

"Exactly." Adam grinned. Then he saw his father's frown and quickly said, "No, no. That's not what I meant. I'm trying to explain that I shouldn't have to do that sort of job in the first place."

"I'm not hopeless," Abraham said. "You're the hopeless one."

"Boys! Boys!" Jacob said. "Enough. I was going to suggest alternating you boys in the shop and at home, but I'm not sure that would work."

The twins looked at their father, wondering what he was saying.

Jacob pursed his lips and mulled the idea over. "This is what's going to happen," he said at last. "Adam, you are going to come and work with me in the shop, and Abraham, you are going to stay home and help your mother with the work around the house."

"Mazel tov!" Adam shouted.

Abraham blinked his eyes. "Papa, I don't understand. Am I being punished?"

"No, no," Jacob said quickly. "It's only temporary until your mother feels better. I wouldn't want you not to learn my trade, but the truth is that you are the best cook of the three of us. You do a far better job cleaning than either Adam or myself. I could make Adam do that work, but then we'd have to sleep in filthy beds and eat slop."

Now it was Adam's turn to look upset. "Papa, just because I tried to boil the eggs and potatoes in the same pot last week doesn't mean everything I make is slop."

Jacob held up a hand. "It's decided. Adam, you will work with me. Abraham, you will work with your mother. And Adam, don't think that you're getting the easier job. I have a new order from Reb Cantor for some jewelry boxes. That's in addition to everything else we have to do. We have our work cut out for us. Now, we'll all do this laundry together, and no more silly faces."

"Yes, Papa," they both said.

The next morning, Abraham rose early, went to the well for water, and fixed breakfast. After saying his morning prayers, Jacob ate with Adam while Abraham brought a dish into his mother's room. He came out just in time to say goodbye as his brother and father went off to work at the carpentry shop.

"Don't feel bad," Adam said, patting his brother on the shoulder.

"I don't feel bad," Abraham lied. "I know that Father is going to work you harder." He smiled. "Get going. I'll bring you lunch before we go to school."

Adam felt as if a huge weight had been lifted from his shoulders. Abraham wasn't sure how he felt. He started scrubbing the dishes and cleaning up the mess his brother and father had made.

A few minutes later, he heard a soft voice from the other room. "Abraham . . ."

He ran in. "Yes, Mama? Is everything all right? Is there something I can get you?"

"No, nothing," Rebecca said. She took his hand. "You're a good boy, Abraham. You work hard. You're smart. You can do or be whatever you want. I just don't want you to get caught up in circumstances surrounding somebody else. You know who I mean?"

At first Abraham nodded. Then he shook his head. "No, Mama. Adam's a good boy, too."

Rebecca raised an eyebrow. "Good? Maybe. Perfect? No. Ha! He starts trouble, and you take the blame. You think I don't know what's what? You're a good brother, Abraham. I just don't want to see you hurt."

Abraham shifted from one foot to the other. He had nothing to say.

"Okay. All right," Rebecca said. "I'll be quiet. I won't say another thing. I just want you to know I love you. Your father told me that you're helping me. Thank you. "

"You're welcome," Abraham said. "I love you, too." He leaned down and kissed his mother's cheek. Shmeenie burped, and they both laughed and watched as she wiggled her tiny fingers.

Chapter Twenty-One

Early One Morning

Weeks turned into months and soon spring was in the air. Even though Rebecca was growing stronger, she was still too weak to do more than hobble around and care for Shmeenie.

By now, Abraham realized that it was possible that his mother might never fully recover. He was also surprised by how much he enjoyed keeping her and the baby company. He liked listening to her recipes, which were one part tradition and three parts whatever happened to be fresh at the market or old in the pantry. Even cleaning wasn't so bad as long as he stayed on top of things. Still, he missed feeling as if he was doing man's work. Every morning while he watched Adam and their father leave the house he felt a twinge of regret.

For his part, Adam was finding out that being a carpenter's apprentice was no easy job. When Abraham had been in the shop there was always someone to laugh or joke with. Now, Adam was frequently left alone, and even when his father was about they didn't have too much to say. Jacob was always criticizing Adam's craftsmanship, showing him what he'd done wrong and how to make it better. Adam tried and tried, but nothing he did seemed to be good enough.

Their parents noticed that the boys seemed troubled. Late at night they stayed awake whispering, and the next morning, an hour before sunrise, there was a sharp rapping at the boys' bedroom door.

"Time to get up!" Jacob shouted.

"Rise and shine!" Rebecca cheerfully agreed. She poked her boys with the end of the stick she'd started to use as a cane.

Abraham and Adam groaned. "It's still night time."

"That's the best time to pick mushrooms," Rebecca said.

"And to find the dawn hardwood," Jacob added.

None of this made sense to the twins, who were barely awake. They got dressed with their eyes half-open, buttoned their overcoats, and stumbled out of the house into the chilly morning.

"G-goo!" Shmeenie chortled merrily. She was warmly bundled in a scarf beneath Rebecca's coat. Only her face was peeking out, enjoying the cool morning darkness.

Adam glared at his baby sister and then tripped over a rock. "Ow!"

"Goo-boom!" Shmeenie burbled.

"You hear that, Jacob?" Rebecca said. "She's talking already."

Everyone laughed except Adam, who limped for ten minutes until he forgot which foot was supposed to be hurt.

The whole family headed north out of Chelm. They walked slowly, allowing Rebecca to set the pace. At the edge of the Schvartzvald, they separated. Jacob took Adam to the east, while Rebecca took Abraham and Shmeenie a little west into the forest and then south.

By now, Abraham was awake enough to ask his mother, "Isn't it a little early for mushrooms?"

"A little," Rebecca smiled. "Mushrooms don't generally grow quite this early in the year. But I am going to take you to a secret hot spring that my mother showed me and her mother showed her. Even in the deepest of snow, the ground surrounding this spring is rich with mushrooms."

"But why do we have to go so early?"

"Because it's a secret." Rebecca's smile widened into a grin. "This is something special. You wouldn't want everyone in Chelm to know about such a treasure. Everyone knows that the Schlemiel family always has fresh mushrooms year round and they want to find out how such a thing is possible. But there are only so many mushrooms, and if everyone went to pick them soon there would be none left for us. So, we leave before dawn, we head in the wrong direction, circle around for a while to confuse any busybodies, and then as the first hints of the sunrise flicker through the trees, we pick only the best and only what we need. Always use a knife to cut the mushroom close to the ground so that you leave the root to grow another mushroom for our next visit. You understand?"

Abraham nodded, but only a fraction of what his mother said was sinking in.

"Never mind," Rebecca said. "Just remember that this is a precious secret, one that I am sharing with you and you alone."

Meanwhile, on the other side of the forest, half a dozen steps behind his father, Adam kept tripping over branches and stumbling over logs.

"Papa!" he shouted as he fell face first and whacked his funny bone. He pushed himself to his knees and rubbed his elbow. "What is dawn hardwood?"

"Pfff," Jacob said, using the opportunity to catch his breath. "There's no such thing. I made it up."

"What?" Adam blinked. "I don't understand."

"Your mother was so gung-ho about getting you boys up and out of the house early that I had to think of something."

"Then where are we going? And why are we in such a hurry?"

"Shh," Jacob said. "You'll see. Come along. We don't have much time."

Adam sighed, picked himself up, and reluctantly trudged along.

"Come! Come!" Jacob urged.

"I know where we are," Adam panted as he climbed. "This is East Hill."

"Two shekels for the boy with a sense of direction," Jacob said. He pulled Adam along. "Over there. Hurry."

"Why over there? Why not just right here."

"Adam, do you trust me?" Jacob asked.

"No."

"Well, it's an honest answer at least. How about I tell you the same thing my father told me when he first brought me here." Jacob paused for a moment. Then he shouted, "If you don't move your lazy *tuchas* as fast as you can, I'm going to think of some horrible punishment and make you suffer for three days! Maybe four."

Adam sighed and hustled after his father. They came to a rough clearing where three fallen trees had been arranged in a triangle.

Jacob sat on one log, and Adam flopped down beside him.

"A triangle on top of a hill in the middle of a forest," Adam said. "Big deal."

"Shh," Jacob said. He reached into his coat and pulled out a small tin flask. "Have some of this and keep your mouth shut."

Adam opened the flask, took a good long draft, and gagged.

"Aaaaagh!" he said, spitting the burning liquid onto the ground. "What is that?"

"Potato vodka. Don't waste it!" Jacob said, grabbing the flask before any more could spill. "If you get cold, drink some. Otherwise, shut up. Listen."

"You're cheerful this morning," Adam mumbled.

Jacob poked him in the stomach with his elbow. "Shh."

"All right, all right!"

"For the last time," Jacob hissed. "Be quiet! I want you to listen."

All right, all right, Adam said to himself. Maybe if I close my eyes I'll get a little rest . . . Just as he was beginning to doze off, Adam felt his father's elbow nudging him. His eyes shot open. "Wha!" he began, furious at being awakened, but his father quickly clamped his hand over Adam's mouth.

"Shhh. Listen."

Adam frowned, thought about biting his father's hand, and then calmed down. A moment later, Jacob peeled his hand away and pointed.

"Look," his father whispered.

The sun was rising. There in the east, just creeping over the horizon, was the edge of the brightest red fireball Adam could ever imagine. Although the sky had been getting brighter for some time, Adam found himself gasping in awe as bright flickers of red and orange flew across the snow-covered forest. The sky above was black and then blue and then orange and even purple. The few clouds shone like white silver. And then in a few minutes or an instant, the red was gone and the world lived in all colors. Green and white and brown and blue . . .

"That's . . ." Adam began.

"Shh," Jacob whispered. "Wait. Listen. Don't say anything else. Please."

So, Adam waited. Five, ten, maybe fifteen minutes passed. He began to fidget. Jacob passed him the flask, and he was about to take a sip when he heard a sharp sound that he'd never heard before. It was the sound of the snow melting. Of the trees breathing, of the ice breaking. It lasted for just a moment, rolling like thunder, in and then away. And then the birds sang and the wind blew and the day was begun.

"Papa," Adam said softly, "that was amazing."

"Drink up," Jacob said, slapping his son on the back. "Now you know what they mean by the crack of dawn."

Adam smiled, took a long pull from the flask, and then coughed uncontrollably while his father laughed and gently squeezed his shoulder.

CHAPTER TWENTY-TWO

Double Bar Mitzvah

When Mrs. Chaipul learned that Rabbi Yohon Abrahms, the school-teacher, had begun tutoring Abraham and Adam Schlemiel for their bar mitzvahs, she shivered with delight.

A bar mitzvah was coming! And not just one, but two!

In Chelm, bar mitzvahs are a big deal. It's a small village, so they aren't that frequent, but when one comes around, it's an excuse for a big party. On the first Saturday after a boy's thirteenth birthday he is called to read from the Torah, and then . . . food and dancing. Everyone in the village contributes. The music doesn't stop until the musicians can no longer play. Mrs. Chaipul was already imagining the double—no, quadruple—layer cake she would bake with butter cream frosting! For their part, Abraham and Adam felt as if they were in the middle of a rising storm, as though a hurricane were building, and all around them people were buzzing and whistling cheerfully.

One day, while Adam was hurrying to his bar mitzvah lesson, Rivka Cantor caught up and fell into step next to him.

"My mother is making me a beautiful dress for your bar mitzvah celebration," she said, chattering away.

He kept walking, trying to ignore her, but she jumped in front of him. "It's made of white silk, and it's absolutely lovely. If you'd like to come over and see the fabric, which came all the way from China, just say the word." Then she winked.

Rivka Cantor, the merchant's youngest daughter, wasn't ugly. In fact, by most standards she was quite pretty, but there was something about her winking smile that made Adam think of a leering one-eyed lizard. So he just smiled. Rivka winked again. Adam felt himself shuddering inside. He nodded, thanked her politely, and hurried on to his lesson.

As usual, Abraham had gotten to Rabbi Abrahms's house first. Also as usual, the rabbi scowled as Adam came in. So, he dropped into the uncomfortable chair next to the fire and sulked while the rabbi and Abraham went over Abraham's Torah portion in minute and exhausting detail.

It isn't fair, Adam thought. I was on time. I would have been. It's Abraham who comes early. Mother lets him out of the house while Father keeps me until the last minute. And then I couldn't just ignore Rivka Cantor, even if I had wanted to. Adam stared into the fire and listened absently as the rabbi showed Abraham just how to chant each and every phrase . . .

"It's time for you boys to go home."

Adam felt someone nudging his shoulder. He shook his head and blinked his eyes open. He must have dozed off. Rabbi Abrahms stood beside him, frowning as always.

"Come, come. I have to see to my dinner," Rabbi Abrahms said.

"But my lesson . . ." Adam said.

"There isn't time today." Rabbi Abrahms shrugged. "Next week be early and we'll start with you."

Adam opened his mouth to argue and then closed it. What was the point? His father couldn't let him out early, wouldn't let him out early. At this rate he would never get a lesson. He pulled on his coat and joined Abraham, who was waiting outside the rabbi's door.

"I'm sorry," Abraham said.

"Oh, be quiet," Adam snapped. "I needed a nap anyway."

Abraham grinned. "So, what does Rivka Cantor have to say?"

Adam gave his brother a furious look. "Were you listening to my mind?"

"No," Abraham smiled. "I just happened to be looking out the rabbi's window. I saw her winking at you."

Adam got a solid punch into Abraham's shoulder before the two of them ended up tussling on the ground in the mud and the snow.

"Look at all this mud on our clothes," Abraham said while they sat catching their breaths. "Mama's going to kill us."

"Nonsense," Adam said. "She'll just blame me."

"Well, you did start it."

Adam looked at his brother. "Do you want to go another round? Now, get up and let's face our punishment—or should I say my punishment."

After dinner, Abraham was told to wash and dry their clothes while Adam was set to scrubbing and polishing the floor in Shmeenie's room until it was shiny enough to see his reflection.

So the weeks passed, the bar mitzvah grew closer, and at last the big day came.

Just after breakfast, Rebecca Schlemiel inspected her boys. They looked so handsome in their new clothes—perfectly matched shirts, trousers, coats, socks, and shoes. She smoothed their hair, kissed their cheeks, and smiled sadly. It took every ounce of her willpower not to burst into hysterical tears.

"You boys look good," Jacob Schlemiel said.

"You can't call us boys after today," Adam said.

"I know." Jacob nodded. He smiled, remembering the first time he had held Adam in his arms. Or was it Abraham?

Shmeenie, who was sitting up in her crib, said, "Bloooger!" and everyone laughed.

The Schlemiel family walked to the synagogue together. With one last kiss, Rebecca took Shmeenie upstairs to the women's balcony, while Jacob and his boys walked in the front door.

The sanctuary was packed. Everyone was there. They watched as the three Schlemiels made their way to the front and took the seats of honor between the rabbis.

For Abraham, it seemed like an eternity before Rabbi Kibbitz turned and called him to come and stand before the entire village to read from the Torah. He rose from his chair and took his place before the great scrolls of law.

For Adam it seemed like just a moment had passed. Had he dozed off again? He glanced up at the balcony and imagined he could see his mother looking down at him, so he moved his fingers in a little wave.

Then Abraham began to sing. His voice was loud and sweet, filling the synagogue with his chant.

Adam, with nothing better to do, found himself mouthing along. He had heard Abraham's Torah portion so many times that he knew it by heart. He moved his lips in perfect time to Abraham's chant and even remembered to hesitate and make the little eyebrow shudder that Abraham always made when he came to a particularly difficult passage.

The congregation observed this strange performance with a stunned silence. While one boy sang, was the other mimicking him? On the *bimah,* Jacob couldn't see what was happening. In the balcony, Rebecca Schlemiel watched in horror with her hand clasped over her mouth.

Then Abraham was done, and there was a pause. Abraham shook hands all around and sat down next to his father, who put his hand on his son's knee and gave it a squeeze.

Then Rabbi Kibbitz turned to Adam with a kind smile.

Adam stood, walked confidently to the Torah, took a deep breath, looked down at the scroll, opened his mouth, and froze.

The words on the parchment looked like squiggles. He stared. It was completely meaningless. All of a sudden he couldn't read Hebrew. He wasn't sure he could even speak. Adam wasn't even sure he knew where to begin. He tried to find the end of Abraham's portion, so at least he could figure out where he should start.

Rabbi Kibbitz, who had led boys through countless bar mitzvahs, took the pointer and aimed its finger directly at the word where Adam was to begin.

Still, nothing came. Even after Adam heard Rabbi Kibbitz begin whispering the opening passage, his mind remained a blank. Adam knew Hebrew, he knew Yiddish, some Russian, some Polish, but his brain was empty of words. His eyes darted back and forth, but nothing came.

At last, Adam Schlemiel did the only thing he could think of. He took a deep breath and began chanting Abraham's Torah portion. He sang it word for word and note for note. He even remembered to hesitate and make the little eyebrow shudder.

And when he was done, there was silence in the shul. Dead silence. Then a prayer book rustled. Whispers began.

Adam turned to slink back to his seat, but Rabbi Kibbitz stopped him.

"You were supposed to read from the Torah," Rabbi Kibbitz said loudly. He paused, squinting at Adam. "And you read from the Torah!"

Then he shook Adam's hand vigorously. "Mazel tov!"

"Mazel tov!" the entire village of Chelm shouted.

Abraham jumped up from his chair, gave his brother a big hug, and the party began.

"Boys, I've got some bad news."

CHAPTER TWENTY-THREE

Bad News . . . The Curse of the Schlemiel . . . A Schlemiel Grows in Brooklyn

Adam and Abraham blinked their eyes slowly. It was the morning after their bar mitzvahs. Neither of them remembered coming home . . .

Their father was standing over their bed, looking down somberly at them.

"Is Mama all right?" Abraham asked.

"Oh, yes," Jacob said. "She's fine. This isn't about anybody sick or dying. In some ways it's worse."

Worse than sick or dying? The boys sat up. What could be worse than sick or dying? Torture, imprisonment? Mrs. Chaipul's potato latkes?

"What is it, Father?" Adam asked.

Jacob Schlemiel shook his head. "Not here. We need to go somewhere else. Get dressed. I'll pack some breakfast."

The boys looked out the window. It was still dark outside. Their heads hurt.

Still, Adam and Abraham grinned as they pulled on their pants.

Their bar mitzvah party had lasted late into the night, or was it early into the morning? Who knew? They had danced and ate and drank and then danced some more. It had been some fun. They had stayed on even after Rebecca had taken Shmeenie back home, even after their father had said that he was leaving. After that, the party had gotten even wilder, as the younger men in the village told stories that made them blush even now. Yesterday they were boys, and today they were men.

What time had they gotten home, and why was their father waking them up so early? After such a night, they had expected to sleep late—at least until dawn.

"What do you think he's going to tell us?" Abraham asked Adam.

"If I knew I wouldn't be getting out of bed," Adam said. "He probably wants us to cut down some tree and drag it half way to Moscow."

Abraham looked puzzled. "Why would he do that?"

"I don't know. I'm barely awake."

Together they went into the kitchen, where Jacob Schlemiel was wrapping half a loaf of brown bread and a big chunk of cheese in a towel. "Get me a knife, would you?"

"Are we cutting down a tree?" Abraham asked, as he found a kitchen knife and wrapped it in another towel.

"A tree?" Jacob's face took on exactly the same puzzled expression as Abraham's had. "Why would we be cutting down a tree?"

"It was Adam's idea."

"Adam? Why do you say such a thing?"

Adam frowned. If their father hadn't been watching, Adam would have punched his brother. "I don't know. It was the stupidest thing I could imagine doing before dawn. I don't know why I said it. Forget it!"

Jacob shook his head. "It's happening already."

"What?" Adam said.

"Let's go." Jacob and his sons went out the door, careful not to let it slam behind them.

In her bedroom, Rebecca Schlemiel heard the door creak open and then shut. She hoped the boys would take the news well. Then she coughed, covering her mouth so she wouldn't disturb Shmeenie.

By the light of the half moon, Jacob Schlemiel led his boys through Chelm's darkened streets. They passed by the market square, where the single street light burned, and headed north through the farmlands.

It was springtime, with some days above freezing and others just below, so the ground was treacherous with mud and ice. For a long time they didn't talk as they walked. Every so often, Jacob cursed as his foot slid into a deep puddle or a pool of slush. The boys were lighter and more careful, but by the time they reached the edge of the Schvartzvald, their boots were soaked and their trousers were muddy up to the knees.

"Welcome to manhood," Adam muttered.

"It's like being in the Russian army," Abraham agreed. "Do you have any idea where we are going?"

Adam nodded. "Actually, I do."

"Really?"

"But I'm not going to tell you."

"You don't know," Abraham said. "You don't really know."

"Oh, yes I do," Adam said with a teasing lilt.

"Stop bickering!" their father ordered.

"Yes, Papa," Abraham said.

"I do I do I do," Adam hummed.

"Do not do not," Abraham hummed back.

"I can hear you boys," Jacob said, without turning around.

"We're not boys any more," Adam said. "We're men."

"All right, then act like men and be still."

Adam pursed his lips. If being a man was all about not teasing your brother—especially when you actually did know where you were going—he wasn't sure he liked it so much.

"We're going to East Hill," Adam said as they began climbing up the gentle slope that led to one of the two hills north of Chelm.

"I can see that," Abraham said. "It doesn't take a genius to figure that out when you're climbing the hill."

Adam frowned. "At the top of the hill is a triangle of logs. We're going to sit there and drink vodka until the sun rises."

"Oh, really?" Abraham said.

"Don't believe me then."

The three men climbed in silence until they reached the clearing at the top of East Hill. There, as Adam had predicted, were the three logs in the shape of the triangle. Panting, Jacob sat down on the east-facing log. He reached under his coat and removed a flask. After taking a drink, he offered it to Adam.

"Told you," Adam said, sticking out his tongue at Abraham.

Jacob scowled. "This isn't funny. You're not boys any more."

"Papa," Adam began, but a look at Jacob's face told him that he'd better not go on. He took a drink from the flask and then made a face. "What is this?"

"Strong tea," Jacob said, smiling just a little. "You were maybe expecting vodka? This is sober business, Adam, not fun and games."

Adam passed the flask to Abraham, who covertly stuck the tip of his tongue out and then covered the move by taking a long drink of tea.

When he was done, Jacob took the flask, drank, and screwed on the top.

He sighed and peered at their faces. They were still so young. They didn't look any different from yesterday, and yet . . .

"Boys," he said at last. Then he corrected himself. "Young men," he paused, "it is time for you to learn the true meaning of being a Schlemiel."

"It's the family name," Abraham said. "Right?"

Jacob nodded, and then he shook his head. "It's much worse than that. Much, much worse . . ." Jacob Schlemiel took a deep breath and then sighed. "So, you wonder, what is the true meaning of the name Schlemiel?"

His children yawned deeply.

"What, you're bored already?" he said. "I haven't even started and already I'm putting you to sleep? You don't want I should tell you about the great Schlemiels throughout history? About Libby Schlemiel and the Egyptians? Judah Schlemiel and the lion? About Samson Schlemiel and the bald barber? No?"

"Papa," the twins protested. "We had a late night. It's barely daylight."

Jacob raised his hands. "I know. I know. History is boring. You're young. You think that there is nothing to learn from the mistakes of the past. Still, what I have to say to you is important. Vital, you might say, to your future. And you need to know it now because it is the bar mitzvah that activates the curse of the Schlemiel. But if you don't want to hear it, go ahead. Take a nap."

"Papa? A curse? What is it? Please. Please tell us."

And so, Jacob Schlemiel began . . .

No one knows the origin of the curse of the Schlemiel. Some say that it is as old as the world itself, that ancient biblical figures such as Cain and Esau were among the original Schlemiels.

Others claim that the first Schlemiel was a fellow named Libby, a friend of Moses, who, as the Israelites fled dry-shod across the Red Sea, decided that his feet had gotten a little too dirty. Libby Schlemiel paused to wash his tootsies just as the Almighty unleashed the flood on the Egyptians. Naturally this poor Schlemiel was caught in the deluge and washed downstream. The Hebrews wandered in the desert for forty years, eating manna from heaven while following a pillar of fire by day and a pillar of smoke by night. Libby Schlemiel, however, ran the other way. For forty years he ate nothing but bugs and weeds and was pursued by pillars of fire and smoke. He wasn't the brightest of fellows. At last, decrepit and dying, he was stumbled upon by a group of Hebrew scouts and brought before Moses.

"You look good," Libby told his friend Moses. "What have you been up to?"

Moses told Libby about his journey to Sinai, about the Golden Calf, about the giving of the Law . . .

"And what have you been doing all these years?" Moses asked his friend.

Libby smiled and patted Moses on the knee. "I've been looking for you. And I'm glad I found you."

Moses stared in amazement at his long-lost friend and shouted, "You couldn't turn around and wait? There's a pillar of smoke and a pillar of fire pointing straight to our camp. Would it have killed you to follow directions?"

But it was too late. Libby Schlemiel had happily closed his eyes and breathed his last.

"That's not true," Adam said.

Abraham laughed nervously. "Papa, I never heard that story before."

Jacob Schlemiel shrugged. "It's family history. Legend if you will. I don't know if it's true, but it is a perfect example of the curse."

"You're making us nervous," Abraham said.

Jacob nodded. "I know. You ought to be. As children, you were protected, but now that you are men . . ." Jacob shook his head sadly. "It's going to start. Better you should know, not that it will do you much good, but at least perhaps you won't take it all so personally."

Jacob took a long drink of tea from his flask and stared out at the red dawn rising in the east.

Adam jumped to his feet, tripped over a branch, and fell to the ground with a thud.

"You see?" Jacob said. "It's right on schedule."

Adam got up and brushed himself off. "Nonsense," he said. "Ridiculous. I fall all the time. Now you're saying that I fall down because we're cursed? That there's some mystical magical hoo-ha that causes bad things to happen to our family?"

"Not to our family," Jacob said. "Just to the people in it. The men mostly."

"That's silly!" Adam shouted. "That's the most foolish thing I've ever heard."

"Shh," Abraham said, taking his brother's hand. "Calm down."

Adam shook himself free. "I can't believe you're listening to this as if it's real."

"I've heard the whispers," Abraham said softly. Jacob nodded.

"What whispers?" Adam asked.

"People talk," Abraham said. "They think that children aren't listening or can't understand, so they say things."

"What kind of things?"

"That I'm lucky for a Schlemiel," Abraham said. "That they were amazed that a couple of Schlemiels could capture the Krabot gang."

"Yes," Jacob said. "That one surprised me, too."

"I don't understand," Adam said, pacing back and forth inside the triangle of logs. "There is nothing wrong with me. There's nothing wrong with you. And aside from this legendary nonsense there is nothing wrong with our father. Why shouldn't we capture the Krabot gang? Why shouldn't we be lucky?"

Abraham fell silent.

"What can I say?" Jacob asked. "It's a curse!"

"Curse shmurse," Adam snorted. "It's a silly story to scare children. I'm not a child."

"No, you're not," Jacob said. "You're an adult now, old enough to start your own family and old enough to know the story of your family. Now, are you awake enough to listen? Will you sit down?"

Adam stared at his father. His nostrils flared, and he slowly sat back down.

"All right," Adam said. "So, talk."

Jacob Schlemiel took a sip of tea, licked his lips, and began. "You think I'm an old fool trying to scare his children with nonsense?"

Adam and Abraham Schlemiel cautiously nodded their heads.

"Feh," Jacob said. "The curse is not just a silly fable. The Schlemiels are not like other families. Maybe it's just bad luck, but I don't think so. It seems inescapable . . . You doubt me?"

"Yes," Adam said. "I do. Frankly, I expected some sort of fatherly talk, but not this."

"And you?" Jacob looked at Abraham. "You think your father ought to be dispensing words of wisdom?"

Abraham winced and then nodded.

"All right," Jacob shrugged. "Fine. One more story, and then I'll give you my wisdom. You think you can sit still long enough?"

My father's older brother, Shmuel decided that his future lay in America. He left Chelm when he was sixteen and it only took him seven years to arrive in New York. At last his ship came in and he saw the miraculous Statue of Liberty holding her torch high.

The immigration official asked for his name and then laughed. Shmuel Schlemiel? He couldn't even pronounce it. So he wrote something else down on the paper, "Samuel Samuels." Of course he didn't bother to tell my Uncle Shmuel, who couldn't read English. Instead, he just slapped him on the back and sent him on a ferry boat.

As he got off the ferry, Uncle Shmuel bent over because he thought he saw a silver coin. The fellow behind him gave Shmuel a kick in the tuchas *and the poor man went flying.*

"Welcome to Brooklyn!" everybody laughed.

The streets in America were not paved with gold. I learned all this because my father read us the letters Uncle Shmuel wrote. The streets were made of stone and mud. There were so many houses that the sewers would overflow regularly, and in the summertime the whole city smelled like a stable.

Brooklyn, as it turned out, was across a wide river from another city called Manhattan. The day after Uncle Shmuel arrived he saw an opportunity and he seized it.

He was walking along the banks of the river when he realized that a bridge connecting Brooklyn to Manhattan would make its owner a fortune. Even better, such a bridge was already under construction. It was a beautiful bridge, made of stone and hung from cables. Uncle Shmuel hurried toward it, admiring the ingenuity. He asked who the owner was. No one understood a word he said. At last, he found a kind man who spoke Polish. This man told him that the bridge was in fact for sale. Best of all, the price was good because it had been on the market for so long. Coincidentally, Uncle Shmuel had just enough in his pockets to buy the bridge. He gave the kind man every ruble he had.

The man slapped him on the back. "How does it feel to be the first man to buy the Brooklyn Bridge.

"Not bad," Uncle Shmuel answered.

The stranger said he'd be right back with the deed. By the time night fell, Uncle Shmuel had begun to wonder if the kind man had gotten lost.

Fortunately, Uncle Shmuel had taken a room nearby and paid a month's rent in advance. For three weeks, he walked to the bridge every morning and waited patiently. At last he went to the police and explained his predicament. He told them he was afraid that the kind man had been robbed because of the enormous sum of money and might be lying somewhere dead or dying. Uncle Shmuel couldn't imagine what the translator and the police sergeant found so funny. Finally, they told him he had better find some way of getting more money to pay for food and shelter before winter came and he was thrown into the streets as a pauper.

Everyone from Chelm knows about poverty, so that didn't frighten Uncle Shmuel. Still, he thought the advice was sound. He went to his bridge and signed on as a laborer. Every day he went to work, and he worked hard. Weeks and months passed. His landlady began to worry because the poor man was wasting away from a lack of nutrition and he hadn't even paid his rent.

"Don't you have a job?" she asked.

"Of course," he said proudly. "I am self-employed as a worker on my own bridge."

"If you work on the bridge," the landlady asked, "where is your pay?"

"I don't know," Uncle Shmuel said. "Every week, I wait but they never call my name."

The landlady took pity on Uncle Shmuel and went with him on the next pay day. When the foreman called out, "Samuel Samuels!" the landlady looked at my uncle. He smiled at her, but he made no move to claim his pay.

"That's your name!" she said.

"Nonsense," my uncle said. "I'm Shmuel Schlemiel."

"You're an idiot," she told my uncle. Dragging him along by his ear, she pulled him to the front of the line and demanded not only that week's pay, but all of his back pay. Even after she and the foreman had split half of what he'd earned, Uncle Shmuel found himself once again a very wealthy man. He thanked his landlady, quit his job, and strolled with confidence across the nearly completed bridge. When at last he reached Manhattan, who did he find but the kind stranger!

"Where have you been?" my uncle asked, embracing the stranger. "I thought you were dead."

Well, the stranger explained, there was a problem. The money my uncle had given him had only been enough to purchase the Brooklyn side of the bridge, not the

Manhattan side. Once again, Uncle Shmuel happily gave the kind man every dollar in his pocket. And once again the man promised to return shortly with the deed.

Uncle Shmuel didn't even bother to wait this time. He went back to Brooklyn and the next day begged for his job back. They gave it to him at half his old salary, and he lived happily. He worked hard and eventually met and married my Aunt Sarah, who demanded that he stop making payments on the bridge. Better to be a partial owner and save some money, Aunt Sarah said, than to own the whole thing and be bankrupt.

So, every week, when the foreman called out, "Samuel Samuels," Uncle Shmuel collected his pay and said, "Call me Schlemiel!"

And they all did.

"Words of wisdom you want from me?" Jacob Schlemiel asked his sons. "Here is what I have—listen carefully for your name."

Abraham and Adam waited for more.

"That's it," Jacob said with a shrug. "I'm not a very wise man. Let's go home before we miss lunch."

CHAPTER TWENTY-FOUR

The Prank

After they got back from the woods, Abraham and Adam didn't have much of a chance to talk about their father's strange warning. By the time they reached the village, they were already two hours late to school, and then there were chores for Abraham and work for Adam. Plus, they were still suffering from the late night bar mitzvah celebrations. By the end of that very long day they were exhausted.

Lying in bed, Adam whispered, "Abraham? Abraham? Are you awake?"

"Hfm?"

"Do you believe what Father told us? Do you think that we're doomed to be failures?"

"Mmmm. I'm asleep."

"Abraham, this is important. Do you think we're failures?"

"No. Now go to sleep."

"I don't either. We need to do something about it."

"That's nice," Abraham mumbled.

"A prank," Adam said. "A nice solid prank. Something glorious that people will talk about for years. If we come up with something good, you'll go along, right?"

"Mmm hmm."

Abraham was fast asleep, but Adam stayed awake late that night thinking, and by dawn he had what he thought was a pretty good plan.

The next morning, he explained it to Abraham as they walked to school. A light snow was falling, and Abraham listened to his brother's idea with growing disbelief.

"You want the king of Poland to come to Chelm?" Abraham said. "Why?"

"Or the czar of Russia," Adam said. "I don't care which. But it won't be the real king or czar."

"You want a fake king . . ."

"Or czar."

" . . . or czar to come to Chelm? And then what? I don't understand."

Adam hopped in front of his brother and stopped. "Just picture this. It's a cold winter morning. Or maybe early spring time. There are birds in the trees, the flowers are just beginning to bud, and throughout all of Chelm there is only one topic of conversation. The czar is coming. When is he coming? Nobody knows. Is it this week? Is it next week? Did we miss him somehow? What are we going to serve him for lunch?

"Everyone will buy new clothes and wear them all the time. There will be a vote to clean up the streets and paint the houses.

"At last, word comes that the czar will arrive on Friday afternoon, just before sunset. This causes great consternation because of the conflict with the Sabbath. But the czar is the czar. If the people of Chelm don't show him proper respect then who knows what will happen?"

Abraham shook his head. "And this is supposed to be funny?"

"It's a prank," Adam said. "It's not funny, it's profound. It's like looking at a chicken and discovering that it's really a horse."

"Chickens are never horses," Abraham said, stepping around Adam and resuming his walk.

"No, but imagine if you looked at a chicken for a day or so and suddenly realized that it wasn't a chicken at all, but a horse. How would that feel? Now, imagine being the young men who managed to convince everyone that the horse was really a chicken. That is something that would be talked about for years to come!"

"I think," Abraham stared at his brother, "that the curse of the Schlemiels has already started working on you."

"No, listen! This is funny!" He hustled after Abraham. "So, we don't do it on the Sabbath. Fine. Another day. Any day. It doesn't matter, because the czar is never going to come."

"But if the czar never comes," Abraham said, "how can we convince everybody he's a chicken?"

"Idiot!" Adam said. "The czar's not the chicken, he's the horse. They just think he's the chicken. But he doesn't exist. Not in Chelm anyway."

Abraham blinked. "That is so much clearer now. Thank you for explaining it to me."

They had arrived at the back door to the synagogue. Abraham smiled, opened the door, and went inside. Adam threw his hands up in the air, stomped his feet in the snow three times, and followed his brother. "Wait, Abraham. It makes perfect sense . . ."

"Late again, Adam," Rabbi Yohon Abrahms said. "I would have thought that your bar mitzvah would have taught you the value of being on time."

The whole class laughed. Adam found his face turning red.

"How is it possible," he sputtered, "that I am late but Abraham is on time?"

The rabbi looked at his pocket watch and shrugged. "A fact is a fact. Before the hour you are on time, and after the hour you are late. It's only the matter of a few seconds, but it is a crucial distinction. It's like circumcision—there isn't much to cut off, but that little bit makes all the difference in the world."

Again the class laughed, and Adam turned even brighter red.

"Take a seat. This is as good a place as any to start our lesson. Who of the younger students remembers where in the Torah the Almighty pledges the covenant through the *bris*?"

At lunch time, as they walked home through three inches of snow, Adam began again. "We can do this, you know. When you create something in the mind, all it takes are a few well-placed words. A little bit of evidence here and there."

"But I think you're going to have to decide," Abraham giggled, "whether the czar is going to be a chicken or a horse."

"Forget about the horse and the chicken!" Adam said hotly. "It's like a magician showing you a coin and then making it vanish."

"Oh, so now you're going to kidnap the czar of Russia?"

"NO!" Adam shouted. "I'm not going to kidnap anyone. He's never going to be here, but everyone is going to think he is."

So involved in his explanation was Adam that he didn't notice Abraham bending down, picking up a large handful of snow, and patting it gently into a firm ball.

"Look over there." Abraham pointed. "It's the king of Poland!"

"Where?" Adam's head swiveled.

This is too easy, Abraham thought to himself, as he fired the snowball into the back of Adam's head.

"Abraham!" Adam roared. "You just wait till I get my hands on you!"

Abraham laughed and started running with Adam following close behind, snatching up handfuls of snow and throwing them after his fleeing brother. The snowball race was on, and by the time the boys reached their house their coats were soaking wet and their fingers were blue from cold.

When Rebecca Schlemiel opened the door to find her two sons, half-frozen with their teeth chattering, she shook her head, chuckled, and said, "I bet you're glad that I made chicken soup."

The boys nodded numbly and stepped inside to get warm.

Weeks passed, and then months. Nothing changed. Nothing happened.

It wasn't that life in Chelm was boring. Far from it. One day the baker's oven would catch on fire, the next month a farmer would find a goat on his roof, eating the thatch. All right, so it was boring. But for Adam Schlemiel, life in Chelm seemed twice as boring.

Every day was pretty much like the next. Every morning Adam woke at dawn and said his prayers. Then there were the morning chores. Then he had to work in his father's shop, but before he could start working, he needed to shovel a path to the shop, light the fire, and tidy up the previous day's mess. He couldn't stand it. Everything was always the same. Time for school, then lunch, then back to the shop for afternoon work and back home for chores, then late afternoon prayers, dinner, and bed. Only the Sabbath was different. Then, instead of work, there were prayers and walks and readings and long discussions about all the important issues of the past thousand years. Adam wasn't sure which he dreaded more, going to work in the morning or staying up late listening to his father, Reb Cantor, and Rabbi Kibbitz argue about which came first: the chicken or the egg, the matzah ball or the matzah ball soup.

It was a mundane and exhausting life. And what was there to look forward to next week, next month, next year? More of the same.

The only thing that kept Adam sane was his prank. It wasn't an idle fantasy. He knew it could happen because he had a model. History was on his side.

Two hundred years earlier, the governor of Warsaw had visited Smyrna, and the villagers of Chelm still spoke of it in hushed whispers. Not only had the governor visited, but he had nearly died in the marketplace! While the governor was making his inspection, a cabbage had rolled down the street. The governor's horse had shied and the governor had plunged to the ground. "Whose cabbage is this?" cried the mud-soaked governor. A meek

"Whose Cabbage is This?"

voice admitted ownership. "And where are you from?" roared the great man. "Chelm," lied the poor Smyrnan. And that was how the infamous cabbage tax had fallen on the poor and innocent village.

It was no wonder that Adam plotted and planned. It was no surprise that an impish glint entered his eyes every time he imagined the chaos. His practical joke would be a topic for conversation in Chelm until the end of time!

Unfortunately, the prank was still in the dream stages. Nothing was happening. The whole process was taking longer than he'd expected. He just couldn't figure out the details. Adam was both overworked and easily distracted. Between the business of his father's shop, his studies in school, meals, and prayers at shul there was barely a moment to think, let alone formulate a coherent plan.

Winter snow became spring mud. The mud solidified and the flowers bloomed. The Schlemiel twins' fourteenth birthday came and went. Crops grew, the harvest was gathered, and again snow fell.

Every so often, Abraham would tease his brother. "So, when are the king and the czar coming to visit?"

Adam would frown or snarl or growl. The truth was, he didn't know how he was going to make it happen.

"What?" Abraham would say, "I thought that the rulers of Russia and Poland kept you fully appraised of all their travel plans."

"Grrrr," Adam would answer.

Then Abraham would laugh.

Adam scowled. Why couldn't his brother understand? A prank like this wasn't something that just happened. It wasn't as simple as putting a bucket over a door. The details were maddening. The biggest problem was that with such a brilliant idea, he didn't even know where to begin to start.

And it didn't help that, in the Schlemiel household, all was not well. In fact, things seemed to be getting worse.

Although little Shmeenie was now two years old, Rebecca Schlemiel had still not fully recovered from the girl's strenuous eight-day birthing. Their mother still had a smile as lovely as an upside down rainbow, but her glow wasn't quite as strong, and her coughs grew louder and more frequent.

"Don't put so much salt in the soup!" she would shout from her bedroom. Standing in front of the soup pot, Abraham would jump in the air with surprise. Then he would put down the salt cellar and wonder how his mother could see through walls. "Oy!" she'd shout. "Now you have to put some more water into the broth."

Jacob was also worried about his wife. If it had only been himself and the boys it would have been easier, but with the little girl running around like an eager mouse always underfoot, he became more and more concerned. He would spend long hours by his beloved wife's side, holding her hand, and whispering the gossip of Chelm.

His father's absence kept Adam even busier in the shop, taking orders, paying bills, and trying to make sense of his father's nearly unreadable blueprints.

"Is this supposed to be a bed or a bureau?" he would mutter. He was astonished when his father turned the paper around—the design was a rocking horse for Shmeenie. A rocking horse?

That was the last straw! Adam tore off his apron and slammed out of the shop.

"The boy is crazy," Jacob Schlemiel said, shaking his head sadly.

Abraham saw his brother stampeding through the village square and called, "So, Adam, the king of Poland is coming when?"

"SOON!" Adam yelled back. "And maybe the czar himself is coming soon!"

Adam fled into the countryside, seeking solitude and quiet.

Meanwhile, nearly a dozen men and women in the village square heard Adam Schlemiel's shout. The talk began almost immediately.

"The czar?"

"Coming?"

"Here?"

"To Chelm?"

"Soon? Really? How soon?"

The rumor was spreading like the belly of a fat man at a wedding feast, but by then Adam was gone, stomping across a rye field into the forest where he half-seriously considered drowning himself in the Uherka River. Fortunately, the flow was low, and the river bottom was mostly frozen dirt. Adam stared into the muck and wondered what it would feel like to breathe in mud. He could become mud. Baah. He kept walking.

Back in the square, Abraham was surprised to see that everyone was excited. All the villagers were eagerly gossiping about the czar's upcoming visit. Abraham laughed and was about to explain that no, there was no such thing as the czar coming to Chelm when he realized that maybe Adam's plan was working. And it could be fun just to watch it play out.

Abraham waited for his turn at the well. He lowered the bucket and pulled it up full of cool clear water, which he poured into his buckets to take back to his house. And again. It took four buckets from the well to fill the two to take home.

While Abraham was hauling up his third bucket, Reb Shikker ran up shouting. "Abraham, Adam—whoever you are . . . Did you hear? The czar of Russia is coming to Chelm next spring!"

"No! Really?" Abraham said, hoping that the grin he was trying to hide would look like surprise.

"Yes," Reb Shikker said. "And he's bringing an elephant with him!"

"An elephant!" Abraham laughed. "You're not serious?"

Reb Shikker raised his hand. "On my mother's grave—may she live a long life."

"That's strange," Abraham said.

"What's strange?"

"You know what I heard?" Abraham looked both ways and then spoke in a low whisper. "I heard that it's not the czar, but the king of Poland."

"Now that's foolish," Reb Shikker said. "What would the king of Poland be doing in Chelm with the czar's elephant?"

"He borrowed it so that he could visit Chelm," Abraham said quite seriously.

"Oh!" Reb Shikker's eyes widened. "That makes perfect sense. I have to tell my wife. She's a big fan of the king of Poland." And off he hurried so quickly that he forgot to pretend he was drunk.

Abraham laughed so hard he nearly dropped the last water bucket back into the well. He could hardly wait to tell Adam.

He lifted the yoke with its twin buckets and started across the square to their father's shop. But then he changed his mind. First of all, Adam wasn't in the shop, and second of all, if Adam didn't realize what was happening . . . that had possibilities too. Maybe it would be possible to trick the trickster . . .

Abraham grinned as he carried the water buckets home. Yes, Mama needed that water right away. Adam would find out in due time.

CHAPTER TWENTY-FIVE

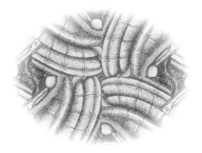

Guess Who's Coming to Chelm

Rumors in any small village, and especially in Chelm, are like the fruit of a ripe cherry tree. One takes a taste, and it's so sweet and delectable that you have to tell someone else, and soon everyone is savoring the flavor.

Reb Shikker kept his promise and told his wife that he'd heard that the king of Poland was coming, but she was hard of hearing and thought he said the king of Prussia. Worse still, she had a bad memory, so when she mentioned the gossip to Mrs. Chaipul she said that her husband had told her that the king of Persia planned to fly into town on a magic carpet or some such nonsense.

"Ridiculous," Mrs. Chaipul said. "First of all, if carpets could fly, do you think anyone would buy a horse? Second, I heard from a very reliable source that it's actually the emperor of China who will be visiting us in secret. Yes, in disguise!"

"Disguise?" Mrs. Shikker shouted back. "How will we know he's the emperor?"

"He'll be wearing a fur hat," Mrs. Chaipul said, tapping her nose knowingly.

"But it's winter. Every cart driver from Berlin to Siberia wears a fur hat," Mrs. Shikker reasoned.

"That," Mrs. Chaipul said, "is why it's such a good disguise."

Within a day, everyone in Chelm knew that someone was coming. By Thursday, it was generally agreed that the important visitor would arrive some time in the late spring, just after the last snow had melted but before Passover.

"What if it snows on Passover?" one child was heard to ask her father.

"Hush," the father answered. "The president of America always knows the weather. Why I've read that he is so wise that he changes his policies depending on which way the wind blows."

The youngster was suitably impressed.

Less than a month later, word reached Smyrna, where everyone laughed. Visiting officials could be expensive to the Chelmener. In Smyrna, two questions were asked, "First of all, why would anybody of importance visit Chelm? And second, what kind of misfortune will fall upon them if they do?"

"You want to know why?" asked Esther Gold, the cobbler's wife, who was in Smyrna to buy shoe leather. "Exactly because no one of importance has ever visited Chelm before."

The shopkeepers glanced at each other and nodded. "And the funny thing is," they said, "that makes perfect sense to someone from Chelm."

Although outsiders continued to laugh, in Chelm plans were being made. After all, it was wintertime, when the snow was shoulder high and a careless sneeze froze before it hit the ground. What else was there to do?

Everyone prepared. Rabbi Kibbitz began writing a speech. Reb Stein, the baker, pored through recipe books for the perfect bread. Mrs. Chaipul wondered if the social hall would be big enough to hold all of the emperor's horses and all of the emperor's men.

Reb Cantor, the merchant, nearly went mad wondering which of two dozen kings, princes, czars, or presidents he could be discussing trade agreements with. And what if they all came? Then perhaps Chelm would become a center of commerce, a hub, with caravans passing through on their way to Cairo or from Sicily. And who would become the most important businessman in the world? Why the ever modest Reb Cantor himself! It was all so exciting that he was bedridden for a week, and after that he began a furious study of Hindustani languages, going on a hunch that the mysterious guest would be a rajah from the Indian subcontinent.

Even in the Schlemiel household the question was raised late at night after the children were asleep.

"You should build something special." Rebecca nudged her husband. "Something wonderful."

"What can I make," Jacob asked his wife, "that any king will not have a million better?"

"A clock perhaps." Rebecca smiled.

"Again with the clocks!" Jacob Schlemiel buried his head under his pillow until he fell asleep, dreaming of a pocket watch the size of a horse carriage. He woke himself up, jotted down the plans, and returned to sleep with a contented smile. In the morning, however, he was disappointed to discover that he had written the following: "Corned beef and onions. Bury it far from the ocean. Tell Rebecca my left nostril is orange. Borscht." He then spent the remainder of the morning peering into a mirror trying to tell whether his nostril really was orange or if it was just the light.

With all of this hubbub and commotion, it seems almost inconceivable that no one would have told Adam Schlemiel. But it was true. Abraham didn't say a word, and no one else in Chelm had any reason to talk with the carpenter's youngest son about the impending event. As a result, Adam had no idea of the excitement and trouble he had been causing.

Since the beginning of time, nothing so momentous or significant had ever happened in Chelm. Nor was it likely to happen again. This was probably going to be the single most important event in the history of Chelm. It would be in the newspapers. Books would be written. And, finally, perhaps those know-it-alls in Smyrna would wipe the sarcastic smiles off their faces. All around him there was joy and anticipation, but Adam was deep in gloom. People were talking, whispering, nearly shouting. He was oblivious, blissfully ignorant. He worked hard in his father's shop, studied as diligently as he could at school, and still was trying to figure out some way to bring the czar of Russia or the king of Poland to Chelm. He even kept a thick bundle of papers on which he jotted each new idea. And, every evening, after Adam fell asleep, Abraham leafed through his brother's plans and giggled softly to himself.

CHAPTER TWENTY-SIX

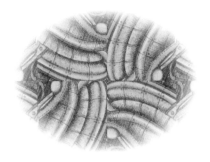

Macarooned

By now, you may have guessed that Rivka Cantor had had designs on Adam Schlemiel. Even though Adam was just shy of fifteen, Rivka didn't think it was too early to begin planting the seeds for matrimony in the poor boy's head. But she had to be subtle about it. Her father was the richest man in Chelm, and if he had his way, he'd marry her off to some importer from Warsaw as part of a trade deal. Still, her father did have a soft spot for the Schlemiel boys, whom he thought were both handsome and heroic. Perhaps if Adam presented the case himself (or even better conspired with a yenta to make the match in secret) then her father could hardly object.

Unfortunately, so far Rivka's plans were all for naught. Every time she spoke with Adam, his face turned bright red, he stuttered, and ran off as soon as he could come up with a polite excuse. Her best friend, Rachel Cohen, assured her that those were signs of true love. All Rivka needed to do was be persistent, keep calm, and above all keep herself in Adam's mind. Don't throw yourself after him, Rachel warned. Just give him food and laugh at his jokes.

A perfect opportunity presented itself when Adam came to her father's house to collect a long overdue bill. Rivka snatched a platter of cookies from the kitchen and, as if by chance, passed through the sitting room.

"Adam Schlemiel!" she said. "What a wonderful surprise. Would you like a macaroon?"

"Yes, thank you," Adam said. He took two.

Rivka giggled. "What brings you to our fine home?"

"Business." Adam blushed. "It's about the chest your father commissioned us to make for the regional governor two years ago."

"Why don't you have a seat and tell me about it?"

"Well," Adam began, "you would think that the merchant would have the decency to pay a hard-working craftsman on time."

"As I understand it," Rivka said, smiling, "the chest was never inspected by my father. When it was inspected, it was only after a gaping hole had been blown in the lid by the robber Krabot. And my father told me he never formally took receipt of the chest. It was confiscated by the regional police inspector, was it not? We never even heard if it was received by the governor."

Adam's mouth dropped open and a few crumbs fell on the Persian carpet.

"Not that I ever pay attention to my father's business," Rivka added quickly.

"But we did the work! Is it our fault that it became a piece of state's evidence?"

"And is it our fault," Rivka asked, "that the Schlemiel boys never showed up at the trial to claim the evidence? Should we pay for your mistakes? Have another cookie sweetie . . . I mean, sweet cookie."

Adam didn't know what to say, so he took another macaroon even though he hadn't quite finished chewing the first two.

"But," he said in a muffled voice. "We tried to . . ."

"Enough," Rivka said, waving her hand. "My father will be here soon enough. Let us talk about something more interesting than money. Tell me, Adam, what do you think about the sultan of Tunisia's visit to Chelm?"

Adam coughed and a piece of macaroon became lodged in his throat. "Thbm sbutan ob Fubgrezia?"

"Are you all right?" Rivka asked. "Can I offer you some tea?"

"Pbfleas."

Rivka poured, and Adam sipped. A moment later he regained his voice.

"What makes you think that the sultan of Tunisia is coming to Chelm?"

"Well, it's either the sultan of Tunisia or the czar of Russia," Rivka smiled. "He's supposed to be coming tomorrow."

"Tomorrow?" Adam was dumbfounded. "Tomorrow?"

Rivka, who had no idea why Adam suddenly seemed so upset, answered innocently. "Yes, but we don't know what time," she said. "Kings, czars, sultans, and emperors always set their own schedules."

Adam's eyes opened wide in fury. His nostrils flared. His lips curled into a frown. "How dare you make fun of me!"

"I don't understand."

"My brother put you up to this," Adam said. "First you won't pay us, then you have the gall to torment me?"

"No, no," Rivka said quickly. "I just thought that the arrival in Chelm of the czar or the sultan, or maybe it's the king of Poland . . ."

"Oh, really? Why not the king of Romania?" Adam shouted and stood up. The tea spilled on the rug, but he didn't care. "It's a good idea! But it's my idea, not Abraham's. Is it my fault that I don't have a moment of free time to myself?"

"Adam, please," Rivka said. "Your heart."

"My heart? My heart is fine, but my head is throbbing. Tell your father I would like to speak with him, if his daughter can be less insulting."

And then he stormed off without even a thanks or goodbye. The door slammed and he was gone.

Rivka Cantor sat in her chair, tears rolling down her cheeks. How is it, she wondered, that I made his head throb instead of his heart? It had all been going so well, and then suddenly . . . What had she said?

"Rivka?" came her father's voice. "Is someone there?"

"No, Father," Rivka said, managing to choke back her sobs. "No one at all."

CHAPTER TWENTY-SEVEN

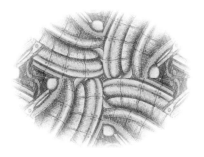

Much Ado

Adam Schlemiel banged in through the front door of the house shouting, "Abraham!"

Abraham, who was stirring a pot of stew, turned around just in time to see his brother's fist coming straight for his face. The punch struck Abraham in the forehead. He stumbled back, tripped, and fell to the floor, barely missing the hot stove.

"How dare you!" Adam shouted, standing over his brother's crumpled form. "Isn't it enough for you to make fun of me without telling every girl in Chelm?"

"What are you talking about?" Abraham said. He could feel a knot rising on his skull.

"My plan," said Adam. His hands were still clenched into fists. "My prank. You've ruined it. And you've ruined my life."

"What's all the fuss?" came Rebecca Schlemiel's feeble voice from her bedroom.

Adam hissed at Abraham to keep his mouth shut and then answered, "Nothing, Mama! A foolish girl told me that the king of Poland was coming to Chelm next week."

"Nonsense," said Rebecca, her voice faint from the effort. "It's not the king of Poland. It's the king of Prussia. He's due to arrive tomorrow morning."

"AAAAAGH!" Adam shrieked. He pulled at his hair. "Is everyone in on this?"

"In on what?" Rebecca said.

But Adam wasn't listening. He had already slammed back outside and was running away from the house.

"Adam, is everything all right? Abraham?"

"Fine, Mama," Abraham said, picking himself up. He giggled softly to himself and then winced as he felt a twinge in his nose. "Adam's just a little excited about tomorrow. He feels personally responsible that the king is coming to Chelm. He thinks it was his idea."

"Oy," Rebecca Schlemiel sighed. What nonsense.

CHAPTER TWENTY-EIGHT

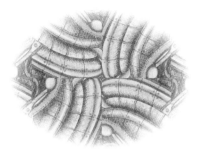

Where Does Rum Come From?

The next morning Adam awoke, stiff and shivering, in the attic of his father's workshop. His whole body ached from sleeping through the still-cold night cramped in a corner under a too-thin blanket. It made him mad. Everything made him mad. He didn't want to talk to anyone. He didn't want to be with anyone. Everyone was making fun of him.

The prank was supposed to have been his. His alone. Why couldn't Abraham see that? It just wasn't fair. He stared up at the crossbeams. Phooey.

Adam sat up, yawned, and stretched his arms. Another day full of nothing but chores and work and school with the promise of even more of the same tomorrow. Oy.

And then he heard something outside. Something was very wrong. There was a noise in the air, a sort of shouting roar. It was rising and falling like a flock of pigeons in the wind. Then it stopped. Then it started again. He couldn't figure it out, but it seemed to be coming from the direction of the village square.

He thought it sounded like a crowd cheering, but that was absurd. The only time crowds ever cheered in Chelm were on Holy Days, at weddings and bar mitzvahs and births, at the arrival of some good news or some important visitor . . .

No. It wasn't possible. Was it?

Adam stood up suddenly and bashed his head against a low crossbeam. He fell back with a wounded yelp. He rubbed his forehead, saw no blood, and then crawled furiously through the trap door and down the ladder.

Abraham! How was it possible? Not only had his brother stolen his prank, but somehow he had made it happen. Was it possible?

Adam ran outside.

It was a beautiful morning in Chelm, that rare perfect day between winter and spring. A few weeks earlier, the snows had begun melting and the roads had turned to mud, but three days of cold air had frozen everything solid, and icicles glistened from the trees. The sky was bright blue, and a few early birds sang.

And the village square was filled from corner to corner with bright cold faces. What was going on? Banners fluttered from poles. Every house in Chelm had been freshly painted. How had he not noticed it before?

As he grew closer, Adam could read signs that said, "Welcome!" He inhaled. It was impressive. Clearly the villagers were certain that they were about to be visited by royalty. It really was brilliant, and at that moment Adam forgot about his jealousy and instead wondered how Abraham had managed all of this.

Adam looked for his brother but couldn't find him. There was a sea of people. He recognized visitors from Smyrna and other strangers. Word had spread beyond Chelm! Brilliant. Beautiful.

Even better, Adam noticed that the conversations around the square were confused. Everyone seemed to be expecting someone different. Some were whispering that the czar of Russia would be arriving any moment. Others argued that it was certainly the king of Poland or the emperor of Ethiopia. Adam grinned. Oy, were they all in for a surprise when the day dragged on and on and nobody showed up.

He had been right. Even though he had nothing to do with the implementation, Adam felt vindicated. It was a fantastic practical joke! So what if Abraham had somehow set it all in motion? At least it was happening. At least it was real.

Adam hugged himself with joy and danced in the street. Nobody noticed. They were all too excited. It was happening. Everyone in Chelm and hundreds of visitors from all of the neighboring villages were about to be fooled. Wonderful!

Or was it?

Adam had a thought that made him frown. It was something he hadn't quite considered. This situation could become dangerous. He hadn't realized it would be so big, with so many people. And no one likes to be fooled, let alone strangers to Chelm. With all of these people milling about there could be anger and fist fights, and that wasn't what he'd had in mind. No, the people needed to be unified, so that when it finally dawned on them that they had been tricked, their disappointment would turn into dismay and laughter, not disarray and rage.

So, Adam thought, maybe this is why I didn't put the plan into motion. My instincts told me that something was missing. There were implications, ramifications, consequences . . . He smiled. Abraham hadn't thought of everything, had he?

But the boulder was already rolling down the mountain. He could see the trouble, but how could he prevent the avalanche? He had to deflect it, find some way to take back some control.

Adam realized that he had to aim them. People were a bit like a herd of goats. If you let them roam about aimlessly then they tended to butt heads, but if you gave them something to focus on you could drive them all together. He had to give everyone a single point of focus. If he could set one final rumor going, then when the bubble finally burst everyone would all be thinking in the same direction. Yes, that was it.

But creating a consensus of opinion in Chelm was like training a mule to play the piano. He would have to be quick and precise. In Chelm, misdirection was the key to creating a consensus. Yes! What Abraham had begun, Adam would finish. It would be perfect.

He turned and spotted Reb Shikker, the town drunk, talking with Reb Gold, the cobbler. "What's going on?" Adam asked innocently. "What's happening?"

"I'm so excited," Reb Shikker said. "As a longtime vodka drinker, I've always wanted to meet the czar of Russia."

"Not the czar of Russia," Reb Gold said. "The czar of Prussia."

Reb Shikker frowned. "Isn't there a king in Prussia?"

"The king of Romania," Adam answered back with authority.

"Oh," said Reb Shikker, clearly puzzled. "But what kind of drink do they make in Romania?"

"Rum," Reb Gold said. "Romania, right?"

A smile blossomed on Reb Shikker's face. "Ahh! Rum is even better than vodka!"

Next Adam targeted Mrs. Chaipul, possibly Chelm's foremost gossip.

"I suppose," he said, "the banquet is ready for the emperor of Ethiopia."

"Not Ethiopia, Adam," the old woman said, "China. I understand they like dumplings in China, so I made kreplach."

"That's good," Adam said, "because Reb Shikker says that the king of Romania loves dumplings."

Mrs. Chaipul's face grew serious. "Reb Shikker says it's the king of Romania?"

Adam nodded. "He should know. That's where rum comes from."

"I know," Mrs. Chaipul said. "Are you sure the king of Romania likes dumplings? I've made quite a lot of them, and I would hate to see them go to waste."

"Absolutely," Adam said. "Now, if you will excuse me, I must talk with Reb Gold."

So it went. Bulga, the fisherman, thought it was the prime minister of Canada, but when Adam told him that Mrs. Chaipul said the king of Romania was coming for her dumplings he agreed that she must be correct.

It was almost too easy. Adam moved quickly through the crowd. With each new conversation, he mentioned the one immediately before, until at last everyone in the square was trying to remember the national anthem of Romania.

"There you are." Abraham's voice came from behind. "Mother was worried when you didn't come home last night. I told her you were safe in Father's attic. She said she wasn't surprised, because that's where all the Schlemiel men hide."

Adam turned and stared at his twin brother. For a moment, his ears reddened with anger, but then it passed. "I'm sorry I hit you."

"I accept your apology," Abraham said. "You are forgiven and absolved. Some day I may return the favor, and I hope you remember that I have been merciful." Then Abraham pointed at the bump on Adam's forehead. "What happened? You were feeling guilty so you whacked yourself as punishment?"

Adam touched the bruise. "Low ceiling."

"So, your idea is working out pretty well, isn't it?" Abraham said.

Adam nodded. "How did you manage it? How did you get them all to believe?"

"It wasn't me," Abraham said. "I didn't have that much to do with it. Really, it was you, although purely by accident. You were upset about something and you were running through the square when I teased you by asking when the king of Poland was coming. I was at the well, and you shouted back, 'Soon. And maybe the czar himself is coming soon!' You remember?"

"Not really," Adam scratched his head. "Was that last summer?"

Abraham shrugged. "Some things take time. What puzzles me is that when everyone gathered this morning people were expecting to see someone different. Now they're all talking about the same person. Everyone thinks it's going to be the king of Romania."

"That was me." Adam patted his chest with pride. "I did that on purpose. I wanted them all to have a single focus so that when nobody shows up it won't start a fight about whose fault it was."

"Really?" Abraham nodded in respect. "That's a good idea. But how did you do that?"

Adam touched his nose. "I'm a Schlemiel. Shall we find a place to watch? I can't wait to see what happens. I was thinking about the roof of the synagogue."

"You read my mind," Abraham said.

"Yes, indeed." Adam grinned. "Sometimes I do."

CHAPTER TWENTY-NINE

Oops, Wrong King

Reb Cantor was pacing back and forth, cursing. "I don't like being made a fool out of," he said. "I've spent months learning both Hindustani to speak with the raja of Punjab and Farsi to impress the sultan of Persia, and now everyone agrees that our visitor will be the king of Romania?"

"Father, calm yourself," Rivka Cantor said soothingly. "I'm sure it was an honest mistake."

Reb Cantor's face grew red. "Fortunes are lost by honest mistakes! Thank goodness I already speak Romanian. I hope he shows up soon."

Everywhere in the village square reactions were similar. They were all tired of waiting. The sun was going down. They'd been standing and sweating for hours and hours as the day got warmer, and still the king of Romania was nowhere to be seen. Mrs. Chaipul was afraid her dumplings were drying out. Jacob Schlemiel wondered if the special clock that he had designed for the queen of England still would work in Romania. Infants dozed. Children and dogs ran through the square. All of the visitors from Smyrna laughed and smirked at yet another example of the foolishness of Chelm.

At last, one traveler, who had come all the way from Minsk, shouted, "Enough already. Forget about the king. It's another piece of idiocy from Chelm. The king's not coming! Let's eat!"

A cheer went up. On the roof of the synagogue, Abraham and Adam Schlemiel grinned at each other.

Only Rabbi Kibbitz managed to maintain his equilibrium. "Friends, friends," he said calmly. "So, the king is late. How many of you have ever tried to get your family up and out of the house on time for the early morning services? Imagine if you have an entire retinue. Horses, soldiers. It's hard to rush a king, but if you make him mad who knows what could happen? We'll give them another ten minutes. Fifteen. Okay? Then we'll eat. The food in the social hall will taste all the better."

"I certainly hope so," Reb Shikker muttered. "I for one could really use a drink."

The rest of the crowd grumbled but conceded.

"All right," Abraham said. "So, that's about it. We should head down to the social hall to be first in line."

"Wait a second," Adam raised his palm. "This is my prank. I want to see how it turns out."

"No, this is our prank," Abraham said. "And I'm hungry." He stood up and was about to slide down the drainpipe when he heard a shout that stopped him cold.

"I see it! I see it! I see the caravan!"

Abraham nearly fell off the roof. Adam grabbed his coat and pulled his brother back from the edge.

"Where did that come from?" Abraham asked. "Who said that?"

"The elm tree," Adam pointed. "Doodle has been up there all day."

"Doodle sees the king? Eh. He's crazy."

"Maybe," Adam said, "but look over there."

Like all of the other boys on the roof, and the ones in the trees, and everybody down in the square, they squinted into the distance.

At first the Schlemiel twins saw nothing. But then the nothing moved. Barely visible in the growing darkness, it bounced. It wasn't people walking. It was horses! There really were horses approaching. And wagons with flags and banners. And they were all coming closer.

"No. It's impossible," Adam said. "I made it all up. This can't be happening."

"I know. I know," Abraham agreed. "You made it up, and I helped. But you can see that someone is coming. A whole caravan! Come on, let's get down there and find out who it is!"

One right after the other, the two boys slid down the drainpipe and ran to the square.

"The king of Romania!" Doodle shouted. "He's here!"

Doodle on the Lookout

"And just in time," Rabbi Kibbitz sighed with relief. He was hungry. Fasting all day on Yom Kippur was one thing, at least you were inside and distracted by prayer . . .

"Romania, phooey," Reb Cantor hissed. But then he put on his best smile, and stepped forward with the rabbi to greet the visitors.

172

The crowd slowly parted as the horse-drawn wagons reached the edge of the square. One wagon, two, three, four . . . Only four wagons? What kind of a king only traveled with four wagons?

Everyone was quiet. It was nearly dark now, and the shadows fell long and deep across the square. The wagons were painted, their drivers dark and somber. The horses weren't exactly royal stock. They looked as if they had traveled thousands of miles for years at a time. There were no soldiers, no jugglers, no long procession of slaves bearing gifts for the villagers of Chelm.

At last, the tiny entourage stopped in the middle of the square. A door in the back of one of the wagons opened, and everyone inhaled, waiting for the red carpet. Instead, a rickety wooden block of steps was unceremoniously dropped.

Out stepped a large swarthy man wearing not a crown but a purple scarf on his head.

"Welcome to Chelm, oh King of Romania," Rabbi Kibbitz said. Then he peered up at the tall man. "You look very familiar."

"Oy," spat a disappointed visitor from Smyrna. "It's just the Gypsies."

"Hush, don't be rude," Rebecca Schlemiel said, nudging the man in the ribs with her elbow.

"Don't be rude," little Shmeenie Schlemiel echoed.

"I am Egon Kalderash," said the man in the purple scarf to Rabbi Kibbitz. He looked out at the crowd. "I have visited Chelm many times before. Yet, never have I been welcomed so."

"Well," Rabbi Kibbitz said, "this time we were expecting you."

"No," corrected Reb Cantor. "Actually, we were expecting the king of Romania. You're not the king of Romania, are you?"

"Not Romania. But you're close," Kalderash agreed. "I am a king now. I am King Egon the Seventh, leader of my people, the Rom. Although the Rom are scattered like dust around the world, we are still a nation. For my whole life I have been a duke, but when we last gathered I was recognized as the true king of the Romany. For the next few years anyway. Then it will be someone else's turn and good luck to them."

"Romany, Romania, Rumania," said Mrs. Chaipul, "I suppose it's an honest mistake."

For once in his life, Reb Cantor had nothing to say. He opened his mouth and then closed it again.

"Mazel tov!" Rabbi Kibbitz shouted loudly. "Kings are always welcome in Chelm. And as far as I know, you're the first king we've ever had. Now, I know that you've had a long journey, and we are all absolutely famished, so I think it would be prudent to go inside and have some of the wonderful nosh."

A stampede of elephants wouldn't have emptied the village square faster.

Only two young men remained in the empty square, standing still and dumbfounded.

"But it was supposed to be a prank," Adam mumbled. "A practical joke. There was no king. There was no czar. It was supposed to be something to brighten the winter, something that would be talked about for years to come."

"It was. And it did. And it will be," Abraham said, patting his brother's shoulder. "Only I suppose the joke is on us. It's the curse of the Schlemiels."

"But," Adam said. "But . . ."

"Come on. I can think of worse ways for a curse to play out. Let's hurry before everything is eaten."

Adam nodded silently. He wasn't sure whether to laugh or to cry.

Without another word, Abraham took his brother by the elbow and led him out of the cold dark square into the warm and sweet-smelling hall, where they found there was still enough food to fill their plates high. The dumplings were moist, the chicken was tender. There was no rum, but the visitor from Minsk had vodka and the Gypsies brought wine. The soft kreplach, sweet noodle pudding, and savory brisket with *kasha varnishkes* tasted wonderful.

CHAPTER THIRTY

A Visitor

Most shops have a little bell over the door that politely jingles whenever a customer enters. Jacob Schlemiel would have no such thing. "This is a carpentry shop," he scoffed. "I'm not going out and buying a brass bell."

So, Jacob had designed what he called "the world's first ratchet-and-hammer wood block chime." When the front door opened, the hammer went up with a "click." When the door closed, it came down with a "cl-ahk." Or at least that's how it was supposed to work. Sometimes it "clicked" open but "clucked" closed, sometimes it "clomped," and sometimes the entire door got stuck. Jacob kept tinkering, but nothing seemed to help. If anything, it just got worse.

On this particular morning, Adam Schlemiel was working in the back of the shop while his father was out running errands—which Adam knew really meant he was at Mrs. Chaipul's having a second cup of tea and schmoozing with the other lazy shopkeepers.

Adam was making a prototype of a seven-sided jewelry box that Reb Cantor, the merchant, said was going to be all the rage in England next year. How Reb Cantor knew these things was anyone's guess, but he promised that once the Schlemiels manufactured an original, he'd place an order for as many as they could build at a fair price. Reb Cantor had finally paid for the governor's chest. That had been enough for Jacob Schlemiel, who said that as long as the merchant paid cash, what he did afterward was his problem.

"Phooey!" Adam said. His thin finishing nail had just split another piece of mahogany. This was his third attempt at nailing the sides on the bottom and he was getting very frustrated. Reb Cantor's design called for exactly thirteen nails along each side of the box. What did a merchant know about carpentry? Nothing! Twelve nails Adam could manage, but the thirteenth . . . Still, money was money and Reb Cantor had supplied the mahogany, so Adam picked up another piece of wood and started over.

He had just finished nailing three sides and twelve nails when he heard the front door "clink" open. He smiled. At least Father would see that he'd accomplished something.

He raised his hammer high to tap in the final nail when the door went "Clank—crump-twang . . ." and then "CRASH!"

The noise startled Adam, whose hand jerked, smashing the hammer down and shattering the nearly perfect box.

"Oy gevalt!" Adam screamed in frustration. Then, waving the hammer like a madman, he ran full tilt into the front showroom. "What do you mean making such a racket like . . ."

He saw the young girl just a moment too late to stop. Bam! He slammed into her. She went sprawling. He tumbled over her. The hammer went flying up into the air.

"Duck!" he said, pushing the girl's head down against the sawdust-covered floor and snatching the hammer in mid-spin just before it could smack her on the back of the neck.

"Okay," Adam said, sitting down in the dust. "All right. It's okay."

The girl sat up with a look of absolute fury. A string of curses in some language Adam had never before heard spat from her mouth so fast that he felt stung. He held his hands up to shield himself, realized he still had the hammer, and quickly put it down.

"Relax," he said. "Relax. I'm okay. You're okay. Are you all right?"

"Yes, I'm all right," the girl said. Even those words sounded like curses. "How can you work in a carpentry shop with a door that falls off the hinges? First it nearly killed me, then you nearly killed me."

Adam looked. She was right. The shop's front door was lying flat on the floor not five inches from where the girl must have been standing. He took a deep breath, stood, and extended his hand to help her up. "I'm sorry."

"Yes," the girl said, "you are sorry." She ignored his hand and stood on her own. "You are Adam Schlemiel."

"No," Adam smiled. "I'm Abraham. Adam's my twin brother." It was an old trick, but at least Abraham would take the blame for this incident.

"You are Adam," the girl insisted.

"No, actually, I'm Abraham. We look a lot alike, so most people can't tell us apart. Are you looking for Adam?"

The girl shook her head. "I know Adam Schlemiel. Although I have not seen him in many years, I believe that I would know him in an instant. I came to see him, but you say he isn't here."

Adam shrugged. The girl looked familiar, but she wasn't from Chelm. She wore a dark fur coat and a bright red scarf over her hair. Maybe she worked in the marketplace in Smyrna, in which case it was probably better that she didn't recognize him.

"All right," the girl shrugged back. "Can you give him a message?"

"Sure."

"Tell him I am sorry that I missed him, and . . ." She beckoned with her finger for Adam to come closer.

He leaned forward.

Then she kissed him on the cheek. It was a gentle touch, like a feather brushing warmly against his skin.

Adam felt his heart pound and face flush red. He looked into her eyes, and then he remembered who she was.

"Rosa? Rosa Kalderash! You're the Gypsy girl. I didn't see you the other day."

The girl smiled. When the caravan had arrived in Chelm, she explained, she'd been too sick to go to the party, but now that she was feeling better she had wanted to say hello to Adam.

"Umm, why Adam? Why not Abraham?"

Again she smiled, and Adam thought about springtime and summer. "Don't take it personally," she said, as she turned to the door, "but I like Adam better."

"Wait." Adam put his hand on her shoulder. "I'm Adam. Really."

"Really?"

"Yes. Really."

Then Rosa spun around and slapped Adam on the cheek she'd just kissed.

"Ow!"

"I will always know when you are lying, Adam Schlemiel," Rosa said.

"But you will never know when I am lying. Maybe it really is Abraham I like better. Now, are you coming for a walk or not?"

Adam rubbed his cheek and winced. "I have work."

"Work will wait. When you come back, you will be able to bang thirteen nails in a row without accident."

"How did you know?"

"I am a Gypsy. Come."

It was impossible to argue. Adam set his apron on the counter and, stepping over the front door, followed Rosa into the sunshine.

CHAPTER THIRTY-ONE

An Innocent Walk

When Jacob Schlemiel, buzzing from six cups of tea, returned to his workshop to find the front door broken down and his son missing he tried not to panic. Keep calm, he thought. There is a rational explanation. Unfortunately, the first rational explanation he thought of was that the murderous thief, Alex Krabot, had finally returned to Chelm to take vengeance. So he immediately panicked.

"Kidnapping! Robbery!" Jacob shouted. "Destruction of property!"

Within moments, a dozen villagers had gathered outside the carpentry shop.

"What's the matter?"

"Jacob, calm down."

"What in the name of Jericho happened to your door?"

"Adam's gone," Jacob wailed. "He was working on a box. Look, one of them is smashed. I don't know what happened."

"Are you sure it was Adam?" Reb Shikker asked. "Maybe it was Abraham . . ."

Jacob spun around. "What do you mean by that?"

Reb Shikker shrugged. "They both look the same to me."

Jacob's eyes widened, and without another word he brushed through the crowd and raced to his house. If anything had happened to Adam, Abraham would know.

"Father," Abraham said as Jacob came panting through the front door, "is everything all right?"

"You're Abraham?" Jacob asked, leaning against the kitchen table to catch his breath.

"Yes."

"What's the matter?" Rebecca's voice came from her bedroom.

"Nothing," Jacob gasped. He stepped closer to Abraham and whispered, "Adam's missing. Do you know where he is?"

"He's missing?" Abraham said. "I didn't know he was missing."

"Shh," Jacob ordered, but it was too late. Rebecca was standing in the doorway, frowning.

"What do you mean Adam's missing?" she said. "Again? You didn't send him off to Smyrna by himself again, did you?"

"No. Don't say such a thing. I just left him in the workshop while I got a cup of tea."

"You left him alone?"

"Rebecca, don't start that with me. Adam is a grown man. I leave him alone all the time. I'm supposed to watch him like a bodyguard? We don't have time for this."

By now, the crowd from the shop had grown and assembled outside the Schlemiel home.

Reb Cantor knocked on the door. "Jacob? Is everything all right?"

"I don't know," Jacob shouted back. "Go away!"

"But Jacob, perhaps we can help."

"Will everybody please be quiet!" the poor man yelled.

"Shh!" Rebecca hissed. "Shmeenie is taking a nap!"

A silence instantly fell. Jacob took the opportunity to explain what he had seen at the shop. "I don't know what to do," he whispered. "Abraham, can you help? That mind-speaking thing you do with Adam. Can you find him?"

Abraham hesitated. He knew that his father guessed that from time to time he and his twin brother were able to communicate without words, sometimes across vast distances. But as they had grown older, they'd begun to lose the knack. It had become uncomfortable and awkward for them to eavesdrop on each other, so they hadn't been doing it. He wasn't even sure that he still could, but what else could he do?

"I'll try," Abraham said. "First of all, Mama, you need your rest. Sit down at least."

Rebecca threw up her hands and then sat in a chair. She shot Jacob a look that said, "You're the one who left my son alone—again—and he'd better be all right, or else."

Jacob's eyes widened in exasperation, and he gave her a look of "What?! The boy is almost sixteen years old and you want me to keep him under lock and key?!"

Then they were all quiet.

Outside the Schlemiel house, the people in the crowd, which was now about half the population of Chelm, were whispering among themselves.

Abraham closed his eyes, and reached out with his mind . . .

Adam . . . Adam . . .

He thought he felt something. So he tried again.

Adam . . . Adam . . .

What? came the answer, faintly.

Adam!

Who is this? Abraham?

Abraham smiled. *Who else would it be?*

"What?" Rebecca whispered.

"He's okay," Abraham answered.

"So, where is he?" Jacob demanded.

"Shhh . . ." Abraham said. He closed his eyes again.

Adam?

What?

Are you there?

Where else would I be? Go away!

Where are you?

I said go away! I don't want to talk.

BAM! Abraham felt as if he'd been smacked behind the eyes. "Ow!" he said.

"What? What happened?" Rebecca and Jacob said as one. "Is he all right?"

"I don't know. He hit me. He's fine," Abraham said. "He said he didn't want to talk just now."

"What do you mean he doesn't want to talk?" Rebecca said. "You tell him that I want to talk with him."

Adam, what are you hitting me for?

I thought I told you to leave me alone. I'm busy.

Wait! Mama wants to talk with you.

Now? Mama? Why?

Abraham sighed. *Papa says that the front door to the shop has been demolished and you are missing. They're worried. Can you blame them?*

Oh. Well, tell them I'm all right.

I already did that. They want to know where you are.

There was a pause. Abraham ignored his parents and listened for Adam. At last an answer came.

Okay, but you can't tell.

What do you mean I can't tell?

Promise me.

They're going to kill me. But all right. I promise.

Another pause. Then . . .

I'm with Rosa.

Rosa?

Rosa Kalderash, the Gypsy princess. I'm with her.

What do you mean you're with her?

Think about it you nudnik!

Then, as understanding dawned, Abraham's face turned red from blushing.

"What's the matter?" Rebecca demanded.

"Nothing, it's tiring," Abraham said.

You see why you can't tell them?

Yes. So, what do I tell them?

I don't care, just leave me alone.

Not a chance! Abraham shouted mentally at his brother. *This is your mess.* Abraham imagined a laugh inside his head.

Rosa says to tell them that I'm learning how to drive thirteen nails in a row.

"Rosa . . ." Abraham began, then he stopped. "Rows of nails. He says he's learning how to bang thirteen nails in a row. Does this make any sense?"

"Yes," Jacob nodded. "The prototype box. But why can't he do that at the shop? And what happened to the door?"

Abraham listened and then reported. "The door fell down when the ratchet-and-hammer wood block chime broke. It startled Adam and he broke the model. After that he had to go for a walk."

"A walk?" Rebecca Schlemiel frowned. "A walk? Tell him next time he should write a note."

Abraham closed his eyes and tried to pass on his mother's message, but all he could get from Adam was giggling and then a contented silence.

Abraham pursed his lips, opened his eyes, and said, "Adam says he's sorry, and he'll be back soon."

Relieved, Rebecca Schlemiel went back to bed. Jacob opened his door and stepped outside and announced that everything was all right.

One by one, the villagers dispersed, most of them mumbling something to the effect of "Trouble. Those Schlemiel boys are nothing but trouble."

CHAPTER THIRTY-TWO

A Very Schlemiel Wedding

"Tell us about your wedding, Mamma," little Shmeenie Schlemiel squeaked.

Abraham and Adam rolled their eyes and said, simultaneously, "Not again!"

"Your brothers are right," Rebecca Schlemiel said. "I wouldn't want to bore our guest." She nodded at Rosa Kalderash, the Gypsy girl who was visiting for dinner.

"Not at all," Rosa said, her right foot kicking Adam under the table. "I would love to hear the story.

"Ow!" Adam said. "I mean, me too."

Rebecca Schlemiel's face brightened and her smile danced. "Well . . ."

I was supposed to marry Reb Cantor. Isaac his name was. We had been betrothed almost from birth. My father was a goldsmith, but I was the youngest of his seven daughters, so there wasn't much left over for my dowry. It was my father's dream that my husband become his apprentice and take over the business.

So, after his bar mitzvah, the papers were signed, and Isaac moved in to the small room over the shop. The plan was that he would live there, eat with our family, and work with Father. After five years, if all went well, we would be married.

Unfortunately, Isaac Cantor was born with five thumbs on each hand. He couldn't pick up a hammer without dropping it on his toe. My father would give him a thin strand of gold wire to make into earring hooks. Simple enough, all you need to do is to cut a small piece and bend it into a U. Two hours later, Reb Cantor would give back a handful of little golden pretzels and knots. And wedding bands? Forget it. You have never seen such an assortment of knobby, bumbled, misshapen rings.

It was getting to the point where Father joked, half seriously, about burning down the jewelry shop rather than turning it over to Reb Cantor.

As to the question of marriage? Four years had passed and Isaac seemed to know even less about making jewelry than on the day he'd begun. How could he possibly earn enough to keep a family? My father was at his wit's end.

"What about you?" Shmeenie interrupted. "Did you love Reb Cantor the way you love Papa?"

Rebecca patted her young daughter on the head. "Never. But, remember, when I was a girl, your father didn't live in Chelm. He had gone to Frampol to become a carpenter's apprentice. Reb Cantor, however, I saw every day . . ."

I liked Isaac Cantor. I liked him a lot. Even though he was a klutz, he had kind brown eyes and he worked hard. Every day when I brought lunch, Isaac would joke with me.

"I can't wait until we're married," he would smile.

"I can wait," I'd laugh back.

After lunch, Isaac would go back to his work bench and demolish fine jewelry while Father held his head in his hands and prayed for a miracle. It wasn't going to work. We all knew it wasn't going to work. But we couldn't say that. We were going to be married. What else could we do?

One day there was an emergency. Mrs. Chaipul had gotten her golden necklace caught in the meat grinder. Even though it was choking her, she refused to cut it. Father was summoned and, reluctantly, he left Isaac in charge of the shop.

It was a delicate operation, but fortunately both the patient and the gold necklace survived. Mrs. Chaipul happily fed Father chocolate and cinnamon babka until he could eat no more.

When he finally returned to the shop, he was surprised to find the door shut and the "Closed" sign hanging in the window.

Frowning, Father unlocked the door and stepped inside.

Everything was gone. Every bracelet, every ring, every piece of fine jewelry that my father had made—years of stock—had vanished from their cases. Staggering under the weight of the blow, Father ran to the back and opened the safe. Only then did he relax slightly. The large bar of gold that he used to make the jewelry and the small box of precious stones were still there.

Isaac Cantor, however, was nowhere to be seen.

Such a scandal, you wouldn't believe! The cobbler reported that he had seen Reb Cantor riding north out of town in a wagon with a foreigner, and that was that.

I was broken hearted. True I hadn't been in love, but my life was over. Father was impoverished, and my fiancé had stolen nearly everything. Who would want to marry me now?

Months went by. Slowly Father rebuilt his business. He even began looking for my new husband, but every time he mentioned someone to me, I shook my head sadly and said, "I'll wait."

Years passed. My mother warned me that if I didn't get married soon then no one would have me. To be sure I felt the same way, but still I said, "I'll wait."

And then a letter from Italy came addressed to Father.

"Prepare the wedding feast," it read. "Arriving in Chelm on Thursday with riches beyond belief. Best regards, Isaac Cantor."

"Best regards?" Father shouted. "A wedding? After all these years he expects a wedding?"

He threw the paper into the fireplace, but before it could burn I snatched it out.

"Father," I begged. "You all say you want me to marry. Please."

"A thief you should marry?" Father frowned. "A man who would leave for years without a single word?"

Glumly, I nodded. I was still young, but getting old fast. I didn't know what else to do.

So the preparations began, but without joy. The social hall was decorated, food prepared, and the wedding cake was baked seven layers high.

On the great day, almost as soon as the cake was delivered, the rain began. It poured, it pelted, it bucketed, it drenched.

"Perfect," Father said, looking out the window of our house. "Just perfect."

And then I, not for the first time that week, burst into tears.

My father took me into his arms and patted me. "Daughter, Daughter, it will be perfect," he repeated over and over.

The rain hid my tears as we arrived at the synagogue at the appointed hour.

"So, where is he?" Father asked.

No one answered. The entire village of Chelm had gathered for the ceremony, but Isaac Cantor was nowhere to be seen. Father fumed and ranted.

"The rain," I said. "The rain has delayed him."

And just then the door at the back of the synagogue opened. Everyone turned and stared. There stood a man covered in mud and soaked from the brim of his hat to the soles of his boots. His beard was full. He had lost weight. It had been five years since we had seen Isaac Cantor, but to my eyes at least he had grown even more handsome.

"YOU!" my Father shouted. "Where have you been?"

"I got lost," came the quiet response.

"Well, you're just in time," Rabbi Kibbitz said, calmly hurrying down the aisle with a towel. "Come in. Come in."

He seemed nervous. He seemed frightened. But who wouldn't be? Not only was this his wedding day, but everyone in Chelm thought that the poor man was a thief.

"This is the man you want?" my father whispered to me.

"Yes," I hissed. "Now be quiet."

The shul was as silent as a tomb as the wedding began. The groom stood stiff and still. He answered by rote, barely moving his eyes as I walked around him seven times. When it came time to give me the ring he froze for a moment and then reached into his shirt, bringing out a chain on which hung a thin gold band.

"Is that all that's left?" my father mumbled.

"It was my grandmother's," he said, slipping the ring onto my finger. Even though he looked scared, his smile was kind to me.

He raised his foot. The glass was shattered. And in that moment all was forgiven as the synagogue resounded with a loud, "Mazel tov!"

I looked at my husband, tears in my eyes, and saw that there were tears in his eyes—blue eyes.

Just then, the doors at the back of the synagogue banged open, and a strong voice shouted, "I'm here! I'm here!"

Oy, what a mess.

All the Schlemiels laughed. Rosa Kalderash looked shocked.

"What happened?" Rosa asked.

"I married the wrong man." Rebecca's smile was as bright as a star.

On the day Reb Cantor vanished, a stranger had come into my father's shop and had marveled at the craftsmanship. The stranger said he would buy everything, but that he had no money with him. Reb Cantor told us that he believed the man, but wouldn't trust him with the jewelry. So he wrote my father a note that we never found and traveled with the man all the way to Paris. There the man paid him, and Isaac Cantor found that his true calling was not as a jeweler but as a merchant. So, taking the long way back to Chelm, he bought and sold and traded his way to a small fortune. Unfortunately for him, he was twenty minutes too late for his own wedding.

Oy, there was screaming and shouting. Once again, I was in tears.

"You said you'd wait!" Isaac yelled at me.

"I waited," I shrieked back. "I waited!"

Not having a clue about what was going on, my new husband tried to protect me.

"Who are you?" he asked Isaac. "What do you want?"

"I'm Isaac Cantor, the merchant. I'm the groom. Who are you?"

In an instant there was silence again. All eyes went to the stranger.

"My name is Jacob Schlemiel," he answered quietly. "I'm a carpenter. And I'm the husband."

At that moment, my heart melted. I looked into my husband's eyes and I saw his kindness. I knew that I was his and he was mine. And that made me so happy. So so happy.

In the Schlemiel house, the only sound was the crackling of the hearth fire. Jacob Schlemiel reached across the table and squeezed his wife's hand.

"Mazel tov!" little Shmeenie shouted.

And everyone laughed.

CHAPTER THIRTY-THREE

The Wisest Rabbi

The marketplace in Smyrna was busy. It was open six days a week, and was at least ten times larger than the small weekly market in Chelm. Still, some things never changed. Whenever they got a moment, the villagers of Smyrna enjoyed making jokes at their neighbor's expense.

"Did you hear the one about how the villagers of Chelm tried to lock the moon in a rain barrel? They saw the reflection of the full moon and decided to hammer a lid onto the barrel and let the moon out later in the month!" The fishmonger's head tilted back with laughter.

Now the pickle man roared with glee, "How about the time it had just snowed, and they thought the snow was so lovely that they didn't want to leave footprints, so they hired a band of Russians to carry them on their backs!"

Abraham Schlemiel's face turned as red as a boiled beet. After filling him with dire warnings about returning straight him, his mother had sent him alone to Smyrna to buy a special kind of paprika. Abraham was already on edge about breaking his promise to Babushka Krabot, and now he had to listen to these men making jokes about his home.

Enough was enough!

"It's not true!" His sixteen-year-old voice squeaked with anger. "Chelm is nothing like that."

The merchants of Smyrna turned toward him.

"And who are you, schlemiel?" the fishmonger asked.

"Yes," Abraham said.

"Yes? Now that's a name from Chelm!" The pickle man giggled. "I can just see his mother calling, 'Yes! Yes!'"

Now the spice vendor and the tea salesman added their guffaws.

"No," Abraham said. "No."

"Ahh," the pickle man said. "That's his last name. Gentlemen, I would like you to meet Mr. Yes No from Chelm!"

The laughter was deafening.

"My name," Abraham shouted, "is Abraham Schlemiel!"

Suddenly, there was a moment of silence, and then the fishmonger said, "Even better, a real Schlemiel from Chelm!"

"He's doomed," giggled the pickle man.

Abraham thought about turning on his heels and storming off. His shopping was done, but he wasn't about to let these men get the better of him.

He waited for the laughter to subside, and then he said, "In Chelm, we have the wisest rabbi in the world!"

"You're serious?" the tea salesman said. "You think Rabbi Kibbitz is wise?"

Abraham nodded, as serious as a cow waiting to be fed.

The tea salesman went, "Braahh hahaha!"

There was more laughter and more waiting. When at last the merchants of Smyrna could laugh no more, Abraham began . . .

When Rabbi Kibbitz prayed, he davened. Now, davening is not rare. Most men daven when they pray, bowing at the waist forward and backward, or from the knees, rocking back and forth. Rabbi Kibbitz, however, davened from left to right, from side to side like a stalk of wheat blowing in the breeze.

So wise was Rabbi Kibbitz that when the other villagers of Chelm tried to copy his davening, he put a stop to it right away.

"You can't daven from side to side," he told everyone. "Your shoulders will bump into each other. I can get away with it because I've got more room up here at the front."

"Ahh," said the people of Chelm. And from that day on, they davened backward and forward while their rabbi rocked from left to right, stamping his feet in a quiet rhythm.

Now, one day a troublemaker thought it would be funny if he played a trick on the rabbi.

For years, for decades, Rabbi Kibbitz had stood in the same place at the front of the shul as he davened, and over time ruts just the size of the rabbi's feet had been worn into the synagogue's wooden floor. Ordinarily, Reb Levitsky, the synagogue's janitor, would have repaired such a defect, but the people of Chelm were proud of their rabbi. In fact, when Rabbi Kibbitz was sick and Rabbi Yohon Abrahms, the mashgiach *and head of the yeshiva took his place, he always stumbled in surprise at how deep and wide the ruts had become.*

"Nobody," said the villagers, "can ever fill the shoes of our rabbi."

Well, one day this troublemaker decided to fill the ruts with wood glue. This particular batch of wood glue was fairly quick drying and when dried it would be the exact color of the synagogue floor. The glue was applied on a Friday, just after the morning prayers. That would give it a chance to set and become invisible, but not harden completely.

The synagogue filled for the evening service. Sabbath greetings were shouted, backs were slapped, and at last Rabbi Kibbitz made his slow way to the place of honor.

As usual, he stepped right into his ruts. A momentary look of puzzlement crossed his brow as his feet sank slowly into the floor. By then, however, the sun was going down and the synagogue had grown dim. It was impossible to see that there was anything amiss, so he shrugged and began the service, davening as was his habit from left to right.

But the more you churn wood glue, the stickier it becomes. This glue, which was almost set, took hold of the rabbi's boots and began to pull.

Side to side the rabbi rocked as he quickly chanted the prayers, but then he slowed. He hesitated. Where were the soft thumps of his feet as they lifted left-right, left-right? In fact, he noticed now that he could barely lift his feet.

"Am I dying?" Rabbi Kibbitz wondered, not realizing that he spoke aloud.

Naturally, this upset the congregation. Mrs. Chaipul, the midwife, hurried down from the women's balcony. She listened to the Rabbi's heart. It sounded fine, but still Mrs. Chaipul suggested that the Rabbi take a seat.

But this was impossible. The glue had solidified, and by all appearances, the rabbi's feet had sunk into the floor. Worse still, because this was a Friday night and the beginning of the Sabbath, no tools could be brought into the sanctuary to free him.

"It is a sign from the almighty!" Rabbi Kibbitz said. "I shall pray all through the Sabbath, and by the end of Havdalah, the blessed one will set me free."

All night the rabbi prayed. Mrs. Chaipul came and brought him sandwiches, but he refused to eat because the crumbs would muffle his voice. In the morning, he was still there, barely awake. He couldn't move his feet, but his body still swayed, lurching with exhaustion like a drunkard on Purim. Through lunch, his rocking continued. All afternoon he prayed, until his voice became hoarse.

At last, the sun went down. The Havdalah candle was lit, held high, and then extinguished in the wine with a sputter.

Finally the rabbi was freed!

"A miracle," the pickle man said, somberly.

"Wait a second," said the fishmonger. "You mean to say that he actually managed to daven his way out of the glue?"

"Well, no," Abraham admitted. "After sunset, the carpenter ran back to his shop and brought back drills, hammers, a saw, and a pry bar."

Then the pickle man said, "How come your rabbi didn't just take off his shoes?"

"Yes, what's so wise about standing there like that?" asked the tea merchant.

"I'm glad you asked," Abraham said at last. "After he sat down, the rabbi said that whoever had poured the glue should be forgiven because that person had taught him the true meaning of the word eternity."

With that, Abraham smiled, picked up his purchases, and began the long walk home.

The merchants waited until he was out of sight, and then laughter once again filled the marketplace in Smyrna.

"A Schlemiel from Chelm," the pickle man said, clutching his sides. "Oy!"

CHAPTER THIRTY-FOUR

The King and the Carpenter

Egon Kalderash, the king of the Rom, peered into the dim carpentry shop. The door still lay on the floor as if it had been knocked down by the police.

"Schlemiel?" The question was softer than it might have been.

A head poked from the back room. "Ahh, your Majesty, come in," Jacob Schlemiel said. "Don't mind the mess. I've been meaning to clean it up for weeks, but the weather's been so nice, and I enjoy the fresh air."

Kalderash strode in.

"Now, your Royalness," Jacob Schlemiel said. "What can I do for you? One of your wagons needs repairs? I'll get my tool box."

Kalderash put a heavy hand on Jacob's shoulder. "The wagons are fine."

"Oh. You need a table? A throne? What?"

"I need to discuss a problem."

"A problem? What problem?"

"With your son."

"Which son? I have two."

"The one called Adam."

Jacob grew tense. "What's the matter with Adam?"

"Your son Adam has been seeing my daughter."

"Oh!" Jacob's shoulders relaxed. "That's nothing. Both of my sons have been seeing your daughter."

A dark line formed across Egon Kalderash's brow. "Both of your sons?"

A nod. "Yes. In fact, I've been seeing your daughter, too."

The Gypsy king's eyes narrowed in instant rage. "You have been seeing my daughter?" he roared.

"Yes! Calm down! My wife saw her too. She came over for dinner recently. You didn't know? We thought she told you."

Kalderash coughed as he struggled to regain his demeanor.

"Rosa is a nice girl," Jacob said. "A very nice girl. Polite. Well behaved. Wonderful table manners. Do you need a glass of water?"

"Enough about table manners. We have to talk." Kalderash took a deep breath and then sat down on the floor.

"Egon, I have chairs."

"Sit," Kalderash said.

Jacob scanned the floor as if trying to gauge whether the layer of sawdust would stick to his black coat because if he came home filthy Rebecca would want him to wash it, and then it would take forever to dry. At last he shrugged, grabbed an apron from behind the counter, and then sat down on it.

"Well, this is uncomfortable," Jacob said with a smile.

"Your son," Kalderash said quietly, "has been seeing my daughter."

"I thought we went through this already."

"No," the Gypsy king said. Even seated he looked gigantic. "He has been seeing her. Not just at dinner. In private. Not in public. In the woods."

"Well, that's where they met, wasn't it? I mean years ago . . ."

"Okay, look," Kalderash said. "Let me be blunt. I don't want them to be married."

"Married? The boy is barely a man. What would he be doing getting married . . ." Then Jacob paused. Now his eyes widened. "You mean they've been *seeing* each other!"

A nod from Kalderash.

"Oy."

"Yes, oy," Kalderash agreed. "So, what do we do?"

The two men sat on the floor in silence. Several minutes passed.

"Can I ask a question?" Jacob said.

"Go ahead."

"So, why shouldn't they get married? She could convert and they could get married."

"You're a Schlemiel," Kalderash said, as if that were answer enough.

It wasn't enough for Jacob. "A couple of years ago you were just another Gypsy. Now you're the king, you think that makes you better than me?"

Kalderash leaned back and roared with laughter. Jacob looked nervous.

At last, Kalderash managed to regain his control. "It's nothing to do with royalty. Neither you nor I are what we might call high-class fellows."

"If you hadn't said that so nicely," Jacob said, "I might have taken that as an insult."

"No offense meant. It's nothing to do with position of leadership. It's tribal. Think about the religious differences. That alone is a void as cold as the steppes of Siberia, and as lonely as the deserts of the Sahara."

"As salty as a kosher pickle." Jacob nodded.

"Plus you're a Schlemiel."

"So?"

"So, everyone knows that your entire family is cursed. The last thing that I want for my little Rosa is for her to become a victim of that curse."

"I . . ." Jacob opened his mouth and then closed it. "Yes, I understand."

"You see my point?"

Jacob nodded. "It's not such a bad curse. I've lived with it my whole life and I'm not miserable."

"No," Kalderash shook his head solemnly. "You want for your children what is best for them. So do I. Rosa would be miserable living here. Even if she took on the appearance of your religion, she would never be accepted by your people."

"Now, that's not true . . ."

"Schlemiel, don't lie to yourself. People are people. Tribes are tribes. Besides, even if your people accepted her, Rosa is a traveler. It is who she is. She is not born to stay in one place. She would become restless. And, I can tell you truthfully that if your son came with us, my people would never accept him. Furthermore, he would be miserable on the road. Finally there is your curse."

"Yes, yes. There's always the curse. Do you happen to know any Gypsy magic to get rid of the curse?"

"No," Kalderash shook his head. "I am sorry, but I don't."

"Too bad," Jacob said. "Ask around, will you?

"I wouldn't hold out much hope."

"Perhaps your mother?"

"She died. That is why I am the king."

"Oh, I'm sorry."

Kalderash touched his fingers to his forehead. "It was her time."

They were quiet a moment, then the Gypsy king said, "So, is it settled?"

"What if they're in love?" Jacob asked.

"Love?" Kalderash rubbed his mustache thoughtfully. "That would be a shame. But young love is sudden and passionate. It's like a torch in a wind storm. It burns bright and hot and then flickers out in a matter of minutes. When I think back to my young days, and my first loves, I regret none of them. And I am only thankful that I did not marry a single one of those young ladies. You see my point?"

"No," Jacob said. "I married my first love, and I don't regret it for a minute."

"Really? That is nice. How rare and precious." The Gypsy paused. "Still, what do you suggest we do about our children?"

"I think," Jacob said, "we should blame each other. You tell your daughter it's my fault. I tell my son it's your fault. At least then they don't hate us."

A smile appeared beneath the bushy mustache. "You're sneaky. I like that."

"It makes me sad," Jacob said.

"They're children," Kalderash said. "Next week they'll find something else to make you sad about. At least this time we can do something for them. Something to help them."

"But what if we're wrong?"

"It would be worse if we're right and we did nothing."

Again they sat. The low afternoon sun peered in through the open front door and began to vanish in the distance.

At last, Jacob Schlemiel spoke. "Can we get up now?"

"I'm stuck," Egon Kalderash said.

Laughing heartily, the two men creakily helped each other to their feet. Silently, they picked up the door and working together hung it back on its hinges. They shook hands, and after Kalderash left, Jacob Schlemiel stared at the closed door for a very long time.

The next morning, both Jacob and Adam were quiet as they walked the short distance between the Schlemiel house and the carpentry shop. Jacob unlocked the front door while Adam took the shutters off the windows.

Inside, Jacob lit a small fire and peered at the day's list he'd written in chalk on the wall.

1) Prototype for Reb Cantor

2) Bread box for Mrs. Chaipul

3) Talk with Adam about problem

Jacob frowned. He glanced over at his son and for a moment thought about erasing the third item, but Adam was too quick.

"What problem?" Adam said. "I told you yesterday that I should have the prototype ready this afternoon. Reb Cantor didn't change the requirements again, did he?"

The merchant had been notoriously fickle about getting the design exactly right for the jewelry boxes that he planned to mass produce and export to England.

"No," Jacob said. "It's not that. It's about Rosa."

Adam looked up. "What's the matter with Rosa?"

"Nothing," Jacob said. "She's a nice girl."

"If you don't like her, just come out and say so."

"I do like her."

"It's her family, isn't it? You have something against her family?"

"Adam," Jacob said. "Relax. And yes, it is her family."

"I knew it!" The young man spun around in a full circle. "I knew that you would be too small. It's just so obvious that . . ."

"Her father forbade it."

"Her father? Her father? I don't believe it." Adam pointed his finger at his father. "I think it's your fault."

"Adam." Jacob put his hand on his heart. "I have nothing but your best interest . . ."

"You hate her, and I love her. It's that simple!" He turned and ran from the shop. The door slammed behind him, and Jacob watched it wobble, wondering if it would fall from its hinges again. The door stayed on, but his son was gone. Again. Rebecca would kill him. Jacob sighed.

CHAPTER THIRTY-FIVE

Breathless

Down the street he raced. Adam Schlemiel ran through Chelm as only a boy in love can—like a hawk in frantic pursuit of a dove. He ignored the stares from neighbors and friends as he zigged and zagged and made his way to the village square where the caravan of travelers had been camping for the better part of a month.

He turned the corner around the side of the synagogue. The square was empty. The Gypsy wagons were gone. Adam searched frantically, as if four horse-drawn wagons could somehow be hidden behind the square's eight elm trees. Nothing. Just matted down grass and the ruts from four sets of wagon wheels heading north toward Smyrna.

In an instant his mind was made up. Adam ran after them.

Only two roads lead from Chelm, the Smyrna Road and the Great Circular Road. When he was a boy, it had taken Adam the better part of a morning to travel from Chelm to Smyrna. At top speed, he thought he might be there in an hour and a half.

He had to see her. He had to. It couldn't just end like that. No.

Help me! he called mentally to his brother.

What? How?

Lend me your strength.

All right. I will try.

Adam felt his resolve harden. He took a deep breath and ran even faster.

"Abraham, what's wrong?" Rebecca Schlemiel's eyes widened.

"Eccccch," Abraham answered.

They had been preparing a *cholent,* a three-day stew that would feed the family over the Sabbath, getting better and better so that by Sunday when only the pot drippings were left the family would almost fight to dip the last of their challah into the wonderful gravy. Then, all of a sudden, Abraham's face had gone red. His breathing had become short and sudden, and he'd fallen to his knees.

"Abraham!" Rebecca shouted. "Shmeenie, run and get Mrs. Chaipul."

The little girl sensed the seriousness in her mother's voice and without hesitation, without even asking a question, she snatched her coat from a hook and ran from the house.

"Abraham, you're scaring me," Rebecca whispered as she knelt down beside her boy. She rolled him onto his back and forced his mouth open, but he wasn't choking on anything she could see.

Abraham's breathing was ragged. His hands were clenched into fists. His arms were feebly pumping back and forth. His feet were twitching as if he were having a fit. And it didn't subside. If anything, it only got worse. You would think that in such a state he would grow weaker and weaker and slow down with exhaustion. Rebecca wasn't sure which scared her more, that the fit might suddenly stop or that it might just keep going.

By the time Shmeenie returned with Mrs. Chaipul and her black bag, Rebecca had managed to get a towel under her boy's head, thrown a soup bone into the pot, and was adding a dozen cloves of garlic plus twelve turns of pepper. The garlic and pepper were the secret. You needed to have exactly the same number of cloves as turns of the pepper mill.

"You're cooking?" Mrs. Chaipul asked as she unpacked her bag. "It smells good."

"You want I should stand here like a lump?" Rebecca snapped. "I would hold him and comfort him, but he won't sit still. So, at least we won't have to worry about supper."

"That wasn't what I meant," Mrs. Chaipul said. She removed a tube from her bag and listened through it to Abraham's chest. "When Shmeenie came into the restaurant, I thought it was you who was in trouble."

"I only wish," Rebecca said. "So, what's wrong?"

The old woman, who was the closest thing Chelm had to a doctor, tapped, prodded, and poked. At last, she shrugged. "I don't know. I can't find anything."

It went on for more than an hour. Jacob was summoned home, but there was little he could do to comfort his son, wife, or daughter. The three grown-ups started a game of canasta while Shmeenie played jacks dangerously close to the thrashing boy.

And then all of a sudden it stopped. Abraham's eyes snapped wide open, he took one deep breath, and then screamed at the top of his lungs, "ROSA!" His eyes shut, all the tension left his body, and a moment later he was asleep.

The shout startled everyone. Cards flew across the room. Jacob leaped to his feet, stepped on one of Shmeenie's jacks, and began cursing.

"Rosa?" Mrs. Chaipul said. "What's a rosa?"

"Rosa," Rebecca whispered, "was Adam's girlfriend."

"Adam?" Mrs. Chaipul said. "I thought you said this was Abraham."

"Abraham and Adam share everything," little Shmeenie said helpfully.

"Hush," her mother ordered.

"Everything?" Mrs. Chaipul looked embarrassed. She knew, as everyone in Chelm knew, that Adam had been visiting with the Gypsy princess in the forest. "They shared everything?"

"No," Rebecca said, shocked. "It's nothing like that. Nothing at all."

"Whatever you say." Mrs. Chaipul bent over her patient. "Well, whatever was happening seems to have passed. Abraham is resting well enough now. Make sure you give him some chicken soup when he wakes up. Let me know."

After the old woman left, Rebecca Schlemiel turned to her husband. "You told him, didn't you?"

Jacob nodded glumly. "Not him, but Adam."

"Papa," Shmeenie said, "Can you give me back my jacks?"

Chapter Thirty-Six

Broken

Three days later, Abraham's eyes finally fluttered open. He blinked twice, saw his brother staring down at him, and smiled.

"What's the news?" Abraham croaked. His mouth was dry, and Adam held a cup of chicken broth to his lips. "So?"

"Well," Adam began, "It looks like there's going to be a war. Russia is building up its army, but it's not really clear who's attacking who."

A crease appeared on Abraham's brow. "I mean with Rosa."

"I don't think she has to worry. They're not conscripting girls."

"Adam," Abraham insisted. "Tell me."

Adam sighed and looked out the window. It was raining. "They vanished. They're gone. She's gone."

Abraham closed his eyes. If he had been any stronger, he would have cried. "I knew it. I knew the moment you left."

"And yet you gave me your strength to run even faster."

Abraham made a small shrug. "It was worth a try."

"I didn't know you cared that much about me," Adam said. He stared intently at his brother. "Or was it Rosa?"

"I . . ." Abraham began.

Then the door to the bedroom banged open. "Talking?" Rebecca Schlemiel said. "I'm hearing talking. You're awake! Jacob, he's awake! Oh, he's not here. Adam, run to the shop and tell your father. Shmeenie, Abraham's awake. Go get him a bowl of soup. Never mind. I'll get it myself. I'm so happy that you're awake. I was worried."

Their mother bent down, gave Abraham a soft wet kiss on the forehead, and then whisked out of the room.

Abraham's eyes glanced around. "I've never seen Mama so excited."

"Your illness is doing wonders for her health," Adam said, standing. "It's been years since she had so much energy."

"Maybe I should get sick more often."

"No," Adam said. "Don't." He bent down, wiped Abraham's forehead, and then kissed his brother in the same spot. "Get better."

"What, you're still here?" Rebecca bustled in with a tray piled high with a soup bowl, a spoon, and a chunk of challah the size of a large hen. "Get your father already."

"I'm going already," Adam said.

"So go already. Skit skat."

As soon as her brother was gone, little Shmeenie bounded into the bedroom and immediately jumped on top of Abraham.

"Shmeenie," her mother warned, "you'll kill him!"

"No, it's all right," Abraham grabbed his sister and hugged her deeply. "I need all the *simchas* I can get."

"Fine," Rebecca said. "But if you spill soup in that bed you still have to sleep there."

Abraham smiled. Everything was back to normal.

Not really. On the surface, all seemed well. Now that Abraham was awake and eating solid foods, he quickly regained his health and was back up on his feet in no time. Jacob and Adam finally finished the prototype jewelry box for Reb Cantor, who promised that after he returned from his next trip to London, he'd take as many as they could build. Now that she didn't have to tiptoe around the house, little Shmeenie was making up for the days of quiet by banging pots and singing loudly until her mother finally threatened to send her out in the rain if she didn't quiet down. Best of all, Rebecca Schlemiel, who had been nearly bedridden herself since Shmeenie's birth, was up and about and as filled with smiles and joy as she had been for years.

Meals at the Schlemiels' house were raucous and exuberant. Bowls were filled, passed, emptied, and refilled. Everything was discussed all at once, from the nature of heaven and the universe to Mrs. Chaipul's opinions on the coming spring planting. Only one subject was not discussed, but that was the most important.

Rosa Kalderash, the Gypsy princess, was gone from Chelm, but not far from the minds of any of the Schlemiels (with the exception of Shmeenie). At work in his father's carpentry shop, Adam fell quiet, straightening bent nails for hours at a time without a single complaint. Jacob Schlemiel watched his son and hoped that the boy's heart would mend.

It was worse for Abraham. Nobody even thought to talk about it with Abraham. Not even Adam. Adam thought that Abraham had collapsed because he had lent Adam his strength. Everyone else agreed that the collapse was a fluke, a sudden illness that came and fortunately went.

For Abraham, though, the world was a suddenly darker and more somber place. You see, he too had fallen in love with Rosa Kalderash. It wasn't something that he had meant or intended. Rosa had been in love with Adam. There was no mistaking that. Still, Abraham had managed to find ways to spend some time with her while his brother was working. At first, he had pretended to be just her friend, as if all was innocent. But then there had been that one day when . . .

He didn't dare think about it. It was just one day. He had no idea how a love so brief could hurt so much. He never would have let himself get so close to her if he'd known the pain it would cause. It was as if the inside of his heart has been removed. Perhaps if he had been kept busy, he could have buried himself in his work like Adam. But now that Mama was feeling a bit better, there was less and less for Abraham to do around the house. She insisted that he rest or go into the forest to look for mushrooms. And so he was alone, more alone than he had been in his entire life.

Sometimes, when he was deep in the Schvartzvald and far from Chelm, he lifted his head to the sky and shouted her name, screaming "Rosa!" until his throat was scorched and his cheeks were wet from crying. Far away, back in the village of Chelm, Adam's hammer would grow still and then tremble in his hand until at last a single tear welled up and fell into the sawdust. Then the hammer would rise and fall with renewed vigor, pounding bent nails straight in one solid blow.

CHAPTER THIRTY-SEVEN

Well, Well . . . A Half-Bucket of Tears

Adam hated doing Abraham's chores. The one he hated most was going to the village well for water for the house. First of all, it was hard work. He'd done his share of lugging water as a boy. Now he was supposed to be the carpenter's apprentice, not some scullery maid. Fetching water was supposed to be Abraham's job, but Abraham was always neglecting his chores. He was always off somewhere, moping and moaning about losing his Gypsy princess.

Enough about Rosa, Adam had told Abraham. Yes, Rosa was a nice girl. For a time, Adam himself had thought he was in love with her, but she was gone. Long gone and far away. Abraham should forget about her. After all, it was more than a year since she'd left. Couldn't Abraham at least pull himself together enough to do his own chores?

And how come Abraham didn't get in trouble for being such a moping pain in the *tuchas*? Neither their mother nor their father seemed to mind. If it had been Adam neglecting his work, then their father would be shouting and slamming doors, and their mother would be shaking her head and clucking her tongue. But when Abraham forgot to go to the well everyone just sighed and said, "Adam you do it."

And of all the chores that Abraham avoided, Adam hated going to the well the most. Drawing the water from the well was work for the women and children, not a grown man. Plus, there was always a line. Adam often had to wait and wait. The girls and women didn't mind the line. They would cackle and gossip like a flock of hens. Adam hated waiting.

And worst of all, on top of all the other indignities and embarrassments, going to the well meant that the Schlemiels were poor. All the wealthier families in Chelm had wells of their own. Some, like Reb Cantor, even had a hand pump inside the house! Add it all up, Adam thought, and going to the well was about as much fun as having a tooth pulled by tying it to a string, tying the string to a door, and slamming the door shut—only slower.

He dragged the two buckets all the way to the village square and then sighed as he saw the length of the line. There must be at least fifteen women standing around waiting their turns. How long did it take to lower a bucket, turn the crank, dump the bucket of water into your pail, and then head home? Hours, it seemed. And because it was a pleasant and sunny day, nobody was in much of a rush. Except Adam.

Worse still, the longer he spent waiting the greater the likelihood was that one of his friends or schoolmates might see him in the line and take the opportunity to taunt him about it. When you're seventeen, you don't want to be called "water boy." Maybe Abraham didn't mind, but for Adam, who saw himself as a carpenter's apprentice, it would be humiliating.

Moreover, their father would be furious at him for coming into work late, but he wouldn't say a thing because their mother had asked Adam so nicely. Instead, their father would silently glare.

It wouldn't even be so bad if he just could sit down on one of the buckets while he waited, but if he flipped it over, then he'd get dirt in the water and his mother would be livid. Adam sighed deeply and took his place in the line.

"How can you be sad on such a beautiful day?" came a voice.

It was a sweet voice, and when Adam turned around he was stunned to look into the face of the most beautiful girl he had ever seen. She had long brown hair tucked into a beautiful red and white silk scarf. Her skin was fair and smooth. Her nose was long and slender. And her eyes were brown and deep, as rich and as full of life as a garden in full bloom. Naturally, he couldn't say a word. His tongue was tied in knots.

"So, Abraham," the girl said. "It's been a long time. I've been away, you see. Traveling. My father thought it would broaden my horizons to see some of the world, so I've been out of Chelm for almost a year now. How have you been?"

"Ff . . . fine," Adam sputtered at last. Who was she? This beautiful young woman looked familiar, but for the life of him he couldn't place her. "I've been very fine."

"Well," the girl said, "you look very handsome, as usual."

Adam felt himself blush. He was mortified. His heart was pounding like a hammer and his knees felt weak and he could barely stand.

"You were always a good-looking fellow," she went on, "but time has treated you well."

"Thank you," he mumbled. He wanted to say "You're the most beautiful girl I've ever seen." But he couldn't. He could barely look at her face. Instead, he looked at her shape, which was slim and tall and lovely, and found himself even more dumbstruck.

"You're always polite, Abraham," she said. "Not like your brother. Did you know I once had a crush on Adam? I don't even know if he knew. But the last time I saw him, the day the king of the Rom came to Chelm, Adam was downright mean to me. He yelled in my face and ran out of the house without saying goodbye."

Adam felt as if he had been struck in the forehead with a hammer. He had insulted this girl? How was that possible? He still didn't know who she was.

"You wouldn't do that, would you, Abraham?" she said, smiling at him.

Adam tried to think, but when she smiled he felt as if a ray of sun had broken through the overcast murk on a gray and miserable day.

"Well," he sputtered, "If Adam did that, then he was a fool. How anyone could be unkind to someone as lovely and sweet as you is beyond my comprehension."

Now it was her turn to pause. She scanned him up and down and nodded, obviously pleased.

"So, Abraham," she said at last, "why do you sigh on such a beautiful day? The sun is high, the air is cool, spring is upon us, the mud is gone, and the world is filled with wonders."

"I, ah . . ." Adam paused. He couldn't tell her a thing that was wrong because all of a sudden nothing at all was wrong. So he said, "All the clouds on my darkened horizon were scattered away the moment you spoke to me."

"A poet too!" she said. "How wonderful."

And so they talked about this and that and nothing at all. All around, the gaggle of women watched with smiles and nods and winks. The line moved slowly, slower than ever, but Adam didn't notice and wouldn't have minded if he did.

When they arrived at the head of the line, he drew her water first and then his own, and then he offered to carry her water back to her house (if only to find out where she lived). She laughed and asked him how would he possibly manage to carry four buckets at once. Two trips, he suggested. She shook her head no and said she would make her way home by herself. It wouldn't do for people to talk.

He nodded glumly and then asked if he might help her at the well again, and she said, "Of course, at least until my father's pump is fixed."

So he smiled and said, "Shalom."

And she smiled back, a smile as bright as a rainbow, a smile that he promised himself would live in his mind forever. And he watched her lift the two buckets and make her way slowly and elegantly across the square.

Adam sighed again, but this time the sigh was one of happiness.

"She's turned into something," said Mrs. Shikker, nudging Adam in the ribs.

Adam blushed. Then he had a thought. "Who is she?"

"You don't remember?" Mrs. Shikker smirked. "That's Rivka Cantor, Reb Cantor's daughter."

Oh no, Adam thought. He remembered his anger and rudeness. How could he have been such a . . . such a Schlemiel . . . Truly he was cursed. He picked up his buckets and made his way slowly home. Rivka. Rivka Cantor. Rivka Schlemiel? Ach, it could never happen. Well, at least the girl liked him when she thought he was Abraham.

From that moment, and for the next few weeks, Adam's attitude changed about collecting water from the well. It was pure bliss. While Abraham moped and moaned and wandered in the Schvartzvald, Adam did this chore without complaint. Every morning he woke up early, put on his best shirt, grabbed the water buckets, and hurried to the village well. ("Without even being asked," his mother whispered to his father. "Without even being reminded. What's wrong with the boy?") There he waited patiently for Rivka Cantor, and when she arrived his face brightened and his whole day turned to light.

They talked about everything and about nothing, about animals and springtime, about the countries around the world that Rivka had seen, and about life in Chelm, which (although often boring and slow) now seemed to both of them so cheerful and filled with promise.

And every day when Rivka left she smiled and said, "Until tomorrow, Abraham."

Her smile made him melt, but her parting words made him grimace. So every day, he trudged home both exalted and diminished.

Then, one day, Rivka Cantor didn't come to the well. Adam waited and dawdled. One after another, he helped the women of Chelm fill their buckets from the well, all the while listening to their praise. "Abraham, you're such a good boy." His mind was elsewhere, his eyes darting around the village square, looking for her quick and lovely shape . . . At last, with noon fast approaching, Adam made his way home, his heart crushed.

"Where have you been?" his mother asked. "It's bad enough I've got one good for nothing son who does nothing but head to the woods when there's a sign of a chore to be done. Now I've got two? Your father was looking for you. He's got work to be done. He says that it's Abraham's job to get the water, not yours, so enough with the nonsense. And where's the water? Three hours you've been at the well, and you forgot to bring back water? What is going on here?"

Adam peered into the empty buckets and immediately burst into tears.

"Okay, okay. It's not such a big deal," his mother said. "So, you forgot the water . . . If Abraham ever gets back, I'll send him to the well . . ."

Adam's sobs grew even louder.

"Madmen," his mother muttered. "I gave birth to a matched set of lunatics. One falls in love with a Gypsy. The other tries to fill the water bucket with tears."

Then, as any mother would do, she opened her arms and hugged her boy tight, patting his back and smoothing his hair. "Shh . . . Shh."

Eventually, Adam's crying subsided and he dried his eyes.

"So?" his mother said. "Tell me."

"It's a girl."

"A girl?" Her voice brightened. "Really?"

Adam nodded and then it all came out in a rush. "I'm in love. I love her. She's beautiful. She's smart. And she's rich."

"Mazel tov! Is she kind?"

"As kind as a kitten."

"Does she have a sweet disposition?"

"Like honey."

"She's not married or betrothed, is she?"

Adam shook his head. "No. No. I don't think so. No."

"That's good. So, what's the problem? Doesn't she like you?"

"Yes." Adam began to sniff. "No. Maybe. I don't know. Sometimes yes. Sometimes no."

"So far, everything you're telling me seems normal, if a bit confusing. We'll call the matchmaker and ask her to set up a meeting with the parents. A six-month waiting period should be long enough to make sure that everything could work. What do you say?"

Adam hesitated. He sputtered. He stuttered. "She . . . She thinks . . . She thinks that I'm Abraham."

"You aren't are you?" Rebecca Schlemiel blinked. "No, I'm not Abraham! I'm Adam." Rebecca looked carefully at her son. "I thought so, but even I get confused. And after all these years, you'd think I'd be able to know. So, it's not surprising she thinks you're Abraham some of the time. You met her at the well? Ah. That makes it clear. Everybody in Chelm knows that Abraham goes to the well for his mother while Adam works in his father's shop. So it's an honest mistake. Just tell her the truth."

"She doesn't like Adam. She hates Adam."

"But you said she likes you."

"She likes me when she thinks I'm Abraham."

"So, you tricked her? You're always with the tricks." His mother frowned. "Did you do this on purpose?"

"No. It was an accident. I didn't know," Adam explained. "I hadn't seen her before. Not in a long time. I didn't even recognize her. Believe me, by the time I found out who she was, it was too late. She already thought I was who I'm not. And she doesn't like who I am."

"So, who is she?"

"Rivka Cantor."

Rebecca Schlemiel's eyes widened. "Reb Cantor's daughter?"

A nod from her son.

"You remember that I was once engaged to Reb Cantor?"

Another nod.

"But that's not the problem, is it?"

Adam shook his head. "No."

"Good," said his mother. "You have enough troubles of your own without adding another generation's woes. So, listen, Adam. Tell her. Tell her the truth."

"I can't."

"What's the worst that could happen?"

"The worst? She could slap me across the face and say that she hates me and never wants to see me again."

"You think that she'd do that?"

"Yes." He nodded. "Yes, I think that she might."

"So, you think she loves you too," his mother said thoughtfully. "But not you. Not exactly. She only loves you because she thinks that you're Abraham? Oy."

"That's about the size of it," Adam said.

"Hmm," his mother said. "It sounds hopeless. But then again, love usually is. Hopeless, but wonderful."

Rebecca Schlemiel put her hands on her hips and frowned. "You're going to sit there and tell me that there is a beautiful girl who is rich and kind and sweet. You love her, but never mind. You're going to pretend it's just another one of your practical jokes? Something that doesn't matter? So, what happens when Abraham finally bumps into this girl and she accidentally tells him how much she loves him?"

Adam stared at his mother and then started crying again.

"More tears? Don't look at me for sympathy. Aim your dripping eyes for the bucket. You've been meeting this girl every day for weeks, but you couldn't be bothered to mention that your name isn't Abraham, it's Adam. And now you think I'm going to help you?"

Rebecca Schlemiel looked at her son, whose shoulders were heaving with every sob.

"All right. All right," she said. "I'll help you. We'll figure out something. So stop already, your nose is running on my nice clean blouse."

CHAPTER THIRTY-EIGHT

Signs in the Forest . . . Two Soldiers

Deep in the Schvartzvald, surrounded by the damp, dark smells of the black forest, Abraham Schlemiel sat on a rock and smiled. He couldn't help himself.

Adam was miserable. Abraham could sense it, and for some reason it was making him feel better. When they were younger, they'd been able to listen to each other's thoughts, but the ability had grown dimmer as they'd grown older. Today, though, Abraham could feel what Adam was feeling, and, strangely, knowing that his brother was upset was making Abraham feel happy. Like the time Abraham had lent Adam his strength to run after Rosa, now Adam was draining the despair from Abraham's spirit.

Of course, Abraham questioned it. "Is it right that I should rejoice at my brother's unhappiness?" But then another wave of sorrow/pleasure lifted him up onto his feet, and Abraham found himself standing up, balancing on the rock, and laughing aloud for what seemed like the first time in months. Despite himself, he began to sing.

For so long, he'd been wrapped up in his own unhappiness. In the whole world, Abraham had believed that there couldn't be anyone more forlorn and miserable. He was the only one who had ever had his heart broken, snapped in two like a dry twig on a cold day. But now Adam was showing him the truth. He wasn't the only one. Sadness was a part of life, the other side of joy. Was it even possible to experience one without the risk of the other?

"This is incredible!" Abraham laughed. "Pathetic perhaps, but incredible." It was pathetic in the sense that he was benefiting so gloriously at Adam's

211

expense. It was incredible because he was feeling so hopeful. "I want to dance. I want to sing." And so, Abraham sang.

"Rosa! Rosa . . . Rosaaaaah!"

As cheerful as Abraham had suddenly become, such cheerfulness hadn't transformed him into a witty lyricist. Nor had it made his voice trill like the song of an angel. When he hit the highest note, a flock of birds lifted out of a nearby elm tree and sped away west, never to be seen in Eastern Europe again.

Birds scattering at the awful tune didn't stop the young man from smiling. Instead, he took the sudden flight of the birds as a sign.

"To the west." Abraham danced. "To Rosa . . . To the west . . ."

It's one thing to stand on a boulder and sing a silly song in the middle of a forest. It's another to perform a jig on a rock. All at once, and without warning, the curse of the Schlemiels kicked in.

Abraham slipped. His weak leg slid out from under him, and he fell and landed with a thud, his head cracking against a nearby log. First he saw stars and then black.

When he finally regained consciousness, it was dark. The sky was filled from horizon to horizon with stars. Abraham blinked twice, winced, and then sat up suddenly. Where was he? A wave of dizziness nearly knocked him back into blackness.

He set a hand down on the damp ground and steadied himself. With his other hand, he reached behind his head and felt a sticky, dry patch of scalp. He'd obviously cut himself, but he didn't seem to be bleeding at the moment. That was one small blessing to be thankful for.

Now came a more important question. Which way was home?

He squinted in every direction, but after nightfall one tree looks pretty much the same as the next. Abraham looked up at the stars. He knew that one was the North Star, but which one? There were so many. Truly they were like grains of sand on a beach.

Ever since he'd lost her, Abraham Schlemiel had been considering leaving Chelm and taking to the road in search of Rosa Kalderash. That was the reason he'd been spending so much time in the Schvartzvald, not simply to get away from his family, but to learn the ways of the woods. He'd practiced walking along narrow trails like a Gypsy. He'd taught himself which tree roots and berries were edible and which should be avoided. He'd become a master mushroomer and had made many a lunch from fat morels roasted with onion grass over a slow fire.

And while he'd walked, he'd daydreamed that he was walking out of Chelm, out in the world. On the road, making his way, living by his wits and skills in search of his true love. But every night he'd gone home. There, he'd eaten his supper in silence, listened to his family bicker and laugh, and climbed into bed beside his brother with barely a word.

Perhaps this really was a sign. It was past dark and he was alone still. The birds had flown to the west. He had heard that when the Gypsies had left Smyrna they had been seen heading toward the west. Maybe it was time.

But could he really go, just like that? Without a word of goodbye?

It would break his mother's heart, and she was so weak. Of course, if he ever got enough courage to tell her to her face that he was going, that would probably break her heart too. In his mind, he could hear her saying, "All right, Abraham, you want to leave me here to get sick and die? Fine. Do what you want."

So much thinking caused Abraham's head to spin. Sometimes he hated his family's curse. Perhaps it was best to give in to it and know that no matter which choice he made everyone would be miserable, so why not make a bad choice for a good reason?

"Idiot!"

The loud word startled Abraham. For a moment he thought that the shout was Adam yelling from inside his skull.

Then Abraham heard it again. The voice was speaking in Russian. "I can't believe that you lost the road."

"What road? You said you wanted a drink of water, and I said that I heard water. It's not my fault that the river is all mud."

"You were supposed to remember how to get back to the road."

"You called that a road?" said the second voice. "Two ruts in the mud? That's like a farmer's cow path. Mud, mud, and more mud."

"Moscow prejudice," said the first voice. "Sergeant Shnuck, if you're not careful, I'll report you."

"And I'll tell them that my Captain Plotz got us lost in the woods."

"You're the one who led us astray."

"But you're the leader."

There followed a volley of cursing so intense that if words were cannon-balls the entire forest would have been flattened.

Abraham sat still, his face red as he listened to the profoundly vulgar names that these men had just called each other.

At last, the shouting stopped, and he heard their footsteps drawing closer.

"So, where's this water?"

"Who can hear water with all the yelling?"

"Sergeant," the captain warned. "You are coming dangerously close to insubordination!"

Just then, the sergeant's boot kicked Abraham soundly in the thigh.

"Yow!" Abraham yelled. He jumped to his feet and was about to run, but the world began to spin and he had to steady himself on the boulder. This was all for the better because a moment later he heard two sharp clicks of rifle bolts being drawn back and two men ordering in a single voice, "Halt!"

Then the captain barked, "Stop! Turn around slowly."

"Come here, boy," ordered the sergeant.

"Stop!" shouted the captain. "Turn around slowly."

"Come here," insisted the sergeant.

Abraham did what any boy from Chelm would do. He began spinning around slowly as he walked toward the soldiers.

The two men, with their rifles raised, squinted in astonishment as Abraham twirled toward them like a drunken ballerina. Then they smiled.

"Stop!" they both barked. Abraham stopped. The men exchanged glances.

"Stand on one foot," ordered the captain.

"Touch your left hand to your nose," added the sergeant.

"Keep turning," said the captain. "Start again."

"And hop, too!"

Poor Abraham did his best, hopping on one foot and spinning around while touching his nose. Round and around. He actually managed to keep it up for a while, but he was starting to get dizzy. Of course, by then the soldiers had changed the rules. Soon he had orders to pat his head, rub his belly, and bounce from one foot to the next while saying, "Boingo-boingo smlutt-nik flokka-flokka-flue!"

Eventually, Abraham's weak foot found a tree root and he fell to the ground with a thud. The Russians also fell to the ground, laughing.

"Sergeant Shnuck, get off me!" laughed the captain.

Abraham tried to use this as an opportunity to crawl away.

"Don't move," the sergeant said, getting to his feet.

Abraham stopped. "Are you going to kill me?" he whimpered.

"I think you are trying to kill us," said the captain as the sergeant helped him to his feet, "kill us with laughter."

"No, no," Abraham said seriously.

The soldiers guffawed.

"Poor kid," said the sergeant. "He has no idea."

"No, you're right," the captain agreed. "None whatsoever. What's your name and where are you from?"

"I'm Abraham Schlemiel. I'm from Chelm."

"Schlemiel, that name sounds familiar . . ." The captain stared at Abraham. "Are you one of the two boys who captured Alex Krabot?"

Abraham blushed and nodded. "Yes. That was me and my twin brother."

Then the sergeant smacked himself on the forehead. "We're near Chelm!"

"Yes, so?" said the captain. "Isn't Chelm on our list?"

"Yes, but we weren't supposed to go to Chelm for another month."

"Yet, here we are wandering blindly through the woods looking for water, sergeant."

The two men argued for a few minutes while Abraham sat on the ground, brushing dirt and dried leaves from his coat.

At last the captain spoke to him. "You must have a well in Chelm, right?"

Abraham nodded. "Yes."

"Let's go then. Get up. No more nonsense."

Abraham rose to his feet. "Ummm . . ."

"What?" the captain snapped.

"I don't know which way to go myself. I'm lost."

"You're lost?" the captain said. "You live here and you pretend you're lost? What kind of fools do you take us for?"

"Sir," said the sergeant, "he is from Chelm."

"So?'

"So, the people of Chelm are idiots. Once, the story goes, the villagers of Chelm were trying to move a mountain by just pushing on it. The day got hot, so they took off their coats and a thief stole them. A little later, they turned around and saw their coats were gone. 'Wonderful!' the villagers of Chelm said. 'We pushed the mountain so far that we can't see our coats anymore.'"

The captain was puzzled. "Is that supposed to be funny?"

The sergeant shrugged, "It is when you've had half a bottle of vodka."

"It's not funny," Abraham said, suddenly feeling defensive. "It's true. It worked. Do you see any mountains around here?" Abraham raised his hands and turned around, pointing in all directions. "No mountains. See?"

The two men stared at the boy, and then they laughed.

"Come on," said the sergeant, poking Abraham with the barrel of his rifle. "Let's find our way back to the road. You'd better remember your way from there."

An hour and two bramble bushes later, the trio were making their way south along the road from Smyrna to Chelm. The two men had slung their rifles across their shoulders and were trudging along wearily while Abraham tried to think of the best way to escape.

"So," he said at last, "what brings you gentlemen to Chelm?"

"Gentlemen?" snorted the sergeant.

"Speak for yourself, Vassily," the captain said. He turned to Abraham. "We are recruiting. The czar needs more soldiers. How old are you?"

Abraham cursed his luck. "Seventeen."

"Perfect! Just the right age. If you're lucky and you sign up willingly, they might even give you a gun."

"I'd enlist," the sergeant said. "When someone is shooting at you, it's better to have a gun than not."

"But," Abraham asked, "what's the point of being a soldier without a gun?"

"You're target practice," said the sergeant with a shrug. "Cannon fodder."

"Oh." Abraham wasn't sure if the man was serious. "Is that what it's like being a soldier?"

"Nonsense," the captain said. "You serve the czar and Mother Russia nobly and with honor!"

"In reality," the sergeant whispered, "the food, when there is food, stinks. Literally. And your uniform probably won't fit. Even if you do get a gun, chances are it will break or be completely rusted. The ammunition, if you have any, only fires once in three times. Your boots will be filled with mud, your hair will fill with lice, and if possible, you should never ever get in the way of a cannon ball."

"You know, I think I'd rather pass," Abraham said.

"You don't want to serve the czar and Mother Russia nobly and with honor?" said the captain in mock horror. "Then we'll have to impress you."

"I don't know what you could say to impress me," Abraham said. "It sounds horrible."

"No, you idiot," the captain laughed. "When we impress you, we sign you up whether you want to or not. That's how Vassily here got in the army."

"I should have run away when I had the chance," the sergeant muttered.

But then Abraham remembered something. "I'm Polish!" he said suddenly.

"Of course you are," the captain said.

"Do you have papers?" the sergeant asked.

Abraham nodded. He reached into his pocket. The men stopped and looked. Even by starlight, it was clear that Abraham's papers identified him as a citizen of Poland.

"You know," said the sergeant, "these papers could be forged. Or they might be accidentally destroyed." He held the papers in both hands and looked ready to rip them in two.

"Don't torture the boy," the captain said. "We'll visit the records office in Chelm and find out who's eligible and who isn't. No point in starting a war with Poland over a boy from Chelm."

"But who would know?" the sergeant asked.

"Give them back," Abraham begged.

"I see a village. Is that Chelm up ahead?" the captain asked.

"Yes, it is," Abraham answered glumly.

"At last! Let the boy have his papers, Sergeant. I'm thirsty, I'm hungry, and I want to sleep in a real bed."

The grinning sergeant held the packet high for a moment or two more and made Abraham jump before finally letting the boy grab his papers. Then the two soldiers left Abraham behind and hurried ahead into Chelm.

CHAPTER THIRTY-NINE

No, You're in Trouble

In the faint light of dawn, Abraham silently slipped in through his bedroom window and nudged his brother Adam, who lay asleep in their bed.

"Wha?"

"Shh," Abraham whispered. "You are in such big trouble."

Adam's eyes blinked open, and he nodded. "I know. And it's all your fault."

"I know," Abraham agreed. "But I didn't do it on purpose."

"I know. If I wasn't such a coward . . ."

"Adam, this has nothing to do with cowardice. It's self-preservation. It's about surviving long enough to build a future. You can't do that if you're dead."

"Yes." Adam rolled over onto his belly. "I wish I were dead." His voice was muffled by his pillow. Then he sat up suddenly, nearly knocking Abraham from the bed. "Wait a moment, dead? What do you mean dead?"

"Shot with a gun. You know. Dead. Bang."

Adam's face drooped. "Her father knows already?"

"Whose father?"

"Who else is going to kill me? Reb Cantor, Rivka Cantor's father. First of all, he hasn't liked me for years. Second of all, he doesn't like you much either."

"Me?" Abraham said. "Why wouldn't he like me?"

"Because you're my brother. And third of all, he's probably the only man in Chelm who has a gun."

"Not any more," Abraham said. "There are two Russian soldiers in Chelm."

"More taxes?" Adam said.

"Worse." Abraham shook his head. "They're conscripting boys into the Russian army."

"So?"

"So, you're seventeen years old, and you're Russian."[*]

Adam's eyes widened and he stifled a sob. "It's the curse. Nothing ever turns out right."

"Shh shh shh," Abraham said. He patted his brother gently on the head. "We'll figure something out. What is this about a girl? Rivka Cantor? I thought you hated her."

"I don't. I love her. But she doesn't love me," Adam bawled. "She loves you."

"Me? How can she love me? She doesn't even know me. Besides, I thought Rivka Cantor was traveling in America."

"She's back now, and she's beautiful and kind and wise . . ." Adam's voice trailed off into tears.

"Well, if she's so wise, how could she be in love with me?"

"She . . . thinks . . . I'm . . . you . . ."

"Why would she think such a thing?"

"I was at the well," Adam explained, "drawing water. Everybody knows that in our house, Abraham is the one who does that. She was there because her household well was broken. So, we started talking. I didn't recognize her at first. She's blossomed, she's bloomed. She's like a rosebud that has opened into a gorgeous . . ."

"Alright already, she's good looking. Why does she think you're me?"

---

[*] *Perhaps you remember the earlier footnote, perhaps not. It was on page 14. It was by a strange coincidence that on the day the twins were born, the province that Chelm was located in had been traded by the king of Poland to the czar of Russia for fifteen pounds of caviar and two boxes of Cuban cigars. This kind of somewhat random territorial change wasn't unusual. During Rabbi Kibbitz's long life, Chelm had been the property of Russia, Poland, Austria, France, and even Finland (for twenty minutes). Thus, as the firstborn, Abraham was Polish, while Adam, who was born twelve hours later, was considered a son of Mother Russia.*

Adam looked glum. "I never got around to telling her I was me, and by the time I realized that she liked me, but she thought I was you, it was too late. I couldn't tell her I was Adam because she told me how much she hated Adam."

"So you told her you were me?" Abraham asked.

"I told her I was you." Adam nodded. "Well, no, not really. I never said so, but I didn't correct her. Ever. You would have done the same. I met her at the well. I was doing your chores. I didn't know who she was. I didn't know who she thought I was until it was too late. Now she says that she'd never marry anybody named Adam."

Abraham laughed. "You've had conversations about marriage already? You're serious?"

"We were joking, but yes."

"Mazel tov."

"Mazel tov?" Adam jumped angrily up from the bed. "You're wishing me luck? I find a girl I can't live without and right away the Russian army comes into town to put me out of my misery? That's luck? It's the curse."

"At least now you know how I've been feeling for the last year or so."

Adam took a half-hearted swing at Abraham, but he tripped over his night shirt and ended up sprawled on the floor.

"Are you all right?" Abraham asked, giggling.

"Fine."

"Then shh. You want to wake Mama and Papa?"

"I'm not the one who didn't come home last night."

Abraham nodded. "You didn't have guns pointed at you all night."

"Really? You're serious?"

Abraham nodded. "Yes, but . . . Look, why don't we just tell her?"

"She'll think that I was trying to make a fool out of her. She's in love with you, why don't you just take her, and I'll go into the army. Then everybody will be happy."

"Don't be an idiot," Abraham said. "I'm in love with someone else."

"Still with Rosa, the Gypsy princess?" Now Adam rolled his eyes. "Abraham, she barely gave you the time of day when she was in Chelm, and that was so long ago."

"What is time to love? Adam, does your heart want to burst with the thought of Rivka?"

"Yes. So?"

"Do you feel like jumping with joy and crying at the same time? As if someone had cut off your arm, like a piece of you is missing? Do you feel as if your life will be over unless you can be with this girl?"

Adam nodded.

"So, okay, I know how you feel, you know how I feel," Abraham said. "Don't tell me otherwise."

"Abraham," Adam said, slowly considering each word. "I spent a lot of time with Rosa. And I hate to say this, but she was more in love with me than she was with you. By all rights, I should have married her."

"No," Abraham shook his head. "Don't say such things. You don't know. You don't know everything. Did you know that I . . ."

"All right, all right." Adam held up the palm of his hand. "Abraham, shh. I know that you love her, or loved her, or think that you love her still, but the fact is that she's gone. Rosa's gone. Her father took her away, and she's not coming back. Right now, right here in Chelm there is a girl who thinks she is in love with you."

"But, Adam, she's in love with you. And you're in love with her."

"Oy, what does it matter?" Adam sighed. He stood and began getting dressed. "It's plainly obvious that the curse is not going to let me get what I want. Why should everyone in the family suffer? You marry her, and I'll join the Russian army and get killed in Siberia."

"Is that where you're going now?" Abraham asked.

"Yes."

"Maybe you should take off your night shirt before you put on your jacket."

Adam looked down and frowned. "You don't think it looks distinguished?"

Abraham grinned back. "No. Now sit down and listen. There's got to be something else we can do. The Schlemiel twins have outwitted demons, criminals, and rabbis. All we have to deal with now are two Russian soldiers and a girl."

Adam sat down on the bed and said, "I'd rather face a Russian firing squad than hear Rivka Cantor say that she hates me."

"You're an idiot, but I can understand that. Now, let's think."

CHAPTER FORTY

Over a Barrel

Shortly before dawn, a loud noise was heard rumbling through the village of Chelm. Puzzled farmers peered into the cool cloudless sky and wondered if a storm was coming. Then, as suddenly as it began, the noise stopped, and it was replaced by a whispered bickering in the village square that was only heard by two young men.

"I don't see how this is going to work," hissed Adam Schlemiel. Catching his breath, he stared up at the gigantic pickle barrel they had rolled from behind Mrs. Chaipul's restaurant. The barrel was huge—four feet wide and six and a half feet high. "What would we have possibly done if the barrel wasn't empty?"

"Do you love this girl?" asked Abraham.

"You know I do!"

"So, the barrel was empty. Stop arguing and get in."

"Why do I have to get in? Why not you?"

"Because I'm the older brother and I say so. Quickly!" Abraham urged. "Someone's coming!"

Cursing loudly, Adam Schlemiel jumped up and grabbed the top of the barrel. As he pulled, Abraham pushed and an instant later Adam tumbled in head first. "Ow!"

"Shh!"

"There are still some pickles in the bottom!" Adam muttered, but by then Abraham had slammed the lid back on top. "It smells in here!"

"That's quite some barrel, Abraham Schlemiel," said Mrs. Chaipul, who visited the well first thing every morning to get water for her restaurant's customers. "Is that my barrel?"

"I'm just borrowing it." Abraham began filling Mrs. Chaipul's water buckets.

"It's for a special project," he said, turning the crank to bring the water up.

"Ahh," Mrs. Chaipul nodded. "Just make sure that your brother can breathe in there. Thank you very much." And away she went.

Abraham pried open the lid. "Are you all right?"

"Yes," Adam gasped. "Aren't there easier ways for you to kill me?"

"Mrs. Chaipul must have seen us. I won't put the lid on so tightly. Be quiet. Someone else is coming."

The morning passed quickly for Abraham, who busied himself hauling buckets of water for the villagers. For Adam, squatting in six inches of pickle juice, it seemed like an eternity until he heard a familiar voice. He immediately stood up so that he could listen better.

"Hello, Abraham."

"Hello, uh . . ."

Adam banged the side of the barrel.

"Rivka!" Abraham said. He smiled. Adam was right, during her year away from Chelm, Rivka Cantor had blossomed. She was stunningly beautiful.

"You don't know me any more?" the young woman said.

Abraham felt himself blushing. "I feel as if I haven't seen you in ages."

"It's only been a few days," Rivka said. "My father finally got our well's pump fixed. Fortunately, last night I accidentally broke it. What is a pickle barrel doing next to the well?"

"Get to it," Adam whispered.

"Well, the barrel is because of an idea I had," Abraham said. Rivka really was much prettier than he remembered her and he found himself stumbling, tongue tied. "I thought, what if we filled up the pickle barrel with water and then filled our buckets from the pickle barrel?"

Rivka smiled. "Then we'd have pickle-flavored water."

Get in here! Adam said, using mind-speech to talk directly to Abraham.

It had been a while since Abraham had heard Adam's voice so clearly in his mind. The sudden interruption startled Abraham.

Get in here!

"No!" Abraham said. "I mean, oh, it's clean."

Right now! Adam began banging on the side of the barrel.

Rivka looked puzzled. "It sounds as if there's a weasel in there."

"No, that's just water settling. Uh, let me look." Abraham pulled himself up to the barrel's rim and whispered, "What?"

Adam grabbed Abraham's collar and pulled. Abraham tumbled down, head first, and landed on Adam's stomach.

They both gasped. "Ooof!"

"Abraham!" came Rivka's concerned voice. "Are you all right?"

"You could have killed me!" Abraham hissed.

"Shh," Adam whispered. "Get up on your hands and knees."

"What?"

"Just do it. Bend over."

"Abraham? Are you all right?"

Adam stepped up onto Abraham's back. His head poked over the top of the barrel. "Fine. Fine."

"Your hair is wet. And you look taller."

"Oh, I slipped," Adam said. "There's a stool in here."

"Why is there a stool inside a pickle barrel?" Rivka asked.

"To stand on," Adam answered. "In case you fall in."

Abraham muttered, "Watch your boot."

"What?" Rivka said.

"It's an echo," Adam said. "I said, you look beautiful."

Now it was Rivka's turn to blush. "Thank you. You're acting very peculiar today."

"What do you mean?

"I don't know," she said. "A moment ago you were so distant, and now you seem . . . Comfortable? Like yourself."

I am not comfortable! Abraham said into Adam's mind. *Ask her!*

"All right!" Adam blurted. "Rivka, would you marry my brother?"

"What?" Rivka said.

Idiot!

"How can you possibly . . ." she began.

Adam quickly interrupted. "I mean, if I wasn't Abraham, would you still like me? Or if my name was Adam . . ."

"I already told you," Rivka said. "I could never marry Adam."

Abraham could listen no longer. He shifted out from under Adam, who fell into the barrel with a thud. A moment later, Abraham stood up on top of his still-squirming brother.

"The stool is slippery," he explained. "I'm sorry. Look, let me be honest. How do you feel about me? Right now?"

"A moment ago," Rivka said nervously, "I was feeling quite settled. But now I'm not sure. You seem, I don't know. Wasn't your hair wet?"

"Would you like a pickle?" Abraham said suddenly. He jumped off Adam, ducked into the barrel, and dipped his hair into the water.

"I . . ." Rivka said. She stared up at the rim of the barrel, confused.

"What are you doing?" Adam said through gritted teeth.

"Shh," Abraham said. *Use mind-speak.*

Okay, so? What are you doing?

She's beautiful, Abraham said.

I know. So, couldn't you marry her?

Yes, but no. I love Rosa. Besides, Rivka loves you. Not me.

But she thinks she loves you, Adam said. *And I'm going to be going into the Russian army . . .*

No, you're not, Abraham said. *Give her this pickle. Ask her to marry you.*

Give her a pickle? Are you crazy?

"Abraham?" Rivka's voice echoed into the barrel. "I have to get my water and go home now."

"Wait, please!" Abraham shouted. "I'm coming. I dropped something."

She's in love with you, Abraham said, *but she likes my name. So, I'll give it to you. You can have it. Who's to say that you're not Abraham anyway? You've heard the stories about how Mama and Papa mixed us up when we were little. Okay fine. Now you'll be Abraham and I'll be Adam. Here.*

Abraham handed Adam a damp bundle.

What's this?

My papers. They prove that you're Polish. You take them.

But what about you? You're going to join the Russian army?

Abraham shook his head. *No. The Russian army I'll run away from. You stay here and marry Rivka. As you said, there's no point in both of us being unhappy.*

Adam stared at his brother in the dim light at the bottom of the pickle barrel.

"You would do this for me?" he whispered.

Abraham nodded. "Of course."

The brothers hugged. Abraham twined his fingers together. Adam stepped into the stirrup. Abraham lifted and Adam was boosted up and out of the barrel.

"Whaaa!" Adam said, flying through the air. He landed, almost gracefully, just in front of Rivka Cantor, who looked extremely startled.

"I thought you said you were getting me a pickle," she said, confused.

Just that moment, Adam looked up, and saw the pickle flying through the air toward Rivka's lovely forehead. He snatched it as if conjuring it out of the air.

"A sour pickle for my sweet one," he said smoothly.

Rivka blushed.

"Rivka, will you marry me?" Adam asked.

"Abraham." Rivka blinked. "You're proposing to me with a pickle?"

Adam shrugged. "I'm not a rich man like your father. I'm not as eloquent as my brother. All I know is that I want to spend every day of the rest of my life with you."

She stared into his eyes, and then nodded. "Of course I will."

"Who hoo!" came a shout from the depths of the pickle barrel.

Rivka jumped. "What was that?"

"I threw my voice," Adam said nonchalantly. "Let's fill your buckets, and tell . . . I mean ask your father."

Two minutes later, the young lovers were gone.

Inside the barrel, Abraham was grinning. He couldn't help himself. So what if he was alone at the bottom of a smelly old barrel. He munched on a pickle and smiled with happiness for his brother.

CHAPTER FORTY-ONE

Home . . . Goodbye, Adam

By the time he finally opened the front door to his house, Abraham was asleep on his feet. Not only had he been up for almost two days straight, but getting out of the gigantic pickle barrel had nearly killed him.

After eating a dozen pickles, he got thirsty and began shouting for someone to get him some water. The women of Chelm who were at the well took him literally and began dumping bucket after bucket of water into the barrel. When Abraham yelled for them to stop they decided that the barrel must be haunted and ran off, screaming. He finally got out of the barrel by slamming back and forth into the walls, pickle water sloshing from side to side, until the barrel tilted, fell, and then rolled two hundred yards across the village square, where it smashed into the side of the synagogue. Abraham felt sick, and it was all he could do not to vomit a mess of half-digested pickles on the steps of the shul.

Now that he was home all he wanted to do was lie down and go to sleep.

"Adam!" his mother said, her voice a cheerful hammer tapping against his brain. "Did you hear the good news? Abraham is getting married. Oh my god! Adam, you look awful. You smell like pickles. Why does everyone smell like pickles? Are you all right? Can I get you something? You want some chicken soup or a little brisket? I have some mashed potatoes. There's a kugel in the oven. It should be ready any minute now. Or maybe some chopped liver? You take a bath and I'll get you some food."

Abraham nodded and burped a green cloud that sent his mother stumbling back.

"Feh," Rebecca Schlemiel said. "Sit down, then take a bath. I can only imagine that this news must be shocking to you. I know that you were fond of Rivka Cantor, but I told you you should have talked with her sooner. Still . . . Adam, I'm sorry."

Abraham looked at his mother. She thought he was Adam. Their plan was working.

He shrugged. "It's all right. Abraham can have Rivka. It's good. I'm just tired." He folded his arms, closed his eyes, and laid his head on the table.

Patting his shoulder, his mother nodded. "There were soldiers here today looking for you. I told them you were probably at your father's shop. But then when I heard the news, I wasn't sure what had happened. You boys get so worked up about girls."

"Already?" Abraham wearily lifted his head. "The soldiers were here already?"

Rebecca nodded. "They said they were drafting young men into the Russian army." Her voice was quiet and serious. "What are we going to do?"

Abraham rubbed his face. It was ironic. For months he'd imagined wandering the world in search of Rosa Kalderash. But now that he knew he had to leave Chelm, he found that he didn't want to.

All he wanted was to lie in his own bed, sleep without dreams, and wake up in time for dinner. Then he'd sit, crowded around the table, elbow to elbow with his brother, new sister-in-law, sister, mother, father, and whatever friends or relatives happened to be in the neighborhood for brisket and soup and mashed potatoes and kugel. Then he and Adam would go for a walk and slap each other on the back. Joke about the future, about girls. About Adam's marriage . . .

"I need to pack," Abraham croaked. "They'll be back. I can't stay."

"Can't you hide?" His mother's voice was nearly begging. "The attic in your father's shop. It's a good hiding place. I'll bring you food."

"No." Abraham shook his head. "I've met these men. They're idiots, but they know how to do their job. They'll expect me to hide. They'll wait, and they'll look, and they'll search. And if they find me it'll be worse than if I volunteered to begin with."

Rebecca Schlemiel nodded sadly, coughed, and suddenly felt very, very old. Her heart was nearly breaking, but she dared not cry. She'd have the two of them in tears, paralyzed, and the Russians would find him there, salty and soaked, and drag him away. So she sighed and began rummaging for a rucksack.

"You take a bath, and I'll pack for you," she said as she bustled from room to room. "Properly, you should leave your parents' house with a wagon filled with clothing and furniture and everything you need to start a house of your own. Instead . . . What, a week's worth of underwear, a few pairs of socks? Several shirts. A sewing kit. Your boots and coat of course. What else? Hats and gloves. An oilskin raincoat that belonged to your great uncle Noah. He always said that it would get him through a flood. A knife, a fork, and this."

Abraham lifted his head off the table again and saw his mother standing before him holding a ten-inch cast iron frying pan.

"This was my mother's," she said, "and her mother's before her." She wedged the pan into the rucksack. "Adam, I know you can't cook, but you'll need something to eat. Here's some garlic and some dried meat. A water skin. Some currant jam. There's just not enough room for everything. You'll have to be able to walk quickly and quietly without getting tired."

Abraham felt the tears rolling down his cheeks.

"Look," said his mother, sniffling, "if you're going to sit there like a lump, the least you can do is go and wash your hair. You stink of pickles. Use my Paris soap, all right?"

Abraham nodded and gave his mother a hug. They held each other for a long time. Then he took a bucket of water from next to the stove and went outside to the bathtub. Rebecca Schlemiel stood still, hugging her arms across her chest.

"Don't forget to wash behind your ears!" she shouted, with only a little catch in her voice.

After Abraham had dried himself and dressed in clean clothes, he felt much better. He still could use a good long nap, but he didn't think he had time. The longer he waited, the more likely it was that the soldiers would return to the house. At last, he gave his mother a hug and swung the rucksack onto his back.

"Here." His mother handed him a cloth napkin with its corners tied into a sack. "There's a brisket sandwich in here. You can eat it while you walk."

Abraham nodded. He was afraid to say anything, afraid he would start crying.

"You have to go and say goodbye to your father," she said.

"I know."

They hugged again and kissed, and through her tears Rebecca Schlemiel whispered, "Come back soon."

Abraham couldn't speak. He gave his mother one last squeeze and slipped out the door.

As she watched her son through the crack in the door, Rebecca whispered to herself the words that the Gypsy queen had spoken so long ago.

"One day here, the next gone . . . The lost son returns, but the son who has vanished has never left. They come together. One becomes two—different, and yet the same."

Rebecca Schlemiel found herself shivering. She shook her head sadly and began to sob.

By now it was late afternoon, and the streets of Chelm were nearly empty. Everyone was either busy at work, at school, or making dinner. Abraham quickly looked around for the Russian soldiers, but fortunately they were nowhere in sight. He glanced up at the sun and guessed he still had three hours until sunset.

What could he say to his father? For years, Abraham had worked in his mother's kitchen instead of at the carpentry shop. Even though he had never said anything, Abraham thought that his father was disappointed in him. What would happen now that he was leaving? Abraham wondered.

"Abraham," said a giggling voice, "where are you going?"

Abraham looked down and saw his sister Shmeenie smiling up at him.

How could he have forgotten her? Such a beautiful little girl. A bundle of joy and mischief.

"Shmeenie, I'm Adam," Abraham said. "And I have to go away for a while. Abraham is going to have to work in the shop with Papa, so you help Mama. I'm going to miss you."

"Abraham, don't be silly," Shmeenie said, poking him in the belly.

"I'm not kidding, little one," he laughed. "And I'm Adam. And I have to hurry."

Shmeenie looked up at her brother's face and saw how sad and serious he looked. She jumped up into her brother's arms and held him tight.

For a moment, it didn't bother either of them that he was wearing a thirty-pound backpack.

"I love you, Abraham," she whispered in his ear.

"I love you too, Shmeenie," he whispered back, kissing her cheek and breathing the smell of her soft hair. "You listen to your mother and your father and your brother. I'll always love you."

Then Shmeenie jumped down, waved, said, "Bye, Adam," and was gone.

Suddenly unbalanced, Abraham stumbled backward and nearly fell. Fortunately, he caught himself. With his luck, it was amazing he didn't land in a mud puddle and get soaked before his journey had even begun.

Before he knew it, his feet had taken him to the door of his father's shop. He knocked, pushed the door open, and peeked in.

"Father?"

There was no answer. He felt relieved. He couldn't go searching all over Chelm just to say goodbye. That would be the surest way to bump into the Russians. So, he decided to write a note, but he couldn't find any paper or a pen or a pencil. At last, he saw a piece of charcoal and found a flat board that looked like the lid to a box.

It's not easy to write with charcoal. You can't make small letters, and the blackened wood begins to smudge if you're not careful. Besides, as much as there was to tell, Abraham didn't know where to begin or what to say.

"Father," he wrote. "I have to go. I love you. Ab . . ."

Phooey. Without thinking, he'd begun to sign his own name instead of Adam's. He looked for a cloth to wipe the board, but there was only the napkin his mother had wrapped the sandwich with. So, he ate the sandwich, which was absolutely delicious, and then tried to erase the word with the napkin. It wasn't working. The charcoal blurred, so he spat on it, and now it became a muddy swirl. He blotted the board with the napkin and tried to write "Adam" on top. Now the signature was completely illegible. All that you could read was the first letter of his name, which he'd written in Hebrew—Aleph.

That would have to do. Abraham sighed. He'd wasted enough time already. He folded the napkin so the blackened part was on the inside and stuffed it into his pocket. He hoisted the pack onto his back, gave the shop one last look, and . . .

That's when his father came in the front door.

Jacob Schlemiel took in the scene in an instant. He'd heard the good news about Abraham's engagement and then he'd gone to Reb Cantor's to celebrate with a little vodka. By the time he'd returned home to hear the horrible news about Adam, it was nearly dark. Rebecca was furious at his tipsy state and horrified that he hadn't seen Adam to say goodbye. So, stumbling out of the house, he'd hurried to the shop, knowing that it was impossible for Adam to still be in Chelm, but hoping . . .

"So," Jacob said, "you're going to leave with crumbs everywhere?" As soon as the words were out of his mouth, he regretted them, but it was too late.

Abraham frowned, took a deep breath, and blew with all his might against the work table. Sawdust and sandwich crumbs flew everywhere. Both men closed their eyes tightly and coughed. Abraham edged toward the door, but his father was in the way.

"Son," Jacob sputtered, steadying himself on Abraham's shoulder. "Adam, I'm sorry. I didn't mean that. You and I haven't always gotten along or agreed. Sometimes I've felt that all we've done for all these years is butt heads like a couple of stupid goats. You're a good boy. You work hard. You try. I know it's been difficult working with me. I don't know what to say sometimes and I yell. I can tell that it makes you crazy, but I can't stop myself. Sometimes I wish I was more like your mother, able to listen and understand. Still, you've learned. You've gotten better. I hope you'll forgive me."

Abraham nodded and listened with difficulty. His father wasn't really talking to him, but to Adam, and this made Abraham feel sadder than ever. But what could he do? He couldn't say anything. Still, he wished that Adam was there, listening to the old man's confession of mistakes made and love misplaced. But, if Jacob had really had said all these things to Adam, Adam probably would have been furious. Perhaps this way was better.

"Papa," Abraham interrupted at last. "I have to leave."

Jacob stopped in mid-sentence and then nodded. "Yes. Did you pack any tools?"

"No. Mama packed my bag. There wasn't any room."

"Women," Jacob shook his head. "Wait a moment." He hurried into the back room and returned an instant later with a tool belt.

"This belonged to your great-grandfather," he said. "I want you to take it."

"But, I can't," Abraham began. He knew how to use a knife, but not the saw and hammer and awl that Jacob was even then strapping around his waist.

"There," Jacob said. "I should have given these to you years ago. You deserve them."

"No," Abraham insisted, pushing the gift away. "My brother will need them."

Jacob Schlemiel smiled at his son. "You're a good boy," he said. "I wish I'd told you sooner. Well, better late than never. I give you my blessing. Good luck."

"Thank you," Abraham said, the words coming out choked.

"Go," Jacob said, opening the door. "It's getting dark. You want to try to make it to Smyrna before it gets too late."

Abraham nodded. He wanted to say more, but Jacob gave his son a fatherly slap on the back, which given the fact that Abraham was already carrying a huge pack, sent him reeling into the street.

"Oy, watch out for the mud puddle!" Jacob cried.

Catching his balance on the edge of disaster, Abraham smiled, waved, and was gone. In the doorway to his shop, Jacob Schlemiel remembered when Adam was a baby, all the trouble he'd been as a boy, and what a good man he was becoming. He watched the empty street until the shadows grew long and then headed home to a house that would seem much smaller now.

CHAPTER FORTY-TWO

Becoming Abraham

The older you become the quicker the days pass. In an ordinary life, a month can seem to pass in a moment. In the village of Chelm, a year can pass as quickly as the turning of a page.

But for Adam Schlemiel, his seventeenth year was the longest of his life (so far) and certainly the most confusing. On the one hand, he was lonely and missed his brother. On the other hand, he was in love, fully and openly in love.

Now that they were engaged, his love for Rivka Cantor grew day by day. It was a wonderful feeling knowing that in just a few months he and Rivka would be together forever. Sometimes he felt like the most blessed man on earth.

Two moments later, though, he would find himself shivering with terror. Sometimes it was his fear. Sometimes he felt as if it was Abraham's fear because he was lost and alone in the world. Mostly, though, it was Adam's own terrors. Adam was afraid of marriage, afraid of his future father-in-law . . . and scared half out of his mind of being discovered as an imposter.

It is said that most young men and women have this fear. They fear that everyone around them will learn the truth that they are not as happy or as smart or as handsome or as successful as they appear. For the most part these fears are groundless or at the very least flawed. Young men and women learn that perhaps their lives aren't as good as they paint them to be, but neither are they as bad as their worst nightmares, so they muddle through.

Adam Schlemiel, however, knew he really was hiding something big. Not only was he going to get married to a girl he hardly knew, but he knew that she didn't even know him at all. In fact, no one did anymore. No one knew who he was.

From morning until night, every time someone called him "Abraham" he tensed. His eyes widened in panic, and he held his breath. He looked left and then right, as if sure that there must be some kind of a mistake. Then, after a moment, he found himself able to breathe and relax and continue the pretense.

He knew that some day he would be found out and called a liar and a cheat. Rivka would desert him, his father would banish him, and his mother would hang her head in shame. Adam was terrified of being found out.

But even worse than that, in the meantime, everyone in Chelm seemed to be going out of their way to tell him what they really and truly thought of Adam and how much better a person Abraham was. If one of the brothers had to leave, they all said, at least it was Adam. They were so glad that Abraham had stayed behind. Now, Adam didn't think he was doing anything differently, but the way his family and neighbors were treating him made him unsure. Only Shmeenie treated him well, telling him how much she missed Adam, and that Adam was always her favorite.

Still, as he woke every morning, Adam had to remind himself that his name was now Abraham. Then he washed and got dressed. Previously, he had considered this ordinary and unremarkable behavior. But now his mother would say, "Abraham, you look so handsome this morning." Then his father would say, "You're looking healthy today, Abraham." Only Shmeenie would wink and say, "Yes, Abraham, your smile is almost as nice as Adam's." By the time he finished breakfast, Adam was already exhausted, ashamed, and confused. He felt as if his eyes had gone dead. Then he and his father went to the shop.

Before the switch going to the shop too had been an unremarkable event. He'd give his mother and his sister a quick peck on their cheeks and then stroll briskly to the carpentry shop. Now, though, everyone made a big production about how proud they were and how he should have a good time.

At the shop it was even worse.

"You know, Abraham," Jacob Schlemiel would say, "it took your brother months to learn how to hammer a nail in straight. You pick up that hammer and ten seconds later you're swinging it like a professional."

That was their father's highest compliment—a professional. Adam had never heard his father call him a professional—only Abraham.

"And you know," Jacob would continue, "the polishing job you did on that last jewelry box? It was professional, better than anything Adam ever managed."

Adam couldn't say a word. He just bit his tongue and held back the rage.

Now that he was engaged, he was allowed to take lunches with his father-in-law-to-be. Adam looked forward to these meals with less enthusiasm than he would have mustered for being buried alive.

The food was splendid. Reb Cantor would meet him at the door. "Abraham! Welcome!" Every lunch was like a Sabbath feast. There was always meat, both chicken and beef. And there was wine. Reb Cantor prided himself on having the largest wine cellar in Chelm. Never mind that he had the only wine cellar in Chelm. He would escort Adam into the basement and say, "Abraham, you see these five bottles of wine? They are from France! A man who owned a vineyard told me that before you open them, you have to shake them up. That's what makes them fizzy. You should see the cork's fly! The last time I opened a bottle, the cork shot out the window into the sky and killed a vulture. Now that's a good wine."

Reb Cantor ate for hours—every meal. "I like to take a half-hour break between breakfast and lunch," he laughed. "And between lunch and dinner I reserve forty-two minutes."

When Adam (as Abraham) wondered aloud how Reb Cantor got any business done, the fat merchant warned him. "Feh. Business is easy. Most of the negotiations take place during the meal. When my associates see how much I can eat and how much I can drink, they are in awe. They know that my appetite is huge and that I will eat them alive. Well, perhaps not alive, but certainly I would eat them roasted."

And then Reb Cantor would laugh and tell stories about all the trips he had taken around the world. Every so often Rivka would peek into the room, and she and Adam would blush.

By the time Adam stumbled back to his work at the carpenter's shop, it would be late afternoon and he would be sleepy and fuddled from too much food and drink.

His father would make excuses, tolerating behavior and laziness that

Adam never could have managed under his own name. "It's not easy becoming a carpenter. It took your brother years. You, though, you're learning on the run, and so quickly. Not only that, you're forming a partnership. This is good. Reb Cantor is powerful and rich. You nap while I finish up this table . . ."

Then it would be time to take Rivka Cantor for a walk. In Chelm there weren't so many opportunities for a young man and a young woman to court each other. Most marriages were arranged almost from birth. The few other weddings were usually performed quickly to avoid an embarrassment at an early *bris* or naming ceremony. To prevent such a misfortune, the courtship of Abraham and Rivka had to be supervised in full view of at least one if not a dozen villagers. So they walked. Mostly around the village square. Sometimes they would walk north and then east, then south, then west. Sometimes they walked the other way. It didn't really matter as long as they were together—and under careful observation. The most humiliating part of the entire situation was that everybody else in Chelm agreed that Abraham and Rivka were a perfect match, unlike Adam and Rivka, they all said, who couldn't manage a civil conversation, let alone a sustained relationship.

Despite all this, for Adam, these walks were the best part of the day. He found he didn't need to talk, that just being with Rivka was enough. He didn't dare hold her hand. He barely managed to glance at her because when he so much as glimpsed her smooth and perfect face he would blush and stop dead in his tracks. It seemed impossible that he, Adam Schlemiel, could be engaged to someone as wonderful in every way as Rivka Cantor.

Then Rivka would squeeze his hand and say in a soft voice, "I can't wait for our wedding night!"

He would feel his heart race. Rivka would giggle, and then, pretending to wipe an eyelash away, her fingers would brush his cheek and she would whisper, "I love you, Abraham."

At that moment, every day, Adam's glorious mood shattered. While any other young man would have been in heaven, Adam would nod silently, his face frozen in a false smile. My brother was wrong, Adam thought, I should have volunteered myself for the Russian army.

CHAPTER FORTY-THREE

Another Schlemiel Wedding

At last, the day of the Schlemiel-Cantor wedding arrived. For a man and a woman, a wedding is the moment when their two fates are twined together. They walk under the chuppah separately and leave as one. For the village of Chelm, however, a spring wedding was as good an excuse for a big party as any. Better. Winter snows were gone, enough grass had grown so your boots didn't sink half a foot, and it was time for a dance! Everyone in Chelm was invited to the wedding. Everyone in Smyrna, too. Even the Russian soldiers were invited to the wedding ceremony and festivals. How could they not be? Shouldn't everyone take pleasure in such a festivity? Besides, if they hadn't been invited, they would have shown up uninvited in front of the door to the synagogue with their guns and scared everyone as they waited for Abraham's twin brother to return for the celebration.

Of course, there had been rumors that it was jealousy, not the Russians, that had chased the younger Schlemiel from Chelm. Adam Schlemiel, it was said, had been secretly in love with Rivka Cantor, even though it was also a well-known fact that Rivka despised Adam Schlemiel for reasons long forgotten. The fact that Abraham was marrying Rivka had driven Adam insane, and he had fled. When Rivka had asked him, Adam (posing as Abraham) had said it was nonsense.

On the morning of his wedding, as he stepped into his brand new formal trousers, all these thoughts ran through the real Adam Schlemiel's mind. He knew they were all nonsense, and yet he knew they were all true as well. He was living a lie. He was marrying under false pretenses. In popular fiction and theater, when a hero takes on a new identity, he always disguises himself. He puts on a false beard, a mustache, or shaves his head. Perhaps he feigns a limp or wears an eye patch. But Adam didn't need a disguise to pretend to be someone else.

At best, Adam knew he was nothing more than a fake. At worst, he was a criminal. He sighed. During the wedding ceremony, Adam would be standing beneath the chuppah with Rivka, but Rivka would be standing there with Abraham. And yet for almost a year, Adam Schlemiel had walked in his brother's name, eaten his brother's meals, accepted his brother's praise and compliments, and of course courted his brother's bride.

No! he told himself. She's not his bride, but my bride. She never was his. She loves me, but not me. Or does she love me? Does she love him? She's never spent time with him, only me. She must love me. Doesn't she? It was all so confusing, and it made him feel terrible.

On the day of his wedding, Adam was shaking in his brother's best boots—and he hadn't even put them on yet. Should he tell her? He couldn't. If he told her then the Russians would come for him and put him in the army. But it was so difficult to keep lying. What would Abraham do? Adam asked himself. What would Abraham suggest? But Adam got no answer.

Time and again, Adam had tried to mind-talk with Abraham, but it just wasn't working. It had once been a wonderful thing, to be able to confide or complain or to call for help. But even in the old days, the farthest their mind-talk had ever reached was from Chelm to Smyrna, and by now Abraham must have traveled far beyond Smyrna.

Adam missed his brother. Abraham was his best friend, his only friend. They had known each other from the moment they were born—sooner perhaps. So much of their lives had been shared. And today especially Adam wanted Abraham to come home and share his wedding.

Come back! He tried to mind-shout it. *Those Russians are idiots. You said it yourself. The famous Schlemiel twins could outsmart them with half a brain, let alone the two that we're blessed with. Abraham? Can you hear me?* But there was no answer. Adam knew only that Abraham was still alive. That at least he could sense.

More than Abraham's company, though, he wanted his counsel. How long could this masquerade go on? At first it had been by turns amusing, disconcerting, unsettling, entertaining, discomforting, and perhaps a little enlivening. Mostly, though, it had been upsetting. Every time someone called him Abraham, Adam smiled on the outside but became numb on the inside. Eventually, this reaction became automatic.

More recently, and worst of all, Adam actually found himself forgetting who he was. Days and even weeks went by when "Adam" didn't really exist. He gave the matter no thought. He was who he was. Whatever name people called him was his. The work that he did was his. The brief moments when Rivka Cantor brushed her hand against his cheek as they walked through Chelm were his.

But this didn't feel like his wedding day. It felt like it was Abraham's. And the funny thing was that the real Abraham wasn't even here to enjoy it.

Everything was new. The trousers, along with the shirt, socks, boots, jacket, and even the felt hat were a pre-wedding gift from Reb Cantor. "To my new son, Abraham," the note in the box had said. Adam would wear them, but he still felt that they were Abraham's.

And of course the letters on the beautiful cake that Mrs. Chaipul had baked spelled "Mazel Tov Rivka and Abraham." So even the cake was really his brother's, not his.

He sighed. Somehow, in spite of all his thoughts and worries, he had managed to slip into this wedding costume, comb his hair, and put on a smile as his father led him into the village synagogue, which was packed to the rafters with grinning, cheering, and laughing family, friends, and neighbors.

Like everyone else, his heart caught in his throat and he felt himself grow warm as Rivka Cantor walked slowly down the aisle toward him. She was the most beautiful woman he had ever seen, and now, brilliant in white silk, she looked even more splendid.

Joy filled the room with a river of tears!

For Adam, however, there was no one else but Rivka. They were alone. The moment stretched into an eternity. Through her veil, he could see her smile glowing just for him. And then he felt a nudge.

"So, Abraham?" Rabbi Kibbitz coughed.

Adam wasn't sure what the question was. He looked from one smile to another, from Rivka's to the rabbi's.

"Well, Abraham?"

Adam! It's me! Mazel tov!

Adam turned around suddenly and searched through the synagogue. He thought he'd heard a voice. Was Abraham out there? Face after face grinned at him. Some nodded, some winked, some rolled their eyes, but Abraham's face was not among them. And then, Adam saw that the two Russian soldiers standing at the back of the room were also looking for Abraham. They knew he would come back. They were hoping to find a face identical to the one under the canopy.

I'm here, Abraham said in Adam's mind. *I'm just outside the social hall.*

Don't come in! Adam called back. *The Russians are still here. They are looking for you. I mean me.*

"Abraham?" Rabbi Kibbitz said.

"What? Who?"

I thought they'd be gone by now.

They're not. You can't come in. Abraham, what am I going to do? Rivka thinks she loves you.

No, she loves you. She's marrying you.

What about the name?

Don't be a cursed Schlemiel. Names don't matter. It's who you are that matters.

There was a commotion in the synagogue. The soldiers knew something was happening. They were moving out of the synagogue.

Quickly, Abraham! The soldiers. Run. Be well.

And you! Just kiss the bride for me.

And he was gone.

"Abraham?" Rabbi Kibbitz repeated. "Is everything all right?"

Adam turned back. The smile on Rivka Cantor's face was flickering with doubt. It looked as if she were having second thoughts. It looked as if at any moment she might change her mind. Adam would not allow that.

"Everything is wonderful," he said with a smile. "I was looking for my brother. I keep hoping he'll show up."

"You know," Rebecca Schlemiel whispered to Shmeenie as she dabbed her tears with a handkerchief, "if Adam walked in right now, I think I'd kill him."

"But then who would get married?" Shmeenie whispered back.

Her mother looked puzzled and then patted her daughter's arm.

"He's not here," Adam said at last. "I miss him."

Rivka hesitated a moment, and then she nodded. The rabbi nodded. Everyone nodded. Eventually, even the soldiers, who had come back into the room, sat down. Then everyone waited.

"Abraham," Rabbi Kibbitz said at last. "Step on the glass already."

A final pang of doubt and fear and anger flashed through Adam Schlemiel's heart as he . . .

Never mind the name!

. . . lifted his leg and smashed his new boot down on the napkin-wrapped wine glass.

CRASH, it shattered.

"Mazel tov!" the village of Chelm roared.

Adam grinned. Then Rivka Schlemiel's lips met his and all thoughts were erased with a warm splash of joy. He was married.

CHAPTER FORTY-FOUR

The Importance of Being Mud

"Abraham."

"Mmmm." Adam Schlemiel hummed in his sleep.

"Abraham," said the musical voice very near his ear. It was a woman and she sounded lovely.

"Mmm?" He smiled.

"Abraham," the voice shouted, "get up!"

"What? Is there a fire?" Adam sat bolt upright, blinking furiously.

Rivka Schlemiel looked at her husband and laughed and laughed.

Adam felt his face widening into a grin. He picked up the pillow and threw it at her. She caught it and hurled it right back. It hit him smack in the face, and he used that as an excuse to lie down again, close his eyes, and pretend to snore. "Zzzzzz."

"ABRAHAM!"

"Mmm?" he grunted, frowning.

Rivka jumped right on top of him and began tickling him furiously. Adam was taken completely by surprise and now found himself laughing uncontrollably.

"Stop, stop!" he begged. "Someone will hear us."

"Who is going to hear us in our very own house?"

"Ahhh!" Adam said, trying to push her hands away. "Ha ha!"

Not only had Reb Cantor given Adam his daughter, he had also given them both a brand new house just on the edge of Chelm, equidistant (and equally far away) from both of the in-laws' homes. The irony of the gift was that Adam himself had helped his father with the construction and carpentry but hadn't realized that this was going to be his own home. If he had, he probably would have used better materials and been a little more careful with some of the hinges and joints . . .

"Stop!" he gasped. "As your husband, I command you."

"Oh," Rivka grinned. "Now you're my husband, are you?"

"Yes, absolutely." Adam tried to keep a straight face. "I am the ruler of this house, and my word is law."

"Law is it?"

"Yes." Adam nodded. "And the first law of this house is no tickling."

"And what happens," Rivka asked coyly, "if someone breaks the law?" She poked him just above the ribs. "Hmmm?" Another poke. "Hmm?"

"Stop. Stop! I'll call the soldiers."

"Call the soldiers indeed," Rivka said as her tickles grew even worse. "You can barely breathe."

"Aaack!" Adam sputtered. Here he was married less than a day, and already his authority was being undermined. Enough was enough. He reached out and began tickling Rivka. "This will be your punishment!"

"I'm not ticklish," she said.

"Nonsense." Adam tried harder, and then differently and then more and then less. No matter where he poked, prodded, or flicked, his efforts at tickling his wife didn't even provoke a smile. How could someone not be ticklish?

"You see?" Rivka said, poking him. "Now, Abraham, who is the ruler of this house?"

"HA!" Adam laughed. He grabbed Rivka and gave her a huge hug and then a soft and gentle kiss. That particular sequence of affection had its desired effect and pushed all thoughts of tickling from Rivka's mind.

A little while later they both sat at the kitchen table, sipping tea.

"You know, Abraham, your breakfast was warm when I came in to wake you up."

"It is delicious cold," Adam said, amazed that the fib came so quickly. The eggs tasted as if they'd been fried in rancid grease, and the rock solid black bread would have been tough food for a goat. At least the tea was still lukewarm, and with a dollop of honey it tasted like sweetened water from a swamp.

Rivka kissed his cheek. "Abraham, Abraham, Abraham," she said. "And to think that we're married."

Adam sighed.

"What is it?" Rivka asked.

"Do you love me?" he said.

"Such a question to ask me at this particular moment," said Rivka. "We just got married. What could have I done that you even think otherwise? How can you say such a thing?"

"Yet you didn't answer," Adam said. "You've done nothing. Do you love me?"

"Yes," Rivka said. Her voice was patient. "I could elaborate by saying that I love you to the core of your being, from horizon to horizon, from the creation of the world to the end of eternity, but that would just be hyperbole."

"Hyper-what?"

"Exaggeration. I love you." She set her hand on his. "I love you as much as a woman can love a man."

Adam smiled. "Then I have a favor."

"Anything, so long as it is legal, moral, and won't hurt."

"Don't call me Abraham any more."

Rivka looked puzzled. "How can one distinguish between a rose and a weed except by its name?"

"Call me 'Husband.'"

Rivka snorted. "As if we are seventy years old already? Should I perhaps call you Mr. Schlemiel? Or 'Your Excellency,' since you are so attached to ruling this small kingdom of ours?"

Although Rivka was being sarcastic, for Adam any name would be better than hearing her sweet lips call him Abraham day in and day out for the rest of their lives.

"Abraham," he said, "is such an old fashioned name."

"I could call you Abe," Rivka offered. "That's got a youthful sound."

"No," Adam shook his head. "It's . . ."

"I'd call you Ham," Rivka said, "but in English 'ham' is another word for pig, which, even though you are acting like one, is hardly kosher."

"Rivka . . ."

"I could call you Braham, or Abra, or perhaps Maharba, which is Abraham spelled backwards."

"Rivka . . ."

"What about Hambra? Or perhaps I should just call you Mud."

"Mud? Why Mud?"

"Because that's what your name will be in my book if we continue this conversation."

Adam sighed. "All right. Mud it is. Call me 'Mud.'"

"You're kidding." Rivka looked at her husband. "Nu? You're not kidding. You'd rather be called Mud than Abraham?"

Adam nodded.

Rivka's face looked like a confused owl's. "Why?"

He wanted to say, "Because I'm not Abraham. I'm Adam." But how could he? The truth was, he couldn't. She'd ask for a divorce in a second. It was insane. So, Mud he would be.

"You don't have an answer?" she said. "It seems to be a simple question. For example, 'Rivka, please don't serve me horseradish because it makes me break out in hives.' This makes perfect sense. 'Rivka, don't call me Abraham because . . . ' Because no reason. It leaves me completely stumped."

"Rivka," Adam said, "you have a brilliant mind. You understand things. You can put words together in ways that leave a simple carpenter like me speechless."

Rivka was flattered. She paused for a moment and then asked, "So, you want me to do it? Just like that?"

Adam nodded.

"All right, Ab . . ." She began to say the name but then pursed her lips. "This is your house, your castle, your domain more or less. Mud it is."

"Do you love me? Even if my name is Mud?"

"I love you, Mud."

Adam smiled. He set his hand on top of hers. "When you call me Mud it fills my heart with joy."

Rivka shook her head. "You are a very strange husband, Mud Schlemiel."

"It's a curse," Adam said. "All the Schlemiels are cursed."

"Really?" Rivka said. "Are you sure about that?"

She kissed him again. And you know, Adam wasn't so sure.

Chapter Forty-Five

Where The Wind Blows

In his dream, Rosa's lips brushed Abraham's cheeks like a light breeze . . . Her kiss landed on his cheek like a wet leaf. Her finger poked into his back like a sharp stick. Abraham's forehead twitched. He frowned and opened his eyes. A wet leaf was stuck to his forehead. He sat up and brushed the stick out of the pile of leaves he had collected to sleep on. Then he lay back to fall asleep again but had no luck.

It was still dark. He could see the sky above through the leaves of the elm tree he had rested under. It was black and clear, star-lit and brilliant. There were more stars than he had ever imagined when he had lived in Chelm. Sometimes he spoke to them, as if they were old friends, but tonight his mind was elsewhere.

Rosa. Always he dreamed of her, and in his dream she was so close. He knew that the Rom, the Gypsies as they were often called, believed strongly in the power of dreams. Did that really mean that Rosa was nearby? Perhaps her caravan was just a mile or two from his poor camping spot. Which direction though? In the woods in the darkness he wouldn't be able to see smoke from their cooking fires. Never mind. As a cursed Schlemiel, he could almost be certain to head in the wrong direction anyway. Still, she was there, and he had nothing better or more important to do than to look.

Abraham sighed. He stretched his arms and legs. He picked up his pack and, while the sun rose behind him, he headed west, searching for the light of his life.